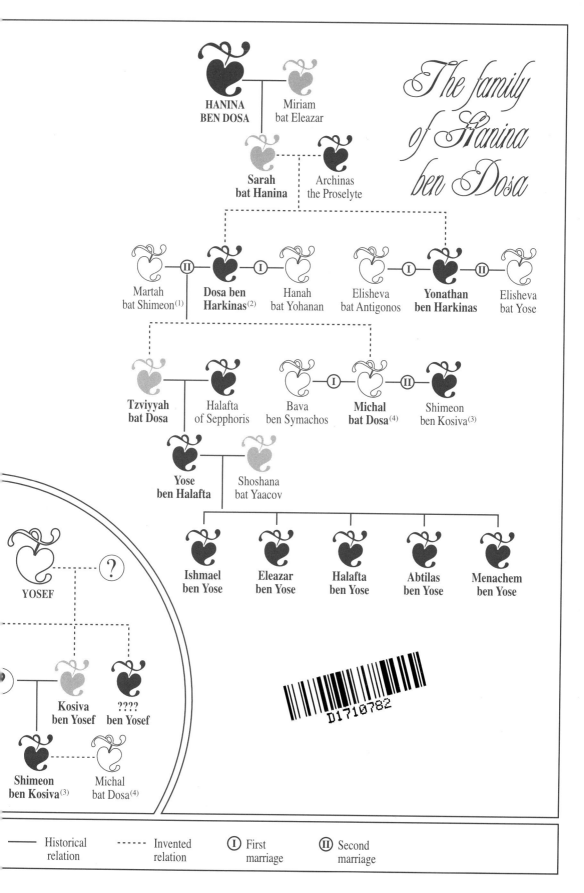

The family of Hanina ben Dosa

HANINA BEN DOSA — Miriam bat Eleazar

Sarah bat Hanina ┄ Archinas the Proselyte

Martah bat Shimeon[1] —(II)— Dosa ben Harkinas[2] —(I)— Hanah bat Yohanan

Elisheva bat Antigonos —(I)— Yonathan ben Harkinas —(II)— Elisheva bat Yose

Tzviyyah bat Dosa — Halafta of Sepphoris

Bava ben Symachos —(I)— Michal bat Dosa[4] —(II)— Shimeon ben Kosiva[3]

Yose ben Halafta — Shoshana bat Yaacov

Ishmael ben Yose

Eleazar ben Yose

Halafta ben Yose

Abtilas ben Yose

Menachem ben Yose

YOSEF ┄ ?

Kosiva ben Yosef

???? ben Yosef

Shimeon ben Kosiva[3] ┄ Michal bat Dosa[4]

D1710782

—— Historical relation

┄┄ Invented relation

(I) First marriage

(II) Second marriage

My Husband, Bar Kokhba

A Historical Novel

Andrew Sanders

gefen גפן
publishing house בית הוצאה לאור
JERUSALEM ♦ NEW YORK

Cover photo of the Bar Kokhba statue appeared in the *Tarbut* encyclopedia,
published by Messada Publishing, © 1963. The image originally appeared
in the Italian edition, published by Fratelli Fabbry Editori.

Typesetting: Raphaël Freeman, Jerusalem Typesetting
Cover Design: Studio Paz

ISBN 965-229-306-7

1   3   5   7   9   8   6   4   2

Gefen Publishing House   Gefen Books
POB 36004, Jerusalem 91360, Israel   12 New Street, Hewlett, NY 11557, USA
972-2-538-0247 • orders@gefenpublishing.com   516-295-2805 • gefenny@gefenpublishing.com

www.israelbooks.com

Printed in Israel   *Send for our free catalogue*

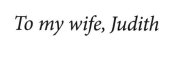

To my wife, Judith

When Rabbi Akiva saw Bar Kokhba
in all his glory, he exclaimed,

"This is the King, the Messiah."

Rabbi Yochanan ben Torta said to him:

"Akiva, grass will grow out of your cheekbones
and the Son of David will still not have arrived."

Table of Contents

BOOK I
Africa

From Yose ben Halafta to Michal bat Dosa, may your peace be great.

My dear aunt, I hope that all is well with you. Thanks to the Lord, my wife Shoshana, my children Ishmael, Eleazar, Halafta, Abtilas and Menachem are all well, and so am I. While I still work in the tannery, I no longer do the very heavy jobs, and I work fewer hours. I have time to devote myself to Torah studies, and also my other projects that I wanted to tell you about.

I have decided to write down the story of the Jewish people, what happened to us, from the Creation to this day. It will be a big undertaking, but with the help of the Lord I should be able to do it. I shall call it Seder Olam.

The easiest part should be those events that took place in my own lifetime, but there are many things that I don't know. I was a young student at the start of the war and was somewhat sheltered from the worst events. But you were, of course, right in the middle of them. Your husband, of blessed memory, was our leader. You must know everything that happened. And not only the events of the last war, but even earlier ones, those of the War of Quietus, just after I was born. And still earlier: Why, you were in Africa during the great war there, and you may also remember some of the events that occurred in Mesopotamia at the same time.

My dear aunt, please tell me about all of those events. I ask that you write a letter to me, or several letters, describing fully what happened to our people, to your husband and, indeed, to yourself, during your long lifetime, and we shall pray for many more healthy years for you. Peace.

Michal's letter to Yose

A SEA VOYAGE

From Michal bat Dosa – to my nephew –
Rabbi Yose ben Halafta, may your peace be great.

You have asked me for the story of the Jewish people during the last forty years or more. That is also the story of my life, and I shall gladly write it all down for you. I know that your work is very important, my dear nephew. I am very proud of you, for your name is known everywhere in Eretz Yisrael, people say that you are now an even greater scholar than your father, of blessed memory.

Writing down events comes easily to me. You may know that I recorded all the happenings of the century before my lifetime, even though that was not my story, but that of my grandfather, Archinas, of blessed memory. And he remembered everything about his father-in-law, the great Rabbi Hanina ben Dosa, of blessed memory, and all the sages who lived in Judaea and here in the Galilee before and after the destruction of the Temple in Jerusalem.

This will be a very long letter, almost a book like the one my grandfather dictated to me. I am now eighty years old; may the Lord grant me enough time to finish it all.

Where should I begin? You were interested in the Africa events; perhaps I shall start with our trip to Africa, a sea voyage.

*　　*　　*

Shimeon and I travelled to Africa from Jaffa on a galley belonging to my father. It was not really a galley, for it needed far fewer oarsmen then the typical ship: my father did not like to hire oarsmen, and was always looking for other ways of moving his vessels over the waves. Our ship, the *Okeanos*, had a new, triangular type of sail, called "lateen." They could move that sail very quickly to catch the wind, the ship flew over the sea...

At first, I took no notice of the ship itself. I did not feel so well, since the ship was heaving a little. Apparently, that was only my impression; people remarked on how smooth the sea was. We had a little corner to ourselves, more than a corner, really, for it was almost enclosed by a canvas partition. We were privileged to have that area, the other travellers all slept together in the hold. Only the ship's captain had an entire room to himself. He was

a very nice old man, a Greek, and he told us that all the sailors and oarsmen on board were Greek, from the islands. He behaved quite deferentially
towards us, due to my father owning the ship, no doubt. He told us on the
first day that he was hired as a young boy by my grandfather and stayed
with the family all his life.

When I felt a little better, I asked the captain about his crew, especially
the oarsmen. You see, I was worried that they might be slaves, as was quite
common. Of course I should have known that my father would never use
slaves. No, the captain assured me, they were strong men who rowed for
money. They received good pay, got time off in the ports, and, after fifteen
or twenty years with the ship, could retire with a generous gift, buy themselves some land or, if they wanted, their own fishing boat. Some even had
family in the home port of Jaffa.

Shimeon and I spent most of our days on the top deck, talking. We
had been married for eight years, but this was perhaps the first time that
Shimeon had nothing else to do but talk with me.

We were sailing towards Cyrene, where Shimeon believed the Jewish
people should start the war of liberation from the Roman Empire. Did
I agree with him? I did raise some arguments, if only because I thought
that he expected those from me; of course, he would not really listen, and
deep down, I felt he was correct in his assessment of the events. And so
he was. Of course, in the end things did not turn out as he expected, but
that did not mean his thinking was at fault. No, the Lord, may His name
be blessed, wanted it otherwise.

And so, on board that ship, he told me all the facts about Cyrenaica, the
country, and I told him all the legends about Cyrene, the city. They were
fine legends; I imbibed them at my beloved mother's knees. From whom
did she hear such stories? I don't know, quite possibly from her grandfather, Rabban Gamaliel the Elder, for he was a great voyager, who sailed all
over the Greek islands.

I mention this to you, so you won't believe that it was my grandfather
Archinas, your own great-grandfather, who taught me such stories. You
see, Grandfather was a Greek, a proselyte. He was very proud of belonging
to the Jewish people, and did not want them to think of him as a Greek.
So he was careful not to tell us any tales from the Greek mythology. Even
when he dictated his life story to me, he said next to nothing about his life
before coming to Eretz Yisrael.

The story I remember most clearly had to do with the foundation of
the city of Cyrene. It went like this:

There was a young nymph named Cyrene who lived in Greece. One day a lion attacked her father's flock of sheep, and Cyrene rushed to defend the animals. In wrestling with the lion, she attracted the attention of the god Apollo, who was smitten by her. Apollo brought Cyrene from Greece to Libya, in Africa, founded a city named after her and made her its queen.

A simple story – totally untrue, of course. But strangely enough, it annoyed Shimeon.

"What's wrong, my dear?" I could see on his face that something seriously bothered him. "I know it's silly, with gods and nymphs, there are no such things, but is it not a charming story? Quite harmless?"

At first he did not answer. In those days, he liked to think things over. He stood by the rail, his long black hair blowing in the wind. Oh, he was so handsome. With his forehead creased, you might have thought that he was angry. But my Shimeon was seldom angry, and almost never with me. Finally he spoke:

"There are several things wrong with it. Yes, there is that god that is not quite as harmless as you think. The Greeks believe in him and in many other gods, and that's why we are fighting them. Then, there are the facts. Cyrenaica was founded by people who came over from Thera, they say it was about eight hundred years ago. But all right, that is not very important…"

He lapsed into silence for a minute or two. Then he turned to me.

"This is what bothers me about the story. That girl who fought with the lion. That is stupid. You don't fight with a lion. You don't choose to fight with anyone or anything, unless you are confident that you can win."

"But how can you be sure? By never fighting against anything bigger than a small bird?"

"No, of course not. You can never be sure, we are only people, no one but the Lord can be sure of anything. But when one decides to fight, he must believe, at that moment, that he will win that fight. And you cannot expect to win if your opponent is a lion."

He was so serious, I almost believed him. But all I said was, "Shimeon, I hope you will always remember what you've just said, especially in Africa. There are many lions there, and not all of them beasts."

"I know, my sweet. I will remember."

Then he started to tell me about the Jewish people in Cyrenaica. I knew some of the story, for I had participated in his recent discussions with Pappus and Julianus – well, I was in and out – but I listened anyway.

"Our people have been in Cyrenaica for hundreds of years. They were originally invited there by the Ptolemies, to help them fight the local people. The Jews became farmers, tenants of public land."

"So I suppose they had lots of trouble with the native people?"

"Strangely enough, no. Not much. But they just can't get along with the Greeks. You see, the local Greeks run the country. They won't permit land ownership to Jews, at least not close to the cities. And we cannot get full citizenship, except for a select few in the last century, and look what happened to them."

"What happened?"

"Well, that's a long story. It started with Greek landowners and Roman contractors. They manipulated land deals and let shepherds move their flocks up the hills and down to the plains in different seasons, and that ruined the land. One way or another, most of the Jews lost their tenancy of public land and had to hire themselves out to Greek landowners. In such a blessed, rich land as Cyrenaica, they became paupers."

Shimeon's voice was getting louder. I patted his hand, indicating that there were others on the deck, for it was nice and sunny. Not everyone was necessarily sympathetic to our cause.

He continued in a lower voice. "The Greeks even prevented them, sometimes, from paying their annual half-shekel tax to the Temple in Jerusalem. You see, they had to pay the local taxes first, and not every man for himself. No, they had to make remittance as a group, and collection was very difficult. Yet until the total sum was paid, money could not be sent to Jerusalem."

"How could such poor people afford to pay local taxes as well as the half-shekel?" I asked

"They really could not, but they had to. And not only that, they had to pay taxes to Rome as well, the *tributa*."

"So what happened to the citizens?"

"I am coming to that. During the War with Rome in Eretz Yisrael, forty-five years ago, there were many Cyreneans fighting in Jerusalem, they were friendly with the Zealots."

"Yes, I am very familiar with them…" I did not continue, for I remembered that he knew about my first husband.

"Well, when the Temple was destroyed and we lost the war, many of the Zealots went to Cyrenaica. These were extremists, not ordinary Zealots, but the Sicariim, you know, the 'daggermen.' At that time, Jews and Greeks hated one another more than ever, perhaps because each group heard about all the clashes everywhere else, in Caesarea and in Syria and, even closer to Cyrenaica, in Egypt, in Alexandria. Also, there was more trouble between those groups because the Jews wanted the Romans to reorganize land tenure. Greeks and Jews were on the verge of attacking one another. And then came Yonathan. Yonathan the Weaver."

"Yonathan the Weaver… I seem to have heard that name before. Was he really a weaver?"

"I have no idea. But he was either a great leader or a great troublemaker. Perhaps both. He was certainly one of the original Jerusalem Sicariim…"

"But I thought that nobody survived there," I interrupted.

"No, but he may have gotten out of the city before the siege. In any case, he arrived in Cyrenaica soon after the war and thought that he would start a revolt there and reverse all the losses."

"Like you." That was a mistake. For a few moments, he *was* angry with me.

"Not like me at all! Don't say stupid things! I told you that I only fight when I know that I can win. He had no chance of winning, but we have. It's a totally different situation."

"All right, sorry, I did not mean it that way. But what happened then?"

"Well, by then there were Jewish citizens in Cyrenaica. Some were wealthy and involved with the leadership of the cities, not only in Cyrene but also in Barka and Teucheira and Bereneike and Ptolemais. There was also a middle group, not rich, but not poor either, many farmers and some craftsmen – don't make faces, they are people, too – and then, all the myriad landless people who had lost their tenancy, or their fathers had. This was the group that Yonathan the Weaver wanted for his revolt."

He continued. "He organized some two thousand of the poorest people and led them into the desert. He told them that they would soon see wondrous things, signs from the Lord and miracles."

"Why, did he say he was the Messiah?"

"I don't think so, but he may have hinted, dropped some suggestions. Jews who had some possessions did not like him much, and the rich Jews, who considered themselves Greeks, just hated him. So when Yonathan went into the desert with his followers, they reported him to the authorities."

"Oh, no!" I was shocked.

"Yes. We Jews should stick together, even when we disagree among ourselves. But, of course, we don't, most of the time. So the Roman proconsul, a man called Catullus, I think Valerius Catullus Messalinus, something like that, sent cavalry and infantry after Yonathan's crowd, and they were dispersed, most of them killed, but Yonathan was captured in the end."

"What did they do to him?"

"They made him talk. Not the truth, though; he saw this as his opportunity to repay the Jewish leadership. So he accused them of supporting his movement. First, he accused a wealthy Jew named Alexander and his wife Berenice, with whom he had some trouble before. So Catullus arrested and executed them, as well as three thousand wealthy Jews all over Cyrenaica, the entire Jewish leadership. Of course, Catullus also confiscated their property."

"That man Yonathan was a rat!"

"Yes, he was. Then he tried to implicate the wealthy Jews outside Cyrenaica, in Alexandria and in Rome. Catullus thought that he could then carry out investigations all over the Roman Empire, but the Emperor Vespasian called a halt to that. He conducted a personal inquiry and found that Yonathan's accusations were a fabric of lies."

"And what happened to Yonathan?"

"Oh, he was killed, of course. Sentenced to death by burning."

"Well, I should probably feel sorry for him, but not now. Maybe later."

"You know whom else they killed in Cyrene at that time? The High Priest Ishmael ben Phiabi. Five years before the war he had traveled from Jerusalem to Rome, to complain against Agrippa and the Roman procurator. That was also interesting: he was not received by the Emperor Nero, but he managed to see Nero's wife, Poppea, and not just once. She became very interested in him and tried to get her husband to act more kindly towards our people."

"She could not have been very successful. They started the war and destroyed Jerusalem."

"True, but they say that she tried. And she insisted that the priest stay there, in Rome. She really liked him. But then, after a year or two, Poppea died. She was pregnant and they say that Nero kicked her down the stairs. Two or three years later, Nero was forced to kill himself, and there was great turmoil in Rome until Vespasian took over. But Ishmael stayed there, in Rome."

"Very interesting. How old was Ishmael at the time?"

"I really don't know. But that trip saved his life. At least for a while, for in Jerusalem he surely would have perished, along with everyone else. Still, in the long run, it did not help. When Jerusalem was destroyed, Ishmael sought refuge in Cyrene. Three years later, he was killed there by Catullus, along with the three thousand, the entire Jewish leadership. He was decapitated."

"Ugh. A horrible death."

"Few forms of death are nice."

We were quiet for a while, watching the waves. There were birds trying to catch fish. We were told to expect to arrive in Africa in a day and a half.

I knew Shimeon was thinking about the political situation in Cyrenaica, how the great rebellion might be started, what role he would have in it... Up to now, he had told me very little about what to expect. I thought that this might be the time to ask.

"Tell me, Shimeon. Is the situation really that much better there now? Do we have a hope of winning?"

He considered for a minute.

"I'll tell you, Michal. Of course we have a chance to win, more than a chance, I am quite certain that we shall win, otherwise I would not have come. And you know why? There are several reasons, but the most important one is precisely what happened there forty-two years ago. What I just told you."

"You mean this Yonathan business?"

"Yes, and the murder of the entire Jewish leadership. Ever since, the Jews have suffered even more than before, because they no longer had any influence with the Greek and Roman authorities. The large middle group has become poorer. They are persecuted. They are desperate. They are ready to start a fight, any fight, and now there are no upper classes among the Jews to interfere, to calm them with promises of getting a better deal from the authorities. If a new Yonathan were to appear now, not two thousand would follow him, but two hundred thousand."

I threw him a quizzical look. He grinned.

"No, don't worry, that is not my role. In any case, they have their own leaders now, Lucuas and also Pappus and Julianus – you have met the two brothers – and they are all reasonable people. I am needed only to help them."

"Help them in what? Exactly what will you do, Shimeon? What are the plans? You can tell me now. You don't have to worry that I will not come with you. You did worry, did you not?"

He held my hands. "Yes, Michal, I did worry. A wife must accompany her husband, if he asks her, but if you had said that you were afraid, I would not have insisted. You are not afraid, are you?"

I tried to smile. "No, I told you. I trust you, Shimeon. But it would be better if I knew exactly what you will do, what to expect."

"But I cannot tell you that, for I don't know myself. Pappus and Julianus suggested that I come, that this is the time and the place, that I would be needed here. That's all I know. When I meet with them, when I see Lucuas, I will know more."

"But listen, Shimeon, what if you don't like what they say? What if you think that they are about to fight a lion? Will you be able to say no? Will you be willing to sail back to Eretz Yisrael then? Will they let you?"

He did not answer for a while. Some minutes later he said, "We'll see."

*   *   *

Next day, the sea was a little rougher, but by then it did not bother me at all. We stood by the railing and watched the clouds, watched the waves. Suddenly I saw a fish jumping up from the water. Shimeon saw it, too. "What is that?" I asked him. To my knowledge, he had never been on a ship before. Yet he assured me that it was a dolphin, a playful sea creature that was a friend of men.

"Men?" I teased him. "Which men? If you jumped in now, would he help you swim? And what if your enemies jumped in? Would he choose sides?"

He did not answer right away. Shimeon did not care for frivolous talk. But after a while he turned to me:

"Enemies? You want me to tell you about our enemies? We have many of them, we'll meet them soon enough." Then he told me more about the situation of the Jews in Cyrenaica, which had become much worse since the destruction of the Temple. Not only have the Romans diverted the half-shekel Temple tax to their own Fiscus Iudaicus, set up to serve the cult of the detested Iupiter Capitolinus, but they have imposed many additional taxes and penalties on the Jews in Cyrenaica and in Egypt, and everywhere else they ruled.

He also told me how the Greeks hated the Jews because our people refused to participate in their silly cults, because we excluded ourselves from all Greek activities. But the curious thing was that, while the Greek masses hated the Jews, the leading classes sometimes became sympathetic.

"Do you mean they actually stood up for the Jews against the Roman authorities?" I asked him.

"No, they would not go that far," he replied. "But individually, some members of those classes actually converted, or came to accept our God as the only one. That has been a major problem in Rome, too, even members of the emperors' families joined our faith at times. They have also been severely punished for this, often executed cruelly."

We were interrupted by the captain, who came over to point out Alexandria on the port side, in the distance. It was too far to make out any of the buildings in detail, but we could see that it was a very large, beautiful city. After the man walked away, Shimeon talked to me about Alexandria. It seems that there were lots of clashes between Jews and Greeks there also. The Jews actually attacked the city's gymnasia some time ago. It should have been a situation similar to Cyrenaica; but there was an important difference.

"You see, in Alexandria the Jewish leadership, the elite, is still there. Yonathan did not succeed in annihilating them, for better or for worse."

"Why do you say 'for better or for worse'?"

"Every time there's been trouble between the Jews and the Greeks, the leadership has tried to calm the tensions, to find compromise solutions, to pacify the authorities."

"Is that so bad?"

"It can be. When it is finally time to take up arms, as it will be soon, they may be in the way."

This was serious food for thought.

*   *   *

The captain came over again to chat with us. He apologized for the rough sea, as if it were his fault. He was solicitous, asked me about the health of my father. I told him that my father had serious problems with his eyesight, and that my mother worried about his heart, which was a little weak, but thank the Lord, his mind was still very sharp, and we hoped that he would be with us for a long time yet.

The man nodded and expressed the same hope, then said something like "Sorry, duty calls" and walked away. Shimeon looked at him, and then remarked:

"I was wondering what to tell him if he'd ask me why we were travelling to Cyrenaica. The man is a Greek, I would not want to tell him about our plans."

"You don't trust him? Would he betray you to the Romans?"

"The Romans. The Greeks. No, I don't think he would betray me. But we are going there to fight the Greeks. His people, after all. The less he knows about such things, the better."

"Does he have no idea, do you think…?"

Shimeon pondered my question.

"He probably has, but he prefers not even to think about such things. He may have heard somewhere that I am one of the Zealots, or something like that."

"Tell me about the Zealots, Shimeon," I begged him.

That was a difficult subject. I always had some sympathy for the Zealots, always felt that because of the excesses of a few individuals, the whole movement was unjustly called an extremist, murderous group. They just wanted freedom for our people, it seemed to me. My uncle also thought so, and so did my first husband. I think he actually participated in meetings and discussions, but I knew that I must not ask questions about that.

Shimeon, I knew, was also close to the Zealots. How close, that is hard to say. He was certainly not one of the crazies, but he wanted to fight off the Roman bondage. Perhaps this was the time to ask him – not about his involvement, but about the group, the people, their beliefs and what they wanted to achieve. He was willing to tell me a little.

"They have five major beliefs." He said 'they,' not 'we.' "First, that the Romans, or any other nation, cannot rule over us, because only God has sovereignty."

"That's obvious."

"Yes. Then, they are committed to liberty."

"Good."

"Third, they believe that God will help, if they are willing to fight."

"Well, I suppose that's reasonable, if…"

"Wait, let me tell you the other two beliefs. They resist any Roman census that is aimed at establishing taxes."

"And the last?"

"They believe that the law obligates personal and direct action against the transgressors."

I thought about that.

"So that, no matter what, we must fight the Romans, right?"

"Right, but there are differences. Some want to take up arms at any moment, while others advise that we should choose our time and place very carefully."

"Like this year, in Cyrene," I said quietly.

"Yes."

*　　*　　*

Later in the day, Shimeon told me about the "Sibylline Oracles." I asked him what they were.

"The Sibyls were supposed to be ancient Greek prophetesses who gave out dire warnings regarding the punishment of unjust rulers and the liberation of the oppressed. So books have been written in the form of these warnings. Nobody takes the Sibyls seriously anymore."

"And who wrote those books?"

"Different people at different times. Lately some have been written by our people, mainly in Egypt. The latest one talks about frightful natural catastrophes. It also predicts that the Jewish people will now re-conquer our land, Eretz Yisrael, and the Temple. It says that a sacred ruler will burn down many cities and slay the wicked."

"What cities, does it say?"

"Yes, Antioch and Memphis and Salamis – that's in Cyprus – and in Cyrenaica, all the major cities."

"Do you believe in that?"

"I don't know. They are written by men, not by the Lord. But who knows, He may have been guiding their hands…"

*   *   *

Next day, our ship turned towards the shore. The wind died down, our oarsmen rowed steadily. We saw a busy harbor and hills behind: a lush, beautiful land.

"Is this Cyrene?" I asked Shimeon.

"No, Cyrene is half a day's journey inland. Up those hills. This is just some harbor town."

Then we were told the name of the harbor town. It was Apollonia.

Shimeon and I looked at each other. I whispered to him:

"Apollonia. The town of the silly god, serving his silly nymph, who fought the lion."

15

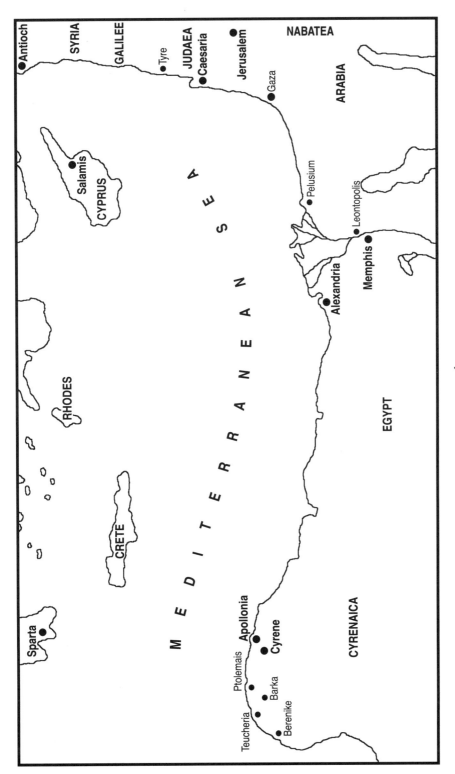

North Africa (1st–2nd century C.E.)

MY HUSBAND, SHIMEON

Yose, my nephew, I don't think that you will understand Shimeon fully the way I have started to describe him. Not with that sea voyage. No, I think that I must tell you a little about his background, things that happened before that event, much before. Perhaps I'll tell you a little of my own background, too, how we met, who we are, and so on. Of course, my sister Tzviyya, your mother of blessed memory, told you all about that long ago, but you may not remember it since she left us six years ago.

And so, to remind you: Your mother and I were daughters of the great Rabbi Dosa ben Harkinas. Yes, your illustrious father, Rabbi Halafta, of blessed memory, was not the only great man among your ancestors. There were many more. Your great-grandfather, my maternal grandfather, was Rabbi Shimeon ben Nethanel haKohen, a disciple of Rabban Yohanan ben Zakkai, may his memory be blessed, a great friend of our family.

Then, when it comes to great-great-grandfathers, two of yours were among the most distinguished sages: Rabban Gamaliel the Elder, leader of the nation, grandson of Hillel the Elder; he was the father of Tzippora, the wife of Shimeon ben Nethanel. And then there was Rabbi Hanina ben Dosa, perhaps the best man who has ever lived, he was my father's grandfather. It is said, as you surely know, that each day a heavenly voice went forth from Mount Horeb, proclaiming: "The whole world is sustained for the sake of My Son Hanina, and Hanina My Son subsists on a *kav* of carobs from one Shabbat eve to the next."

Through Hillel you can trace your ancestry back to King David.

But it is your great-grandfather Archinas that I wanted to write to you about. He was my grandfather, the father of Dosa ben Harkinas and his younger brother Yonathan. He was also the husband of Sarah, the daughter of Rabbi Hanina ben Dosa.

I always loved my grandfather, Archinas (the only one I knew, for my other grandfather, Rabbi Shimeon ben Nethanel, may his memory be blessed, died in the war against the Romans forty-five years before these events). Our mother, Martha bat Shimeon, told us many wonderful stories about her father, but I don't really know what he looked like. Archinas, on the other hand, lived until ten years ago; he died at the age of 102. He was a beautiful old man, tall, with very sharp features; he had lots of hair, thick white hair and a white beard, and he was always smiling. He retained a sharp mind until the end. He dictated his life story to me during his last years. It was not really his life story, at least he did not intend it to be such:

he insisted that it was the story of his father-in-law, Hanina ben Dosa, and Hanina's family, and so it was. But he could not hide the fact that he was a great man, not a scholar perhaps, but without his support many of the great scholars, great leaders of our nation would have remained unknown. Archinas was a businessman, very wealthy. My father inherited his business talent from him, and his Torah scholarship from Hanina.

The reason I am writing so much about Grandfather Archinas is that I want to start my story where he finished his. In the last days of his life he thought a lot about me and my future. He gave me good advice, which I have not followed. I must tell you why, for that is essential to the understanding of my husband Shimeon and of how I came to know him.

You see, I married early, married Bava ben Symmachos, against the wishes of my parents. They did not forbid the marriage but were not happy about it, because Bava was not a scholar but a translator of books. In our family that kind of thing was unheard of. I did not care. I loved him.

But the marriage was not successful. Bava was not really a man. So he gave me a *get*, and I came back to live in my parents' house. I must have been a good-looking young woman, or perhaps it was the wealth and position of my father that attracted men, for the house was always full of visitors who wanted to see me. And those are the men that I wanted to tell you about.

Your father, Rabbi Halafta, often invited his teacher and best friend, Rabbi Yohanan ben Nuri, to our house, even before he married your mother Tzviyya. After the marriage, Yohanan ben Nuri continued to come to our house all the time. Halafta would have loved it if his best friend were to become his brother-in-law. Yohanan was a lovely person, intelligent, good-looking in a friendly, soft way, not tall, but not short either, really, there was nothing wrong with him in any way. I would probably have married him, if I had not met Shimeon.

There was also another Shimeon, the young son of Rabban Gamaliel, of course he is known today as Rabban Shimeon ben Gamaliel himself. He was two years my junior, and somehow I could never take him seriously. He turned out to be serious enough in his mature days.

My grandfather wanted me to marry Rabbi Eleazar ben Azariyah, perhaps the greatest sage of those days. You see, Rabbi Yehoshua ben Hananiyah was already getting old; for a while they called him the Father of the Nation. Rabbi Tarfon was well liked by all, but he preferred to be the power behind the throne, while Rabbi Akiva, recognized by all as the real leader of the Jews, had not yet reached his prime. Eleazar ben Azariyah had. When the sages were so upset about the autocratic rulings of Rabban Gamaliel, about the way he treated Yehoshua ben Hananiyah, they thought that he should be impeached and replaced. Who should replace him? They agreed that Eleazar ben Azariyah would be the ideal person. Strange, he was actually five years younger than Akiva; but he had studied Torah from his earliest days, while Akiva remained an illiterate goatherd until age forty.

Eleazar was the nicest person in the world. It is hard to explain now, at my age of eighty, but in those days, especially after Bava, I did not want the nicest person in the world for a husband. I wanted a man. Eleazar was probably a man, but one looks at it differently at age twenty-seven, twenty-eight. And so I would have married Yohanan ben Nuri, if Akiva had not introduced Shimeon to us one day. (You know, Yose, that must have been the reason Yohanan ben Nuri caused so much trouble for Akiva later, complained about him to Rabban Gamaliel, who punished him publicly, several times. No, that's silly; I attribute too much importance to myself. All those suitors must have made me into a very conceited girl.)

*   *   *

Now, why did Akiva introduce Shimeon? This is not just a personal matter; to understand the situation, you must recall the great debates, fights really, between the House of Hillel and the House of Shammai.

Sects! Always sects. Before the war there were the High Priests' circle and the Sadducees and the Pharisees and the Essenes and the Zealots and the Notzrim. The Sadducees disappeared along with Jerusalem and the Temple, and so have, of course, the High Priests. You don't hear much about the Essenes these days. Zealots? Yes, they were still around, that was my group and Shimeon's.

But within the main Pharisean group there were, as you know, those who followed the teaching of Hillel and those who were the disciples of Shammai. My father was of Bet Hillel; my Uncle Yonathan, he was a committed member of Bet Shammai.

Well, Bet Hillel was victorious in the Sanhedrin after the war. There was a heavenly voice that said: "Both are the words of the Living God. But the Halakha follows the rulings of Bet Hillel."

Of course the Halakha is the law directing our lives. And so, along with the great Rabbi Eliezer ben Hyrkanus, my Uncle Yonathan was finished. Or should have been, if Shammaism was truly dead; but you see, it refused to die.

For not everyone in Yavneh felt the same way about Shammaism as

Rabban Gamaliel, the direct descendant of Hillel. Rabban Yohanan ben Zakkai, the man who saved the nation after the destruction of the Temple, was ambivalent about the two schools. Remember, he was the teacher not only of the Hillelite Yehoshua but also of the Shammaite Eliezer. And a follower of both of those great men, the best disciple of both Yehoshua and Eliezer, was also ambivalent about Shammaism: Rabbi Akiva. He never formally supported Bet Shammai – you could not survive in his position in the Sanhedrin at Yavneh without being a vocal Hillelite – but deep down Akiva often sympathized with the Shammaite position, especially as he grew older.

Grandfather told me of an occasion when they discussed a case in the Sanhedrin, and somebody mentioned that ben Harkinas ruled according to Bet Shammai. They were all surprised, knowing that except for Gamaliel nobody was a stauncher Hillelite than my father. They sent a delegation to my father's house to consult him about the matter. He was almost blind by then and seldom attended the sessions.

The delegation included Eleazar ben Azariyah, Yehoshua ben Hanani-yah and Akiva.

Akiva asked him: "In a particular case, it was stated in your name that the Halakhah was in accordance with Bet Shammai!"

Father seemed pleased.

"What did you hear? That Dosa said this? Or that ben Harkinas said it?"

There was a look of surprise on their faces. Eleazar spoke.

"By the life of our Master, we have not heard the name specified."

"Aha!" Father stood up and pointed towards the part of the house where Yonathan was living.

"I have a younger brother. That's what I call him, *ah katan*."

Father grinned and continued:

"What is he like? He is like the *firstborn of Satan*."

He looked around triumphantly and completed his little poem:

"And his name? His name is *Yonathan*."

They all laughed. Father explained about Yonathan being a Shammaite and suggested that they seek him out; Yonathan and his wife Elisheva shared our house.

They agreed to look for Yonathan. Akiva eventually found him and confronted him with this question, which concerned levirate marriage, I think.

Yonathan was reluctant to talk about his Shammaite position to Akiva, for then he would surely hear about the heavenly voice; and then he would have to counter with the other heavenly voice that supported Rabbi Eliezer but was ignored by the whole Sanhedrin, and they would get into a shouting match. So he decided to insult Akiva instead.

"So you are that Akiva whose name rings from one end of the world to the other. Well, it seems that you are surely fortunate, to have achieved fame, even though to this day you have not attained the rank of oxherd."

Akiva grinned. "No, not even that of shepherd." He patted Yonathan on the back.

Grandfather told me about that story, but he did not realize that Akiva liked Uncle Yonathan and came back to talk with him seriously about his Shammaite views. They talked and talked and became good friends.

Well, that was a long detour to explain the background of Akiva's introduction of Shimeon to our house. But now I hope that what happened next will make sense to you.

One day, Yonathan told Akiva that he would be traveling to Modi'in on business. Akiva asked him:

"Where will you stay in Modi'in?"

"I don't yet know. I shall ask around. Perhaps there is a prominent Shammaite scholar there…"

"Don't ask. I'll tell you the name of the right person. Go to the house of Rabbi Kosiva ben Yosef, he is exactly the one you are looking for. A Shammaite scholar. Tell him that I sent you. He'll be happy to put you up, you will be comfortable enough. Mind you, you won't be surrounded by the luxuries you like…"

"I don't need luxuries. Dosa wants luxuries in this house, not I."

"He is not forcing you to wear clothes like that," smiled Akiva, pointing to Yonathan's elaborate finery. "Don't mind me. I am not criticizing you. Maybe I am just envious."

"Why, Akiva, now that you head an important academy, surely you could afford…"

"Yes, yes, I could afford nice clothes, but I don't have your taste. You inherited that from your father. My father, of blessed memory, was a simple man, and a proselyte. True, your father was also a proselyte, but there is nothing simple about him."

So Yonathan travelled to Modi'in and introduced himself at the house of Kosiva ben Yosef. He told Kosiva that Rabbi Akiva had sent him and that he was a Shammaite scholar himself.

"You don't need to explain who you are," said Kosiva. "Your name is known throughout the country. But tell me, what else did Akiva say about me?"

"Nothing else. Said he knows you and thought that you would not mind putting me up."

"Nothing else? Good. I will be happy to welcome you as my honored guest."

Yonathan stayed in Modi'in for a few days and got to know Kosiva and his son. Kosiva's wife was no longer alive, and there was only the one boy, Shimeon. Not really a boy, a young man of twenty-two. The same age I was. During the evening meals, they would discuss the state of the nation, and Yonathan was struck by Shimeon's astute observations.

They were talking about the town of Modi'in. Young Shimeon was very proud of the history of his birthplace.

"Of course you know that Yehuda ben Matityahu, the man they now call Yehuda haMaccabee, was born here. Not only he, but Shimeon and all the other important Hasmonean leaders. You can safely say that the revolution started in Modi'in."

"Yes, and what a revolution that was. I wish we had leaders today such as the Maccabees were," Uncle Yonathan commented.

Thus encouraged, Shimeon talked more about the revolution of some two hundred and seventy years earlier. He admired their victories, their achieving independence for the nation, their purifying and rededicating the Temple, striking coins and making the Land of Israel one of the important military powers of the world.

Yonathan gently reminded the young man of the successors and descendants of the Hasmoneans, including some very nasty rulers, such as Herod. Shimeon waved that aside.

"Yes, in every dynasty you have better kings and worse ones. They brought in the Idumenean group, which was not good for the land. But that does not diminish the achievement of the founders of the revolution."

Yonathan was basically in agreement with the young man's views. Generally, the Shammaites were close to the Zealot position regarding the necessity of freeing the land from foreign occupation; it was the Hillelites who always strove for compromise, letting well enough alone.

He asked Kosiva about the education of the young man.

"I have been teaching him to the best of my ability," answered Kosiva. "He had been also attending the academy of my brother-in-law here in Modi'in…"

Yonathan was surprised. "Do you mean Rabbi Eleazar haKohen?" For that was the only academy at Modi'in. Kosiva nodded. "I didn't know he was your brother-in-law."

Kosiva sighed. "Yes, he married my dear sister, of blessed memory. They had no children, and Eleazar had taken a keen interest in young Shimeon. But eventually, I had to take him out of his academy, for the man started to fill his head with Hillelite nonsense."

Yonathan mulled this over.

"Should not the young man go up to Yavneh to study?" he asked Kosiva.

"Some years ago, I hoped that one day Rabbi Eliezer ben Hyrkanus would take him," Kosiva sighed again. "But Eliezer has now been rejected by the sages, and I hear that he no longer accepts students…"

After a pause, he added:

"But perhaps yourself…? If it were not an imposition?"

Yonathan was taken aback, for he had no disciples.

"Well, it would certainly be a great honor to accept such a bright student. But you could do better than that. Why not have your friend Akiva teach him?"

Kosiva and his son looked at each other. Yonathan was not sure what was it that passed between them.

"But doesn't Akiva teach Torah according to Bet Hillel?" Kosiva wondered.

"Don't be so sure of that. As he gets older, he desires to emulate the teacher of his teachers, Rabban Yohanan ben Zakkai. He will teach the law according to both Hillel and Shammai. He will tell you what the Bat Kol, that Heavenly Voice, said. He will also impart to you his own interpretation of the Law. He is not closer to Hillel than to Shammai."

Kosiva did not respond to that. Again, he exchanged knowing glances with his son. Eventually, he told Yonathan that he needed time to think.

But before Yonathan left for Yavneh, Kosiva sought him out and told him:

"Rabbi Yonathan, will you be kind enough to have a talk with Akiva and ask him if he would accept young Shimeon? But tell him how I feel about Hillelism. If he will not accept him, or if he insists on teaching Torah according to Bet Hillel, then perhaps you will accept him yourself?"

Yonathan promised the one or the other. And so he talked to Akiva upon his return to Yavneh.

Akiva smiled and told Yonathan that he was not entirely surprised. He wanted to know what else was said about him.

"Nothing, except they worried that you might want to make a Hillelite out of the young man."

"He is twenty-two? If he is not a Hillelite by now, he will never be one," said Akiva. "I shall send a message for the boy to come."

And so Shimeon came to live in Yavneh. It seems that Akiva was very impressed by his enthusiasm and patriotism, if not by his scholarship. Shimeon was a bright, talented young man, don't misunderstand me, but in that town, those qualities were very common. No, Shimeon was not an outstanding light of the Torah. But he was clearly a leader, a man who would, perhaps, bring about national liberation. (Of course, I have the advantage of hindsight.)

*   *   *

One thing is for sure, Akiva liked him. And he wanted to introduce him to our house. Why? Perhaps so he could spend more time with Yonathan. I don't think there was any other reason.

But why would Shimeon need to be introduced by Akiva, when he already knew Yonathan well? It seems that they had a discussion about it. Yonathan told Akiva:

"Look, Akiva, the young man can come and see me as often as he likes. But he will not be very welcome in the rest of the house, not if he is known as a budding Shammaite scholar."

"So what would you like to suggest, Yonathan?"

"Why don't you introduce him yourself? Tell them that he is a student of yours, that you would like him to meet some of the members of this household, perhaps Dosa on occasion, myself every once in a while, and all the other young people who habitually gather and meet here."

So that's what Akiva did, and Shimeon became a regular visitor at our house. Shimeon was tall and strong, with a face that could have been chiseled from stone. He did not smile much, he was always serious, but he was so manly. Not at all like Bava, my first husband. We noticed each other and looked at each other more and more, hoping that no one else would see. My grandfather certainly noticed, and he did not like what he saw. He was afraid of Shimeon. He said that Shimeon had some strange fire in his eyes.

*   *   *

I told you that Grandfather was dictating his life story to me. During the very last day of his life, he was trying to advise me on whom to marry. He could not make up his mind on whether it should be Yohanan ben Nuri, whom he considered ideal, or Eleazar ben Azariyah, his friend; I think that he felt slightly guilty for not arranging a marriage with Eleazar much earlier.

Eleazar was a wonderfully nice man, as well as a great sage. During the *shiva* for my grandfather he was there every day, and I was forced to think about him. By the end of the week I decided that whomever I would marry, it would not be Eleazar. And I thought that I should tell him that.

But how to tell a man that you won't marry him, when he had never asked you to do so?

I pondered that question. I was almost ready to approach my mother, to ask her to talk to Eleazar – after all, they were first cousins. I would have preferred not to talk to her about this, for that would take us into another argument about my future.

My task was suddenly made easier. Eleazar finally decided to approach my father, ask him formally for my hand. They both knew that he could not make the decision for me; so, soon after the *shiva*, he asked me to come into his elegant study, full of gold furniture. I never liked that room. There he told me:

"Michal, listen. We have received a great honor. Our friend, our best friend, the great Rabbi Eleazar ben Azariyah, would like to marry you."

I was surprised, but only for a moment.

"Father, he is of the priestly caste. Is it not true that he cannot marry a divorced woman?"

"No, my daughter, not in your case."

Of course I knew what he meant. A priest is allowed to marry only a virgin. I was certainly that.

He waited. I had to tell him.

"Father, please don't be angry with me. I don't want to marry Eleazar. I shall eventually marry somebody, but not him."

He looked at me, and I was afraid that he would ask me whom I wanted to marry. But no, he did not. Perhaps he was afraid of another row, such as we had at the time I told him about my plan to marry Bava.

Then he nodded and said: "Yes, I knew that you would say something like that. Despite all your education, you are not a very clever girl. But I won't force you. I have discussed this with your mother, and she is willing to let you make a second mistake, if that's what you want to do."

Did they notice how I looked at Shimeon? How he looked at me?

They told Eleazar, and we saw a lot less of him during the coming months. Soon there was news about his asking for the hand of a certain Miriam, daughter of one of the sages. He was gladly accepted, and they were married a few months later. Eleazar was fifty-one years old at the time, unusually late for a first marriage.

That still left Yohanan ben Nuri and Shimeon ben Gamaliel among my suitors. And Shimeon. My Shimeon.

*   *   *

My grandfather was a wise old man, but he did not know everything. He knew that I had studied some Torah – my father had encouraged me in my younger days – but he did not know that I had continued my studies with Uncle Yonathan, especially after my return to the house. Yonathan was not so busy, and when I showed some interest, he was happy to tutor me.

He taught me the Law according to Bet Shammai. Did that make me a Shammaite? I don't think so. I became quite knowledgeable, probably knew as much Torah as my mother's cousin Imma Shalom, the wife of Rabbi Eliezer, or Beruriah, the wife of the young Rabbi Meir; of course she is the daughter of Rabbi Hananiyah ben Taradyon. But I did not really worry so much about the niceties of Bet Hillel and Bet Shammai. What interested me was the Zealot cause.

Even as a young girl, I heard a lot about the Roman oppression and what should be done about it. Then, when I married Bava, he hardly talked about anything else. There were meetings; once Bava took me, it was a little bit embarrassing, I was the only woman there. They also knew that I was the daughter of Rabbi Dosa ben Harkinas, the staunchest of Hillelites, and they did not like me there. So I never went again, but Bava often told me about the discussions. They were always talking about uprisings and collecting arms and the weakness of the Romans and when the revolt should start and who should do what. But it was just that: talk. I thought that nothing would ever come of it.

Then Bava had to divorce me and I came back to my father's house. For a while I had no contact with anyone talking about throwing out the Romans. But then, one day, when I went to Uncle Yonathan for my daily Torah lessons, Shimeon was there.

"Michal, I think that you may have met this young man?" he asked. He had a mischievous smile on his face.

I was a little taken aback. Shimeon and I had looked at each other surreptitiously, quite a lot really, but we had never talked to each other directly.

"I thought that you might want to talk to Shimeon, because he has a great interest in a subject about which you have talked to me from time to time."

I tried to keep my eye on Uncle Yonathan's face, so as not to glance at Shimeon.

"Yes, Uncle? What subject?"

"Why, the subject of Zealotry. Shimeon is such a keen Zealot, he does not seem to care for anything else."

"Not another one!" But at the same time, Shimeon protested:

"Yes, I do care for many things."

"Indeed. What, for example?" Yonathan teased him.

Shimeon flushed. "Oh, many things. Of course, I care for Torah, certainly. I study Torah with Rabbi Akiva and also with Rabbi Yonathan here...," he turned to me, he was telling these things to me! "And I study the events of the past, the deeds of the Hasmoneans, the Maccabees..."

I turned to him directly, for I never cared for the niceties of polite society.

"And the Zealots?" I asked him.

"Yes, those too." Again, he answered me directly. As I found out later, he cared even less about the rules of society than I did.

"So do you go to their meetings?"

That question surprised him. He did not know how to answer. I continued, to encourage him.

"I used to go to their meetings. Well, I really went only once. But my husband went regularly. You know that I was once married?"

His face became quite red.

"Yes, I was told..." He hesitated. "I do go to the meetings sometimes."

"How do you like them?"

"Not so much. Lots of talk, little action."

"That's what I thought when I went."

"But that may change now."

"Really?" I looked at him. "How?"

"Oh, I don't know. We shall see." I kept looking at him, and so did Uncle Yonathan. Shimeon mumbled: "There may be a new leadership."

Yonathan smiled: "With a certain Shimeon bar Kosiva playing an important role, perhaps?"

Shimeon averted his eyes from both of us.

"We shall see."

*　*　*

But from that time on, Shimeon and I found opportunities to talk to each other briefly, in corners where we were not observed. We had a common interest, and without Uncle Yonathan there, he was willing to tell me more about his friends.

"They want to make me their leader," he confided in me. "Seems that I am the first to talk in terms of practicalities."

"What kind of things?"

"Well, you know, not only what should be done to the Romans, but, specifically, what are we going to do next year, next month, next week."

"Next week? Don't tell me you are going to attack the Romans next week?"

"No, no, of course not. But if we want to do something next year, or even in two years, we have to start preparing for it now. With specific actions, not just talk."

"Give me an example."

He hesitated. Then he nodded, apparently deciding that I could be trusted.

"Arms. We must collect arms, build up a vast storehouse of arms."

"Where can you get arms?"

"Do you know that many of the arms the Romans use are actually made here, in Judaea, by our own people?"

I did not know that.

"Yes, and sometimes the Romans reject them, if they are not satisfied with the quality. Then our arms-mongers melt them down and start again."

I looked at him "Do you mean that we should…"

"Yes! We should keep them! And we should make many arms with defects, to make sure the Romans reject them. You know, it is enough if they don't like the finish, if they find a blemish, even though the weapons may work perfectly. The Romans reject them, our people take them back, and we store them in a warehouse. Perhaps underground," he added.

The way he talked, I knew that now we were discussing real things, not ideas. The arms-smiths were already making the faulty arms, Shimeon was already taking them somewhere, there might already be underground facilities.

And I knew something else.

I knew that Shimeon would be my husband.

*   *   *

He talked to me about the Zealot movement in Eretz Yisrael and in the Diaspora.

"What do you think, Michal, what happened to all the Zealots who fought the Romans, after the war?" he asked me one day.

"Why, have they not all perished in Jerusalem?"

"Certainly not. Have you not heard of Masada?"

"Of course, I heard. Do you take me for an uneducated girl? They took over a fortress of Herod's."

"Yes, and defended it for three years after the fall of Jerusalem. At the end, the Romans surrounded the hill and built a ramp, and there were so many of them, there was no chance of resisting."

"Yes, and so all the Jews perished. Or was anyone taken into captivity?"

"No, they all killed themselves. The Romans found nothing but dead bodies."

I shuddered. "Tell me, why is this such a great secret? Why is there nothing about it in the Gemarah?"

"Ask your father. Maybe they want us to forget what the Romans did to our people."

I did not reply to that but thought that he might be right. Then I turned to him.

"So you see, the Zealots did all perish, after all. Either in Jerusalem, or at Masada."

"No, my daughter, not all. Many Zealots survived. They left Eretz Yisrael, they escaped, all of the original ones."

"Where? I suppose to Babylonia?"

"Babylonia? No, why?"

"Why? Is that not the place where everyone escaped, everyone who could, Babylonia, Mesopotamia, places in the Parthian Empire? Where the Romans could not lay their hands on them?"

"Maybe the wise old sages escaped there, some of them, but not the fighters." He said this quite proudly, as if he were one of them. "They all went to places where the Romans were in charge."

"Where?"

"Mainly, to Africa. To Alexandria, other places in Egypt, and further west, to Cyrenaica and so on. Also, to Cyprus. Some went to Greece, but not many. Even to Rome."

"And what are they doing there? Are they still alive, still active?"

"Yes, indeed. They are doing more than we are doing here. I am constantly in touch with them, and it could be that the real action will start somewhere in Africa, before it starts here. Or, if we do our work well, perhaps it will start at the same time…"

I knew that I could look forward to an interesting life.

*   *   *

But don't think that Shimeon spent all his time organizing a revolt. No, he was still a Torah student, spending much time with his master, Rabbi Akiva, learning Torah and interpretation from him and, strangely, perhaps teaching him something, too. Teaching Rabbi Akiva? you ask, incredulously. Well, not really teaching, but Shimeon, through his constant harping on the theme of rejecting Roman rule, may have encouraged Rabbi Akiva to reject the Hillelite orthodoxy as well, at least as far as Roman rule was concerned.

It was in those days that Rabban Gamaliel insulted Rabbi Yehoshua ben Hananiyah again, one time too many. The sages, Akiva first among them, decided that enough was enough, Gamaliel had to be deposed. They invited Eleazar ben Azariyah to take over. Eleazar was safely married by that time, a rich scholar of eminent stature in learning and in aristocratic lineage – he was a descendant of Ezra. His hair was already white, he was fifty-one years old. He asked for time to consult with his wife, Miriam, who was not enthusiastic about the prospect. She warned that he who can be promoted may also be deposed later. That did not bother Eleazar, though, and eventually he accepted the offered position.

Curiously enough, Gamaliel behaved more nobly than could be expected, and this surprised the whole leadership. He continued to attend the sessions, meekly, as a simple member. After one further debate with Yehoshua – a debate that the poor but wise Rabbi won – Gamaliel realized how much respect Yehoshua commanded in the Sanhedrin; he decided that formal apologies were due, and offered them to Yehoshua. That kind, ugly, old man was reluctant to accept them, and did so only in honor of Gamaliel's illustrious ancestors.

After that, Yehoshua suggested that the role of Nasi be restored to Gamaliel. The sages, too, gradually came around to that view, Akiva resisting it to the last moment. Was that Shimeon's influence? Honor was maintained for Eleazar ben Azariyah, who was offered the opportunity to teach one Shabbat out of four, while Gamaliel taught on the other three Shabbat days.

Akiva was, in any case, quite busy with matters of politics, and certainly did not involve himself with zealotry; but he must have been aware of Shimeon's activities. Perhaps he did not fully approve of them.

But Shimeon liked the turn of events.

"See, Michal, they are coming around to seeing the situation the right way."

"Who is? What situation? What way?"

"Why, the sages. Your father and his friends. The Sanhedrin."

"They see something differently?"

"I think they do. They won't be so willing to appease the Romans. Maybe your father would, but he no longer has influence there."

That was brutal, but certainly the truth. He continued.

"And Gamaliel is finished, even if he has the title again. The person really in charge will soon be Akiva."

"Don't be so sure," I retorted. "What about Yehoshua? What about Eleazar? What about Tarfon? And Ishmael ben Elisha?"

"Well, Yehoshua is getting on. And he is a modest man. So is Eleazar. They are all modest. Tarfon may be the power behind the throne, as they say, but I have the impression that in their clashes with Akiva, increasingly it is Akiva who comes out ahead. They are the best of friends, anyway."

After a short pause he added:

"Ishmael ben Elisha, yes, he is now considered one of the greatest sages. All right, he does not like the Romans, no problem there. But I think that Akiva is stronger. They find so many ways to oppose each other. Yet, somehow, they still have great respect for each other."

"But Akiva likes Rabbi Tarfon more?" I asked him.

"Yes, he loves Tarfon as much as he loves Yehoshua. You know, it's interesting about Bet Shammai. Tarfon used to be closer to Bet Shammai than Akiva. He was even punished for that. But these days it is Akiva who is getting closer to our views."

"*Our* views?"

"My views, then. And of course, that of your uncle. And Rabbi Eliezer's."

*   *   *

When Shimeon asked me to marry him, two years after my grandfather's death, I did not know what to do. Of course I wanted to marry him, I wanted that since I first set eyes on him six years earlier. But he asked me, not my father. So did Bava, but at that time I was a strong-headed girl, and now I should have been a calm and wise woman. Yose, you must know that your aunt may have been well-educated, but she was not wise.

Still, I had to say something to Father, Mother. I asked for permission to speak to them.

"Father. Mother. I have been asked to marry. I know that he should have asked you, but I think he is afraid of you. And I love the young man. I ask for your permission to marry him."

"Marry whom?!" my father roared. Mother patted his hands. Of course he knew.

"Shimeon bar Kosiva. The nephew of Rabbi Eleazar of Modi'in," I added.

"And who is this man?" As if he did not know.

"He is a scholar, a student of Torah. He is a disciple of Rabbi Akiva." That should have been the final argument.

"And a disciple of Rabbi Yonathan ben Harkinas?"

"Yes, that too, Father."

"And what does he learn from Rabbi Yonathan? The 'Law' according to Bet Shammai."

"Which is 'the voice of the living God,' even if the Halakhah is according to Bet Hillel," I interposed impertinently, quoting the Heavenly Voice once heard, or so they say. My father glared at me.

Mother whispered into his ears. He was quiet for a while.

"And what would you do after marrying this... this Shimeon?" he asked.

"With my father's permission, we would live here in this house for a while, until Shimeon will have some money to buy our own." It was a big house. He did not seem to mind that. Maybe he thought that he would have some influence over Shimeon. Of course, he should have known better.

"Well, what do you want from me? You did not ask my opinion when you married the first time. I would have told you what I thought (actually, I *did* ask him, and he *did* tell me what he thought, but there was no point reminding him of that), it would have saved you from all that trouble, all that embarrassment..." I interrupted: "But you could not have known...", but Mother shut me up quickly.

"Don't speak, girl, when your father is talking. He is right, he would have given you the right advice. But you are grown-up now."

There was quiet in the room. Father sighed.

"You have my permission. You can both live here. And may the Lord bless this marriage of yours."

And so He did. I think that our marriage was blessed, even if not with children.

*   *   *

Shimeon continued to study. He and Akiva became ever closer friends, but Shimeon was never recognized as a major scholar. I don't think that he ever craved that distinction. He was building the resistance, collecting arms, preparing underground storage facilities and talking with his friends about the upcoming revolution.

He was getting nowhere.

It seems that there just were not enough people in Eretz Yisrael willing to take up arms. The Roman army was strong, and no matter how much weaponry we collected, how many hiding places we dug, it seemed foolish to think that a successful war could be waged.

Shimeon had many discussions about this with his mentor, Rabbi Akiva. He was not unrealistic, he accepted the older man's advice. But he was frustrated. On one occasion, I overheard part of their discussion (Akiva did not want me in the room when they debated such matters).

On this occasion they were talking about the Messiah, about when he would be coming. Shimeon asked Akiva:

"My Master, but are you sure that the Messiah will come in our life-time?"

And Akiva answered confidently:

"Shimeon, I am certain of that. He will come and liberate us while you are still a young man."

Yes, that was the answer Shimeon wanted to hear. But he wanted to draw Akiva out still further.

"And you don't think that we are supposed to wait, sit back and do nothing?"

"We must not hasten the coming of the Messiah. You know that. But there *are* things that we can do, that we should do."

Shimeon asked eagerly.

"Yes, master? What things?"

"The more we observe the Law of the Lord, the more we study Torah," Akiva answered, "the better people we become, so the faster he will come."

Shimeon sounded disappointed.

"But are we not supposed to start fighting the oppressors on our own?"

"No, my son, not now. You have to know when to fight and when to negotiate."

"And now is the time to…"

"To negotiate. To allay their fears. Don't expect the Messiah to come and help you when you can do no more than collect a ragtag army against the might of the Roman Empire. The Lord will perform miracles for you, but only if you make such miracles possible."

*   *   *

We had a good marriage, over the years, Shimeon and I, but our life was not entirely fulfilled. For one thing, I was not blessed with a child.

That worried me to no end. I remembered the stories about my father, how he sent his first wife away for being barren. More than once I asked Shimeon:

"You will want another wife, won't you? One who can give you a son?"

And he always assured me:

"Michal, I want you for my wife. Only you."

"You won't send me away then? Like my father sent his first wife away?"

"No, Michal, never. I want you with me, always."

"But the Shammaites don't object to a man having a second wife. Maybe you'll get another woman, perhaps a younger one, for a second wife, and she will give you lots of children."

"No, Michal, no. Understand that I don't want anybody else. I want you, always. I love you." And he held me strongly in his arms.

Every time he calmed me down. Slowly, I came to believe him.

But he was unhappy because the revolution was somehow not material-izing. He could not find enough people to support the cause. The Romans appeared to get stronger, not weaker, at least in Eretz Yisrael.

Gradually, it became clear that the liberating war must start in the Diaspora, probably in Africa. Shimeon had discussions with two leaders from Cyrenaica, two brothers, Pappus and Julianus, who came to visit us one day. Very pleasant men, both of them, though quite unlike each other. Julianus was tall, thin, good-looking, while Pappus was shorter, stockier, with an easy smile on his face. They wore expensive clothes, acquired, I think, in Alexandria. They were the ones who eventually convinced him that he must travel to Cyrenaica, to Libya, be instrumental in starting the action there.

Pappus explained:

"Look, Shimeon, it will be very difficult to start it here. The leadership in Yavneh is very strong, and it supports the Roman occupation fully."

I found myself commenting on that. I know that I should not have, I should have been grateful that they did not send me out of the room, but by then Shimeon considered me a full partner.

"You misunderstand them. They don't support the occupation. They detest it as much as any Jew, anywhere. But they are trying to make the best of a bad situation, and they hope that time will be on their side."

The men were slightly surprised; Julianus responded, looking at Shimeon, not me.

"I understand the family connections. Still, they are wrong. Don't misunderstand me, I don't consider them traitors, like some people in Egypt. But if we'll just wait for the Romans to go away, they never will."

Pappus took over.

"You could not start the war in Egypt, just as you could not start it here, because of the influence of the wealthy Jews. They collaborate with the Romans and with the local Greeks. They will report you to the authorities, to make sure that there will not be trouble, and that the Romans will see what good citizens they are," he added bitterly.

"And in Cyrenaica?" asked Shimeon.

"In Cyrenaica there is no wealthy Jewish leadership. There everybody is against the Romans. Everybody is ready to fight."

Julianus added:

"Most people in Egypt are also on our side. Even in Alexandria. Once the war begins, the leadership is finished, the people will join us. Only it cannot start there."

Shimeon did not disagree with them, and neither did I, for I liked the two brothers. I did not stay in the room all through the discussions, after all, somebody had to bring in refreshments, and I felt that they would be more comfortable with Shimeon alone. But after they left, Shimeon was very thoughtful.

I waited a long while, then went over, embraced him and asked:

"Are you thinking of going there?"

He looked up at me and slowly nodded.

"Maybe I should. Maybe that is where my place is."

I asked him:

"Do you want me with you?"

He seemed surprised.

"If you would come, if you are not afraid…"

"No, I am not afraid of anything. If I can be with you, I am not afraid."

"Michal, there will be a war. Real war. Killing. Blood. Suffering."

"And you will be there. Then, so will I."

*   *   *

All we told my parents was that we wanted to see that part of the world. Even Uncle Yonathan did not really know why we were travelling to Africa, though he may have guessed.

Only Rabbi Akiva knew.

IN AFRICA

It was a beautiful spring day, Yose, when the galley docked at Apollonia. Shimeon managed to send a message about our coming to the two brothers by an earlier boat, so they expected us. When we disembarked, we were met by Julianus, the taller of the two young men. He embraced Shimeon. Then he turned to me with a broad smile.

"Did you have a good trip?" he asked me.

"Very pleasant. Surprisingly smooth."

"And that is even more surprising than you think, Michal. You have not heard, I think, about Antiochia."

"No, I have not heard anything," I replied, while Shimeon asked eagerly, "What about Antiochia?"

"Ah, that is a big question. I'd rather tell you later, when you are nicely settled in. Let's just say that I would have expected a rough crossing, because of Antiochia."

"You want to be mysterious?" Shimeon asked him "No matter, I can wait."

"Good. Let the men load your things on the cart, you sit up front with me, and we'll be on our way."

And soon the mules started to pull the carriage up the hill.

*   *   *

A hot wind was blowing from the south, from the mountains. It was pleasant at first, but as we moved to higher ground, the dry hot air began to bother me. I commented to Julianus:

"Is it always like this? With the hot wind?"

"Yes, I am afraid it is, in the spring. Also, in the fall. It is the Ghibli. You will get used to it."

Well, if I have to, I shall, I thought, and concentrated on the landscape. It was very beautiful. Everything was green. In the distance, not too far, green hills rose; halfway up on one of them we could easily see a lovely city.

"Is that Cyrene?"

"Yes, it is. Nice, beautiful. Pity that it will have to be destroyed."

I looked at Julianus.

"Does it have to be?"

He in turn looked at Shimeon. Then he said:

"We shall have to talk about all of these things. I am glad that you are here. We need someone with new ideas, fresh thinking."

Then he added:

"Let's not talk about such things now. Today is for enjoyment, rest, getting used to this country. Tomorrow, we shall meet and discuss everything."

I used this opportunity to make a point that I had already raised with Shimeon:

"Julianus, would you mind if I were to sit in on the discussions? Will Pappus mind?"

He did not quite know how to reply. He was slightly embarrassed.

"No... I don't think that I'll mind. Or Pappus. It is unusual, but I know that you are an educated woman. We don't have educated women here."

"Because if it bothers you, I don't have to..."

"No, no, do sit in. Do participate. It will be good to have a woman's view."

"I don't really want to participate, just to hear what is said." Shimeon and I had agreed that I should sit in, but I would try to keep my mouth shut.

Julianus then said: "You know, when I said that there were no educated women here, I should have added that there are not many educated men, either. The only people with education these days are those who were at one time sent over to Alexandria, or to Eretz Yisrael. To Yavneh, your town."

"Are there no schools around here?"

"Not for Jews. In the old days, before Yonathan the Weaver, all the rich Jews sent their sons to the best schools. But they were all killed, and ever since, education is only for the Greeks."

"What about the locals? The Libyans?"

"No, not for them, either. Just the Greeks."

*   *   *

The mules pulled our carriage up the hill; in a few hours we were in Cyrene. And what a city it was! I have never seen anything as lovely in my life. Of course, I never saw Jerusalem in its glory: it was destroyed before I was born.

Cyrene was – still is, I suppose – located on a plateau, surrounded by ravines on two sides. There is a cliff to the north, from the bottom of that flows a spring, they call it the Spring of Apollo (again, Apollo!). It meanders over a terrace which was then the Sanctuary of the city, with a very large bath and many temples, most of them sparkling white, honoring all kinds of Greek deities, such as Artemis, Hecate, Isis (was she not Egyptian?), Pluto, and whom have I forgotten? No, you cannot forget him there, Apollo, there was not one, but three temples for him, and one more in the Agora. There were many public buildings, the Augusteum, the Stoa of Zeus, the tomb of Onymastos, the tomb of Battus with a shrine over it, the Caesareum, the Basilica; there was a monumental portico; and further up, on another hill, an unbelievably large temple to Zeus.

Not one of these buildings was for our people. In days to come, I walked on the streets of the city, and the more I walked, the more I hated it. Sure, it was all very grand, very beautiful, but all alien. Worse, all pagan, all devoted to false gods.

Julianus and Pappus had arranged to rent a house for us. It was to the east of the city, just outside the city walls, not far from the Temple of Zeus. Not an especially large house, just six rooms, including a large one for eating and reclining, cooking facilities, all the necessities. It was very clean, with a shining marble floor, very simple mosaics, nothing elaborate. We were quite comfortable there, but Shimeon warned me not to consider the place permanent. I knew that.

Next day, we met at the home of Pappus and Julianus, a much larger house close to where we were located, a house for rich people. I was invited to sit in but made an effort to say almost nothing. There were only the four of us, for neither of the brothers was married.

Julianus was very good-looking, though not nearly as handsome as my Shimeon. Pappus was much shorter, I told you that already; he was not as thin, not as dark, he had a curly brown beard and hair, while Julianus' was almost smooth and black. Yet now I saw that they did resemble each other, the way they laughed – and they laughed a lot.

After we exchanged pleasantries, Pappus told us about Antioch.

"About a week ago, just before you left Jaffa, there was a terrible earthquake there. The entire city is destroyed."

There was a gleam in Shimeon's eyes.

"But that's exactly what's predicted in the 'Sibylline Oracles'!"

"Yes, a first step. But there is more. Rhodes was also hard-hit, perhaps not as severely as Antioch. And other cities in that area. But wait, it gets better still. Do you know who was in the city, in Antioch, at the time? No less a personage than Trajan. Yes, the emperor of Rome."

"Was he killed?"

"Unfortunately, no. He was injured, the first news we had said seriously, but apparently he is going to recover. He had just returned there from his Parthian campaign."

Shimeon was moving around the room, very excited.

"Pappus, these are great news. Don't you think that it might just be the signal we need?"

"That's exactly what we thought. And perhaps that's what our people in Parthia think also."

"Why, has Trajan succeeded in occupying Parthia?"

"Some of it, yes. He has taken Armenia and Northern Mesopotamia. I understand that this year he is trying to take Adiabene and the rest of Mesopotamia, the southern part as well. He may succeed, or might if he had not been wounded. I don't know if that will slow the campaign."

"You think, then, that the Jews in Parthia are ready to resist him?"

"I believe that they are."

"If we could just coordinate our efforts."

"Yes, but that's almost impossible, a special messenger on the best horse cannot make the trip in less than a week, if he gets there at all. We seldom use such a messenger. Sending letters by the caravan routes takes a month or more."

Shimeon thought. "You know, there is a lot to be said for centralizing the command in Eretz Yisrael. From there, you can get messages to Meso-potamia or Babylon in two or three days, and to Alexandria in one day or so. Less than two days to here."

"True," said Julianus, "but you still have a problem with other key areas. Take Cyprus. Horses won't help you there, you have to travel by sea. Even if you are lucky and there happens to be a fast galley just ready to leave, it will take two days to get there. But sometimes you have to wait for days before you find a ship."

"Are you in touch with our people in Cyprus?"

"Indeed, we are. When we'll attack, they'll attack."

"You certainly seem to be well organized, my friends."

"We think we are," said both of them in unison and grinned smugly.

"But let's get practical. You say that your people here are ready to attack. So are those in Cyprus. I assume that the same goes for Alexandria?"

"Yes, and the rest of Egypt, although there are difficulties there. Some of our people are hotheads, we have to hold them back, to prevent them from doing something foolish. And, at the same time, the leaders are desperately trying to talk us out of it, they prefer to maintain the status quo."

Pappus added: "They like the Greeks, if not the Romans. They behave like Greeks. You look at them, you would not know that they were Jews."

Julianus continued:

"Why, even their names are all Greek now. Jason and Isidorus and Theophilos. Isidora. Zosimeter."

"And Pappus and Julianus," I cut in with a smile. "I am sorry."

"Yes, but those are Latin names, not Greek," commented Julianus, but he smiled too. "Our parents hate Greeks as much as any Jew does, but perhaps they don't hate the Romans so much. Or did not when we were born. Yet both of us were born after the war."

"And, of course," said Pappus, "our parents are from Alexandria. They are not from here."

That explained things for me, such as their aristocratic demeanor: such families had all been murdered in Cyrenaica some forty years earlier, and in forty years new upper classes could not have developed.

"For that matter, what about Lucuas?" asked Shimeon.

"Yes, that's another Greek name. He is our leader. Believe me, there is nothing Greek about him. You shall see," Pappus assured us.

"But he is from here, is he not? From Cyrenaica?"

"Yes, he is the real thing. You will be impressed by him."

"When shall I see him? I thought he might be here today."

"He is away, talking to our people in Ptolemais and Teucheira. He should be back in a few days."

Shimeon drummed his fingers on the table. I knew that he was impatient, but did not know how to get around that problem. Then he said:

"I really want to see him. We must discuss timing. Don't you think that this Antioch situation, the wounding of Trajan, should be utilized? Perhaps we should act faster than originally planned?"

"Perhaps. We shall discuss it with Lucuas."

Julianus added: "Meanwhile, tomorrow, we shall go for a ride in the countryside."

"A ride?!" Shimeon seemed almost angry. "Surely there are more important…"

"No, no, this is part of the program that we planned for you. There are things we want you to see. Believe me, it is important."

*   *   *

Next day the mule-drawn carriage was brought up again, and we were taken to the countryside. It was a very pleasant ride.

Most of the fields were lush green, yet some were conspicuously fallow, wasted. I asked Julianus about those.

"I think they have recently been ravaged by sheep."

"Sheep? I have not seen any sheep."

Julianus turned to our mule-driver.

"Nehemiah, where are the sheep?"

Nehemiah shrugged.

"They are now all up the mountains. We don't care, not any more."

That interested Shimeon.

"Why do you say that? But before you answer, tell me: are you a Jew? With a name like Nehemiah, you must be."

"I am a Jew like you," replied the man. "I was a farmer, tenant farmer. But the Greeks stole away my tenancy, and now I do what I can to make a living for my family, and I don't always succeed in getting them enough food on the table."

We waited in silence for a while. Then Nehemiah sighed and continued.

"We used to have lots of trouble with the sheep, they were down here in the winter, their owners were rich, bought up the best fields and the sheep ate up everything. But now it is no longer our concern, let the Greeks worry about that."

He was a weather-beaten man, looked eighty years old, yet I thought that he might not even be fifty. Eventually I learned that he was forty-seven.

We were riding by houses, little houses built of mud brick, a few of stones such as we were used to seeing at home. None of them were large enough to contain even two rooms. I asked who lived in these houses.

Nehemiah answered again.

"These are the houses of the Jews. We all live in small houses in the countryside. Almost nobody has a big house."

Shimeon asked Julianus:

"What about the middle group? I know that the richest Jews were massacred, but there must have been a middle group?"

"You are right, there is still a small group, a few thousand people who live in the cities. They are tradesmen, and they are great supporters of our cause. Really, all the Jews are, at least here, in Cyrenaica."

Nehemiah added:

"And we all support our country, Eretz Yisrael, when we can. Which is seldom, for nobody around here has any money."

"Yes, that's true. They all support the Land of Israel, and Nehemiah, I know that you have sent money there before," Julianus commented.

"Well, maybe once or twice. We have sent in the Poorman's Tithe during the Sabbatical Year, so that the needy in the Land of Israel might be sustained."

Shimeon asked:

"Tell me, Nehemiah, about the loss of your tenancy."

He thought a little.

"Well, you know, we all lived in the countryside, Jews from Eretz Yisrael. Well, not all, as Master Julianus here says, some live in the cities, but I don't count them. They are just craftsmen. We are different. We were brought here, our fathers were, to defend this country, I don't know who is the enemy, but then we all became farmers. You see, new immigrants could only acquire land tenancy far out from the cities. Those who lived in the cities were all craftsmen of some sort, as I said, you know that kind of person," and he spat.

Then he went on. "Working the fields, a man could eventually ask for citizenship. Quite a few of us got it. We thought that citizenship would make us equal with the Greeks. Ha!"

"What went wrong?" asked Shimeon.

"We did not own the land. The owners always bought and sold, always played tricks. There were the rich Roman landlords, they made deals with the owners of the huge sheep flocks, half the land became unusable. For the rest, when the land changed hands, they took the tenancy away, gave it to the Libyans. And the Greeks were just laughing."

"Was there no place one could turn for help?" I asked.

"Help? Ha! There were the Roman authorities. They set up a commission to study our complaints. They made a few changes, some of our people regained their tenancy. Then our people were attacked by the Greeks. That's when they really started to hate us. No, I think we've hated the Greeks and they've hated us much longer than that, for a hundred years or more. But that made the hatred much worse."

Julianus added:

"The tension is quite intense now. You know that there have been clashes between us and the Greeks everywhere. Here and in Alexandria and in Syria…"

"And also in Judaea, for instance in Caesarea."

"Yes. But here, when a Jew and a Greek pass each other in the city, you can feel the tension, both fear that something might happen."

"Well, perhaps something should happen, quite soon."

"Perhaps." Julianus nodded. "The Jews are getting desperate. Tell them about the taxes, Nehemiah."

The man up front thought again, before speaking.

"Well, you know that we all have to pay the Jewish tax."

"Yes, I know that."

"Yes. It's what used to be the half-shekel we paid every year, for the maintenance of the Temple. But when they destroyed the Temple in Jerusalem, they insisted that we keep paying a tax, but to them! The Romans. They called it the *didrachmon*, but now it is simply the Jewish tax. But wait, that's not all."

So we waited.

"The Temple tax was paid only by men, only when they became twenty years old, and only until the age of fifty."

"And this new tax?"

"We pay it until we die. Even women have to pay it, until age sixty-three. And we all have to start, you know when? At age three!"

"And how much is the tax?" asked Shimeon.

"Yes, that's the other thing. It is not how much the tax is, it is that we earn so little money. Why, to pay the tax just on himself, a labourer must work for four or five days. Then there is the tax on his wife, and all of his children, at least those who are still alive at age three. So don't be surprised that many of us are starving."

Julianus nodded. "And it is not only the financial burden, bad as it is. This tax marks our people as despised foreigners who are constantly punished for something that we did not do."

"Citizens, too?"

"Yes, citizens, too. We are a defeated nation, whatever citizenship we have, and we are constantly humiliated. Those who insisted that they were first and foremost proud Cyrenaican citizens, and Jews only second, were the leading classes, and they are now gone. Murdered these many years."

"Yes, I know."

We moved on. There was quiet in the carriage for a while.

We watched the rolling hills.

Julianus spoke after a while.

"Pity. This is a beautiful country. It is so fertile. All kinds of produce grow here, with very little effort."

"Yes, and lots of animals, they seem to be doing very well." Shimeon commented.

"Now, that you mention it," I observed, "yes, there are plenty of cattle, horses, poultry, and I suppose many sheep up the hills. But I don't see any camels."

Nehemiah answered: "No camels here. Every once in a while a caravan passes through, with camels, but they never stay here. I don't know why."

I remembered some discussions from my childhood.

"You know, all the produce, all the animals, they are quite well known in Judaea. My father – you realize that he does a lot of shipping business, at least he did when he was younger – he always talked about Cyrenaican livestock, Cyrenaican grain, Cyrenaican dried fruit and so on."

"Yes," Pappus nodded, "we have everything here. It could have been a wonderful country."

Nehemiah spoke again.

"You know, sir, I think that there must be a war. We all think that."

I knew that Shimeon did not disagree with that sentiment, but he was still surprised to hear it from our mule-driver.

"Why do you say that, Nehemiah? Don't you think that the problems could be solved some other way? Negotiations perhaps?"

"Bah! You can't negotiate with arrogant people like that. We must fight them, show them who is stronger."

"And are you sure that we are stronger?"

"We are stronger if we do this right."

"How do we do it right?"

"You tell us. That's why you are here, is it not?"

How can you respond to a statement like that? Shimeon reached forward, took the man's hand and said:

"I shall try to do my best, my friend. We all shall."

THE STRATEGIST

Well, Yose, we met Lucuas two days later.

We were invited to Pappus' and Julianus' house. We arrived, and there was the great man himself.

Lucuas was tall, not quite as tall as Shimeon, but broad-shouldered. His face was very hard, his forehead high and lined, and his beard dark, with just a few white hairs. He was friendly enough. I did not like him, but I could not say why.

Pappus introduced us.

"Lucuas, this is Shimeon bar Kosiva, from Judaea, and his wife Michal bat Dosa."

"Welcome, welcome." His voice was booming and self-confident. "Did you have a good trip?"

"Very pleasant, thank you."

"Good. Well, we are going to be busy here. Things are going to move faster than we planned originally, so we have no time to lose. Are you all settled in?"

"Yes, we are very comfortable," answered Shimeon.

"Good. Are you ready? Can we start our discussion immediately?"

"I am ready."

"Good." He said that a lot. "We shall sit in the next room. We won't be long today, Michal, an hour or two. Will you wait, or go home?"

I swallowed.

"Would you mind if I sat in with you? I won't interfere."

He looked surprised.

"I don't think that's a very good idea. There will be things that we want to discuss freely. No, you better stay out. I am sure you won't mind."

He did not wait for an answer, but went straight to the next room. The others looked at me, embarrassed, Shimeon spread his arms apologetically, but they all followed Lucuas and closed the door.

What was I to do? There were no other women in the house, none that I could see, although there may have been some women servants. I felt hurt. I thought that I would wait until they came out; then I would look at him in such a way that he could see how unfairly he'd treated me. But then it occurred to me that he would notice absolutely nothing in my looks, no matter how hard I stared at him.

No, it was better to go home and wait there, and that is what I did.

When Shimeon came home, many hours later, he was a little confused.

He did not know whether to apologize to me, explain, or rave about his new boss. He chose to do the latter.

"Michal, you should have seen this. Finally, here is a man who can make decisions. He is not afraid, he is not worried about what the Romans will say, or do. He knows what needs to be done, and he is willing to go ahead and do it."

"Perhaps pulling his assistants down with him, along with the entire people."

"No, he is not stupid. Certainly not stupid. I know that you are annoyed, but it is true that he really would not have been able to discuss things the way he did, if you were there. Maybe later, when he gets to know you better…"

"That will never happen. But it's all right, don't worry. I'll manage. Are you willing to tell me what you discussed? Or is it a big secret?"

"No secret at all, not from you. He did not make me promise to keep these things from you."

"How nice of him."

"Yes, well, he is different from the people we have known before. In any case, you asked what we discussed. It went like this:

"Strangely enough, he did not start by assuming that the revolution is inevitable. He threw the discussion open as to why there should be a revolution at all."

"Why, is it not obvious to everyone?"

"I would have thought so. Of course it is. But he says that he wants to make sure that we all see things the same way. So he asked each one of us why there should be a revolution."

"So what did you all say?"

"First, Julianus stressed the Zealot beliefs. You know, that only God has sovereignty, our commitment to liberty, our belief that God will help us if we are willing to fight, our resistance to any Roman census imposed on us to establish who pays taxes and, most important, that the law obligates every one of us to undertake personal and direct action against the oppressors."

"But those are your own arguments. So what did you say yourself?"

"In a moment. But Pappus spoke next. He also stressed the current situation in Africa and elsewhere, the suffering of the Jewish people under the Romans and the Greeks. He said that because of that, revenge is absolutely necessary. Revenge and liberation."

"Of course, but that is not a strong enough argument."

"Not by itself, no. But with everything else, together… Well, in any case, then it was my turn, and I had a whole set of arguments not mentioned before. I told them that we must always remember what is written in the Scriptures. We did remember Daniel's prophecy before, we knew that the Temple would be destroyed, we knew exactly when that was going to happen, and lo, it did. Now there are other prophecies, those of Amos and Hosea, Isaiah and Ezekiel. Each talks about the Lord helping our people to reestablish our land in freedom, under the House of David, the King. Each talk about the ingathering of the exiles. Many talk about the Messiah, Son of David, who will be with us in those days. We all believe that those days are here, these are the sufferings, these are the final days that the Prophets have described."

"Was there any disagreement?"

"No, none at all. I added that I was convinced the Messiah is here with us today but will not help us if we won't help ourselves. We must show that we are willing to fight. We must take the initiative."

"They all agreed?"

"Yes, they did. Then Lucuas asked us if there were arguments for starting the war right now, this year, as opposed to, say, two or three years hence."

"Were there any?"

"Yes. First Pappus talked about utilizing the current fervent, the unusually strong sentiment against the Greeks, here and also in Egypt. Then I brought up the special situation regarding the latest news about the Romans."

"You mean the Emperor in Antioch?"

"Yes, his being wounded in the earthquake. The city being destroyed there. Other Roman cities being devastated. And their preoccupation with the war in Parthia. Lucuas added that he heard of one of the Roman legions, or at least some detachments of it, being withdrawn from Egypt and sent to Parthia. So this must be the ideal time."

"And again, they all agreed?"

"Yes, they did. And then Lucuas summarized by saying that he thought the current situation, if we handled it right, would not only lead to the liberation of Eretz Yisrael, but to the total defeat of the Roman Empire."

"Do you believe that?"

Shimeon thought for a while.

"You know, when he talked, I believed it fully. Now I am not so certain. But that does not matter. The main thing is that they should be gone from our land. What they do elsewhere is not our business. But it is interesting how Lucuas carries one along with his convictions."

"Yes, a strong man, no doubt. Then what happened?"

"Then he assigned responsibilities. Pappus will have to make sure that there is a sufficient supply of arms and all the other provisions needed. Julianus will be responsible for training all the people."

"And you?"

"I shall be the main strategist."

"What does that mean?"

"It means, I shall have to plan the entire war in detail, step-by-step, working together with Lucuas, of course. And with everybody. I shall also help Julianus with the training, you know that I have experience with that kind of thing. I also have some experience with obtaining and stockpiling arms and supplies…"

"Would you have preferred to do that?"

"No, for my job is the most important of all, I think. But I shall be involved with all aspects of the war."

Shimeon was glowing with pride and excitement. I decided to forget about my resentment, at least for the time being.

* * *

Shimeon usually worked at Pappus' and Julianus' house. It was so much larger than our house, with lots of room for a strategist to surround himself with papyrus and people and who knows what else. The brothers also had a few servants, while we had none. We could have afforded some, but I felt that hiring servants – necessarily Jewish ones, if only to make sure that no secret gets out – would create a bad impression. I had no other occupation, so I did all the cleaning and washing and cooking, it was not very difficult.

We became very friendly with Julianus and Pappus (I have to make an effort to call them so, everybody always said 'Pappus and Julianus,' even though I believe that Julianus was the older one). We were their guests quite often. They also came to our house many times.

Through the brothers we got to know the other members of the local Jewish leadership, half a dozen men looking after day-to-day activities, such as teaching the children, collecting taxes (on behalf of the community, not tax farmers like in Judaea), a medical man and two who knew their way around the government sufficiently to arrange difficult things or help minimize the effect of unfavourable edicts. Each of these people also had a role in organizing the war effort.

We also met the wives of these men. They were nice women, pleasant and very simple. None of those women was educated or involved in political activities the way I would have liked to be. They were busy with their families. Such is life.

Of course I sat in on all the meetings with the two brothers. Once I wanted to participate in a discussion with a couple of lower-ranking leaders, but Shimeon discouraged me, told me that these people would not feel comfortable with a woman there. I did not argue much.

One strange thing: Shimeon talked more and more about Messianic times. The subject came up in almost every discussion. He insisted that we could take risks, because the Messiah would be fighting with us. Pappus and Julianus (it's easier to write it this way) did not, of course, disagree, how could they? But they seemed to feel that Shimeon put too much reliance on the Messiah. On one occasion they argued with him.

Julianus said: "Shimeon, of course the Messiah will help us. But you should not take risks unnecessarily."

"What's unnecessary?" Half-smile, arms spread out wide, in a questioning gesture.

"I tell you what. Would you lead your troops to the edge of a high precipice, and tell them to jump off, along with yourself, because the Messiah would be there and would teach you to fly?"

"Of course not. That's silly. Men cannot fly, with the Messiah or without."

"But to rush into battle against a force maybe ten times as large as yours, is that reasonable?"

I remembered what he had said about the nymph Cyrene fighting with a lion, about not entering battles if you were not convinced that you could win. He remembered, too, I am sure. He said:

"No, again, I would never do that. I would never lead my troops into battle unless I was confident of winning. But that does not mean we have to be always as many as, or more than, the enemy. If we are better prepared, better armed and better motivated, we shall win against a larger force. Surely you can see that?"

Pappus hesitated: "Yes, I accept that. But how far can we put our faith into arms, preparation, motivation? How much more numerous can the enemy be and we can still prevail?"

"Ah, but that's where the Messiah comes in. We must have faith in him and in the Lord who sent him."

"But not unreasonable faith, surely?" asked Pappus. "Not against an enemy with ten times more men. So where do you draw the line? Twice as many? Three times as many?"

Shimeon had a certain way of jerking his head to one side when he was annoyed. I recognized that movement now, Pappus perhaps did not.

"Friends, don't force me to give you such a number, because I would regret it later. It depends on so many things, the location of the battle, the access roads, the surrounding area, the population there, hundreds of things. But more than that, I think it depends on how the leader feels, if he senses that the Lord is with him. Then he does not need to worry about counting troops."

The brothers were not quite convinced, but they did not want to argue the point further.

We also discussed how war could be avoided, how a peaceful resolution might be achieved. Actually, I initiated that discussion. I was not afraid of war (yet I should have been, if I had only listened to my grandfather more closely, when he told me about the horrors of the earlier war). But I thought that all alternative plans should be explored. Just to please me, Shimeon let me ask such questions in meetings; he would not ask them himself, did not want to appear hesitant or weak.

Several times I asked questions like, "Would the Romans not stand up for the Diaspora Jews, protect them from the Greeks, if they knew how high the stakes were?"

And they would explain that it was just not possible to forewarn the Romans in any way, the element of surprise must at all costs be maintained.

And I asked about the fate of the enemy, if we succeeded in conquering him. They did not say what would happen to individual soldiers, but I thought they were sure all would be killed.

Then I asked about the children, and one of the brothers, I don't remember which, said that they would not kill children just because they were Greek; but if they got in the way, in a battle, anything could happen, we would not have time to watch out for them, protect them. When I asked them why children would be in the battlefield, they looked at me with surprise in their eyes and said, "What battlefield?"

*   *   *

So the summer went by, with strategy meetings, often with Lucuas (but without me), collecting of arms, food storage and training. Shimeon was often away for days, assisting Pappus with military training.

One day a messenger brought sad news from home. My father, Rabbi Dosa ben Harkinas, had passed away. May his memory be blessed, I loved

him. We knew that he was not a well man; he had lost his eyesight years
earlier, and gradually he lost most other faculties as well; but he was still
able to arrange some business matters before we left. Now Yonathan, my
uncle, will have to look after those things, and when – may that time be
far off – he will also go, then who? I supposed, correctly, that it would be
my father's son-in-law, Halafta (your father, Yose).

My heart ached for my mother. Shimeon knew, and asked me:

"Would you not like to travel back home, Michal? To be by your mother's side?"

It took some effort for me to reply the way I wanted it to sound:

"No, Shimeon, my beloved, my place is by your side. I shall stay here.
Let Tzviyya take care of our mother."

*   *   *

Mid-summer saw more intense discussions, increased tensions, raised
voices, excitement. The men still loved one another, but the stakes were
high.

On one particular occasion they stopped by at our house, on their
way to who knows where, the brothers and even Lucuas. They came in for
a moment, and ended up having a heated argument right there. I stayed
in the other room, but heard some of it. They were debating land route
versus naval route.

Julianus was arguing for the naval route. He said things like this:

"By splitting up among many vessels, we shall be less vulnerable."

I did not hear the answer to that, but he said again:

"It will be much easier. We won't be all weakened, all spent by the long,
exhausting march."

Then he argued:

"Alexandria shall be ours. We can command the harbor."

I did not hear what Pappus had to say, nor Lucuas' comments, I think he
just listened. It was Shimeon who raised most of the counter-arguments:

"Our people are not used to the sea. They are land fighters."

Later he argued:

"The right ships might not be along at the right time. It might be impossible to organize it that way."

And still later:

"Something might just go wrong in Alexandria. You cannot count on
all steps going smoothly."

Lucuas stopped the debate at that point, suggested that they discuss

Alexandria separately, the following day. They all left then, I don't know where they went.

When Shimeon came home in the evening, I asked about the arguments. He told me that the land route was chosen, at least as far as Alexandria.

"But please explain. How many people will go by land? And why do you say 'at least as far as Alexandria'? I thought that the target *was* Alexandria, but are we going to board ships there?"

"Everybody is to go, first to..."

I interrupted.

"Everybody?"

"Yes, a new Exodus. From Cyrenaica and also from Egypt. We are going home. To Eretz Yisrael. All the Jews in Cyrenaica. All the Jews in Egypt. Eventually all the Jews from Cyprus!"

I had to sit down, that was a momentous announcement.

"How long have you known?"

"For a few weeks. I did not want to talk to you about that, not until I was sure it was going to happen. But now it has been firmly decided."

"And when will all this take place?"

"We shall leave here by late fall. Should be in Alexandria by winter and then, with the help of the Lord, reach Judaea in the spring by the sea route."

"But how many people...?"

"Two hundred thousand, three hundred thousand. Maybe half a million. Not all shall travel by sea, many will continue on foot."

"But Shimeon, what will happen to that many people in Eretz Yisrael? Where will you house them? How will you feed them?"

"Not 'them,' Michal, 'us.' We shall be there all along. We shall live in tents, eat whatever food we can gather. We shall live exactly as our forefathers did, when the Lord, blessed be His name, brought us out of bondage in Egypt."

"And how long do you think...?"

"A few years. Until, gradually, the people will be absorbed by the society. But don't forget, it will not be just peaceful sitting around in the tents. We shall have to fight there, too. There are still Romans in Eretz Yisrael. If our battles will go according to plan, the Romans will be greatly weakened, but there are many of them, we shall have to achieve many victories before they decide to give up."

"And if we don't win those battles?"

"Don't say such things, Michal. Of course we shall win. Don't forget that we shall have hundreds of thousands of fighters, most from here and Cyprus, all trained and armed. The Romans are not used to that kind of resistance in Judaea. They will get the shock of their lives. They will suffer defeat after defeat, and in the end they will decide that the cost is just too high. Our land will be liberated."

"Amen."

"And the King Messiah will then rule on the throne of David."

"But where is this King Messiah?"

For the first time Shimeon was slightly unsure of himself.

"He will appear at the right time."

"You don't think that Lucuas…?"

"No… no… not really. Probably not. I have heard such a thing mentioned, once or twice, but somehow that's not how I envision the Messiah."

"How do you envision him, then?"

"More kingly, more just, perhaps more gentle. Yes, gentle, but strong."

"Lucuas is strong."

"Yes, but not gentle. I may be wrong, of course. Time will tell."

*　　*　　*

As the strategy became crystallized and accepted, Shimeon spent more and more time with Pappus, helping him train the people. Until he talked to me about it, I had not realized what a large operation it was. He told me that they were half a day's journey away, in a huge camp, divided into twelve companies, each consisting of about ten thousand fighters. They had been training now for up to three years.

Not all of them were there all the time, of course. They still had to earn a living for their families; and they could not conspicuously disappear for a long time: that might be noticed. But each company was there for two or three days every two weeks, at any one time three companies were training. Thirty thousand men!

"How do you feed them?" I asked him.

"We have a huge amount of food accumulated. Grains, mainly, some dried fruits and nuts. But the people are encouraged to bring their own food with them, what they would eat at home. The poorest ones, who cannot bring their own, request food from the storage and get it. Most of them don't request."

"That many people." I marvelled. "And you said that they are not only from around here, but from all the areas of Cyrenaica?"

"Yes, the largest number of Jews live around Cyrene, but there are also many from Teucheira and Barka and many other places. Ptolemais. El-Bagga. Even Bereneike, and that is quite far."

"That takes some organization. Who looks after that? Pappus?"

"Yes, but mainly Lucuas. He has some good people at every place, they send in the trainees, and await the word."

"The final word?"

"Yes. When to go."

I thought about that for some minutes, while I was busy with preparing his clothes and other necessities for the next training session. I would have liked to see the camp, but that was out of the question.

"What about the Egyptians? What about the Cypriots? Are they also there? At the camp?"

"Actually, the Egyptians are there. At least, many of them, tens of thousands. The Cypriots, no. I understand that they do their own training at home. Lucuas is constantly in touch with them."

"And they will get the signal, to start at the same time as our people here?"

"Exactly. And, of course, the Egyptians will, too. Fighting should start in Alexandria, at the same time, otherwise news of our attack might reach the Romans, who would then take protective measures. It is better if the attack comes as a surprise."

I pondered, tried to imagine how the battles would go. It was a little difficult to picture our people, simple peasants, waging a successful fight against the mighty Roman legions. I said as much to Shimeon.

"No, but you are wrong there, Michal. These are not simple peasants. They are soldiers."

"You mean, by training…"

"Not only that, no. They have been soldiers for generations. Their forefathers were settled here by the Ptolemies, they were in those armies, paid to defend these lands. Those Ptolemaic armies were strong, they knew how to fight. And part of the upbringing of every boy is military training. They are soldiers, believe me. And they not only know how to fight, they also know how to endure."

"You mean deprivations? Hardships?"

"Exactly. Think of the march across Cyrenaica, across Egypt, into Eretz Yisrael."

A thought occurred to me.

"Shimeon, but what about their families? What about the women and children? The old people?"

"Of course we have thought of that. There are many carts available, thousands. Each can take twenty, thirty people, if necessary. Anybody who can walk, shall. The small children, the sick and the old will ride."

He added:

"I wanted to ask you to train yourself in walking. It would not be seemly for the wife of one of the leaders to ride."

"Oh, but I can walk. Of course I would not ride."

"Yes, but this will be heavy walking. All morning, maybe all afternoon, with just a short break at noon. No stopping at all."

"I can do it."

"Do exercise. Walk every day, more and more each day. Make sure that your sandals are strong, that they won't hurt your feet. You know, I am not the only one asking his wife to do that. Tonight, all the men are asking their wives to start walking exercises. The older children as well. Tomorrow, there will be lots of women and children walking in the countryside."

And so there were. Thousands of us walked into the hills, avoiding farms where the Greeks and the Libyans could notice us. We smiled at one another, some women walked in groups of twos and threes. Some single walkers started talking to others. I walked with one woman, then a third joined us. I did not tell them who I was, but listened to stories about their children and their troubles. We did not talk about the coming fight or the march that was rapidly approaching. We just made conversation about nothing in particular, and we walked.

*   *   *

By the fall, about three weeks before the attack, we received disturbing news from Alexandria. A messenger came running, ordering Shimeon to Lucuas' headquarters.

Shimeon came back a couple of hours later, clearly upset.

"What's wrong?"

"The Alexandrian Jews have begun an attack."

"On their own? Prematurely?"

"Yes. And, of course, not everybody, just some of them. It is not clear to us what has happened. There may have been just a few thousand people, maybe ten thousand. They attacked the Romans."

"And then what happened?"

"What do you think? The Romans killed them all. And now there are Roman patrols all over the Jewish neighborhoods, and anybody who is suspicious is arrested. They may have arrested a thousand or two, some of our best people. The idiots!"

I knew that the idiots were not the Romans.

"Shimeon, will this change the plans? We are weaker now in Alexandria, and the Romans may be forewarned. Perhaps the whole thing should be postponed?"

"We talked about that. But it is not practical. Everything is prepared. The people are ready to start. We couldn't just stop the whole thing now. There are still plenty of good people in Alexandria and elsewhere in Egypt. It will be all right."

"But are you sure...?"

"It will be all right," he repeated. "Don't worry."

But I did worry.

REVOLT!

Yose, I shall never forget that Sunday.

Our people poured into the city. They attacked fiercely, cruelly, ferociously. I did not see it myself, for the night before, we were evacuated into the camps. But eyewitnesses came with reports. It was horrible.

They burst into the houses and killed all the men. I was told that often the women, sometimes even the children, fell victim.

They destroyed the houses, even the larger ones. They had ropes and chains and levers, they tore down the walls.

The local Roman detachments came running and riding, but they were no match for our fighters. They were all killed.

By the third day, when there was no more resistance, we attacked (did I write 'we'?) the public buildings. With levers and chains, our soldiers pulled down the walls of those marvellous but pagan temples and monuments. They managed to pull down the huge inner columns of the Temple of Zeus. They even managed to destroy much of the Temple of Apollo in the Sanctuary. I don't quite understand how they could do that. How, not why. Of course, they had to do it, of course they had to destroy all the pagan temples. We Jews have always hated idolatry, always detested those altars, those temples, those images. Well, perhaps not always, but, thank the Lord, for a long time now.

No, I had no quarrel with the destruction of the temples. But why all the houses, and all the men in it? Why even women and children at times?

After the first day, when Shimeon came back to the camp, exhausted, dirty and sad, I was ready to confront him. If he had come with a happy face, victorious, proud, I don't know what I would have done, screamed at him, perhaps. But he looked just tired.

I got him anyway.

"Shimeon! You told me that innocent women and children would not be harmed."

He bowed his head.

"Michal, I could not help it. There was so much hate. They went in to repay centuries of mistreatment, oppression. You should have seen them. The most common word was 'revenge.'"

"Revenge against small children?"

"Actually, it is not true that small children were killed. Maybe a few, but most were just left alone. What bothers me is that where the mother was killed, the children will perish, anyway, with nobody looking after them.

Surely you can't expect that our troops now go around and collect all
orphans, start some kind of institution to look after them? In the middle
of the war?"

"But why were the mothers, the women, killed?"

"Some were. Some of them fought back."

I sat and cried. This was not right. It did not have to be done that
way.

*   *   *

After that first day I got Shimeon to talk with Lucuas, so as to make him
issue orders to spare all children and all women, too, if they didn't fight.

He told me about the meeting, when he got home late at night.

He had confronted Lucuas. Three other leaders were present, people
I did not know. He demanded that orders be issued for the lenient treatment of women and children.

Lucuas was reasonable at first.

"Shimeon, but don't you realize that this is war? You work fast, you
want to save your life, you go from house to house, kill the enemy, and if
someone else happens to be in the way, that is just bad luck."

"Happens to be in the way? They live there."

"Well, what do you want us to do, collect the children and put them
in a protected compound of some kind, before killing their father? I have
never issued orders to kill children."

"But never issued orders to save them, either!"

Lucuas just shrugged. "That's up to the individual fighter. But I tell you
something, Shimeon. What happened today is nothing. Wait until we are
finished here. The whole country will lie in ruins. There will be scorched
earth. Wait until we get out into the countryside."

"You mean, it will be worse?" Shimeon was shocked. This was not part
of the strategy.

"Worse? That is the place which everyone knows, everyone understands.
That is where the real oppressors are, those who stole our lands, those who
made our people work for next to nothing."

Shimeon grabbed his hand.

"Lucuas, my leader. Stop the carnage. Tell them to spare whoever is
not fighting them."

The three others there sniggered. Lucuas turned to them.

"What do you think?"

"Stupid," said one.

"It cannot be done," said another.

I think the deciding comment came from the third:

"Lily-livered," said he.

Lucuas faced Shimeon, looked deeply into his eyes, and said:

"Well, my friend, you will just have to decide. Are you with us, or are you against us?"

Shimeon did not tell me what words he used to assure them that he was with them, but assure them he did and came back to me an even sadder man than earlier that evening, a beaten man.

He explained to me that such things were regrettable, but that in war, one cannot be oversensitive, one cannot worry about details.

And I explained to him that these details were important to me.

"Listen, Shimeon. I cannot do this. I cannot be responsible for senseless killing and cruelty."

He looked truly surprised.

"But you are not responsible, Michal."

"Yes, I am. If my husband kills, I am also responsible. The killing must be stopped."

"But it cannot be. I just explained to you…"

"Find a way. Because I shall not be the wife of a killer."

He just looked at me, not understanding. I explained.

"If you go along with this massacre, I shall have to leave you."

Before he had a chance to reply, I added:

"I shall spend the night with the maidservants of Pappus and Julianus. You can tell me tomorrow what you have decided."

*   *   *

Next morning he came over. I could see that he had not slept. He called me aside and said:

"Michal, you are unreasonable. I thought over what you said. The thing cannot be stopped. This is war. I tried to stop it last night, but it cannot be done."

"Well, then…"

"Wait. Please remember what the Holy One, blessed be He, commanded to our people, in Deuteronomy."

"I remember it very well. He said that you should first offer peace. And if there is no peace, you should go in there and kill all the men, but spare all the women and children. Did He not?!"

"Yes, but He also said something else. He stipulated that with certain nations, closer to home, you must be harsher. You must kill every living soul there. Don't you remember? The Hittites, the Amorites, the Canaanites, the Perizzites, the Hivites and the Jebusites."

I did remember. The Lord did so command; but that was a long time ago. Things change. People change. We were no longer the cruel, war-like nation of old. I told him that.

"And then, there were also the Amelekites: the Lord commanded Shaul, through Samuel, to go in there and slay every man, woman and child, and every animal they owned."

"Did the Lord give such an explicit command to Lucuas?" I asked Shimeon.

Then he chose another approach.

"In any case, you must understand that my loyalty is with Lucuas. He is my leader. He is leading this war against the Romans. We are liberating our people and our land. I must not interfere, for I must not jeopardize the effort. This is the war of the Messiah. This is not a time to be oversensitive."

"Again 'oversensitive'? All right, Shimeon, I loved you, but this is the end."

I walked away from him, went over to the servant women and did not look back. I wanted to cry, to weep, but kept it all in.

When I was at a safe distance, so he could not easily have seen me, I looked back. He was not following me. I sat down, if not to cry, at least to think.

But yes, to cry.

I did that for a long time. I thought even longer.

What could I do? Where could I go?

I sat there all day, and could not think of any solution to my problem.

That evening, after all the men had returned to the camp and the sentries been posted, I sent one of the servants over to the leaders' group with a message: Find one of your masters, either Pappus or Julianus, tell him that I would like to talk with him.

After a while, Julianus came. I went out to meet him. He was a little surprised by my request to see him.

"Julianus, my friend, I need your advice."

"Of course, Michal, anything I can do."

So I told him about my clash with Shimeon. He listened to the end.

"Was I wrong?" I asked him.

He considered it.

"You know, Michal, I think that you were. Not in your argument. I must admit that Pappus and I were quite unhappy with the way things went… Wait a moment, let's discuss this with Pappus. Come with me."

We walked over to the men's compound, outdoors, where the single men slept. Julianus went in and soon came out with Pappus.

"I already told my brother briefly about your problem with Shimeon."

"What do you think, Pappus?" I turned to him.

He did not answer right away. They looked at each other. Pappus sighed and motioned me to sit down on a rock.

"Julianus and I have talked about this for hours, Michal. We are just as upset about the killing as you are. But there are several things to consider."

"Yes, I know. We must not interfere. We must not jeopardize the war effort. I've heard that."

"No, there is more to it than that. One thing is, we are not natives here. You are from Judaea, we are from Alexandria. We are all sensitive, refined people who hate killing."

"Why, don't all Jews hate killing?"

"Apparently not. You have to remember who these people are, the people who live around here. They are all military Jews."

"That's a strange expression."

"Yes, but true. You know that they were brought here as soldiers by the Ptolemies. They are mercenaries, they have been trained for generations to fight, and that means to kill. They don't have the revulsion about blood that you and we have."

"That's sad."

"Sad, yes, but true. Once we get back to Eretz Yisrael, and if things go well and we shall have peace, then in a few generations they should also develop the sensitivity, the abhorrence of killing."

"Or so one would hope," added Julianus.

"Yes. But there is another thing. Or two. They read the Torah. Some cannot read, so others read the Torah for them. And there is plenty of killing in the Torah."

"But those were the old days. I would have thought that we were more humane, less cruel by now."

"It seems that you thought wrong, Michal," said Pappus bitterly. "In any case, they take their Torah seriously."

"But Pappus, the Torah is full of injunctions against cruelty, against killing, against doing to your neighbors that which you would not want them to do to you..."

"Not in a war. No, war is different. The laws are very different."

Julianus added: "And why do you think that these people are so enthusiastic about this war?"

"Why, I suppose for the same reason all of us are. For the opportunity to liberate ourselves and our land, Eretz Yisrael."

"Perhaps. But there is another reason, Michal. The thing that drives them, I fear, is revenge."

"I know. And I don't like it very much."

"Neither do we. This is what Julianus and I discussed for hours this evening."

Julianus added: "You see, one understands the desire for revenge, perhaps. But we don't feel that the punishment is in proportion to the crime."

"You mean the revenge is unjustified."

"Yes, perhaps. These people have been treated unfairly. They have been discriminated against, they were not given citizenship, their children were not admitted into the best schools. Worse, their land, their tenancy was stolen from them, they were forced into penury, deprivation, even starvation at times. They have no rights at all. Every one of them is despised and mocked by the Greeks. But..."

Pappus took over. "Yes, but... But they have not been the victims of killing, massacres. So we feel that the revenge is unjustified. At least unjustified in this form. So we feel like you do. But..."

"Again 'but'?" I asked.

"Yes. The thing is this. You may disagree with your commander, but you cannot interfere with the war effort."

Julianus corrected him: "That does not mean that you have to act as you are commanded in every instance. For instance, if I was told to enter a house and kill everyone there, women, children, old people, I would refuse. But I should also be ready to suffer the consequences of such a refusal."

Pappus continued: "And if you were to disagree totally with the direction your commander took, then you should withdraw from the war, even risk being called an enemy, or a spy. But we don't totally disagree, and neither does your husband."

"So he must go along with the orders of the chief commander, like it or not?"

Again they looked at each other, then slowly nodded.

"I am afraid that may be the case. Shimeon and we shall not commit any cruelty. Neither shall we order our men to do any such things, and, to the extent of our power, we shall prevent unnecessary killings. You know Shimeon well enough to realize that he will do so. But we shall not sabotage this war."

"So you suggest that I accept Shimeon's stand."

"Yes, Michal, accept it. Talk to him. This is his most difficult hour. He does not need your problems added to his own."

We did not get any farther with the discussion. I did not want to hold them back, since it was late. I slept with the servants again and did not see Shimeon the next day. But in the evening I went back to where he was expected, and when he came in, he found me there.

I embraced him.

"Shimeon, my love, forgive me. I know that you could not have done anything else."

He had tears in his eyes and kissed me – he did not say anything, just held me.

*   *   *

After the third day the Roman legions arrived from Egypt.

Two legions were normally stationed there, but part of one was ordered into the Parthian war earlier. A detachment was dispatched by sea – it must have been a fast messenger who alerted them.

They arrived, but we were ready for them. Disembarking at Apollonia, they were met by our fighters. They lost their commander and many others; the rest jumped into the sea and swam to their galley.

By that time, there was little left of Cyrene, the beautiful. All its public buildings lay in ruin, all the temples and statues. I was told that, of all Cyrenaican cities, Cyrene suffered the most complete devastation – of course, most of the Jews lived around there, and the camp was located in that area.

The buildings did not really concern me, but the people certainly did. It is estimated that there were close to three hundred thousand Greek men living in the province, and only about fifty thousand managed to escape, most by sea, towards Alexandria. So over two hundred thousand must have perished during that week – not all of them during those first three days, and not all in the cities.

After the third day, groups of fighters rode out to the countryside, wreaking havoc on the Greeks and Libyans, everywhere. They truly scorched the earth. Whatever was flammable, they burned. They did not leave one man alive, if they could help it. Years later I was told that Hadrian, the emperor who succeeded Trajan at the end of the war, found that he had to import new settlers to marry the women and till the land, because there was almost no one left.

Our people were thoroughly trained, expertly taught. They knew that they were going home, and would not need any land to work on in Cyrenaica. Why there could not be any for others, I am still not quite sure; as they explained to me, when there is a war, you don't ask such questions.

*   *   *

We were ready to start out, but Lucuas wanted to wait for word from Cyprus. It came after one week.

It seems that under Artemion, the Cypriot Jews acted very much as our people did in Cyrenaica. They attacked the Greeks mercilessly, killed all the men, some two hundred and forty thousand. But they did not leave the island; the plan was for them to await the arrival of the African Jews in Eretz Yisrael before ships would be dispatched for them from there.

Frankly, while I hated Lucuas, I also respected him for his coordination of activities on such a large scale. He organized the Jews in all of Cyrenaica, all of Egypt (even if some Alexandrians acted too hastily), and all of Cyprus. He spearheaded the operations from Cyrene, and hundreds of thousand of his people went to war as one.

Yet I made some nasty comments when some people started to call him 'King Lucuas.' King, indeed. I was told that he did not anoint himself king but did not object to the appellation either.

After the news from Cyprus was received, we were given orders to get ready for the march. We were leaving the next morning.

I was shivering with emotion. Hundreds of thousand of Jews were marching through the land, to the east, to Egypt and then home, to Eretz Yisrael. Old people and children on carts and on mules, some on horses or asses. The carts themselves were pulled by mules, or sometimes by the men in the family. It must have been very similar to the original exodus from Egypt!

Indeed, but in the Exodus we were persecuted, yet did not do any killing ourselves. Now we did. As we progressed, we saw that the remaining countryside was devastated, crops burned, farmers massacred.

*   *   *

The march was very hard. We were slowed down by people needing to rest, several times every day. I was very tired but would not sit on one of the carts offered to me. Many of the women did, but that slowed us still further.

It took us twenty-seven days to reach Egypt, another forty days to get close to Alexandria.

ALEXANDRIA

I regret to tell you, Yose, that we left behind a devastated land and arrived in Egypt, to do the same to that country.

When we reached the border, it was already winter. I was told that in Cyrenaica there generally was not much rain, but that year it poured. That made travelling even more difficult. We were slogging though mud, very slowly. When it rained heavily, we stopped and huddled under the carts and canvasses; there was usually not enough time to set up the tents properly.

Yet the people did not complain. They trusted their leader Lucuas, and they saw that everything was progressing as he had promised. At the border of Egypt a number of local Jews, agrarian workers, too, joined us, and we held a celebration. It was Shabbat. We had a day's rest.

In the evening, a leadership council was called. Shimeon went, I waited. When he came back, he told me that there was some concern about what was happening in Alexandria. It was decided that Pappus and Julianus, both from Alexandria, should ride ahead, find out about the situation, and report back as soon as they could.

They needed two days to reach the city, two days to learn everything about it, and two more days to get back. They managed to rejoin us by the next Shabbat, and reported to the council after the holiday was over. There was also a debate. Shimeon told me all about it.

"First, Pappus reported on the attack against the Romans there. It seems that it was a relatively minor skirmish. The Romans maintained order. They handled it with a firm hand. Many Jews were executed. Yet it was not clear what started it and which group was at fault. The Jewish leadership complained afterwards to the Senate in Rome about the overly harsh punishment, and the Emperor Trajan sent a judge to investigate. Probably nothing will come out of that.

"Then they told us about the feelings of the Jews there, both the ordinary people and the leadership. There are vast disagreements.

"According to them, the people in the city, as well as in the countryside, feel just like the Cyrenaican Jews did. They hate their Greek neighbors. Then, of course, they are closer to Eretz Yisrael and hear about the Roman oppression there; so they hate the Romans, too."

I was listening to this with lots of concern. Where will all this lead? Back home, I hoped; but shall we really get there? There was so much trouble everywhere, so much hate.

"But why all this hatred?" I had to ask. "What do they have against the Greeks?"

"Well, first of all, in the country it is exactly the same situation as in Cyrenaica. They have lost everything to the manipulation of the Greeks. Then, the religious differences are very pronounced. The Greeks practice their so-called religion and detest the Jews for not joining them. They build statues and temples and are upset by the Jews' indifference to them. Indifference? No, it is more. The Jews don't make a secret of their contempt of those pagan deities. Then our customs are quite different, our food, our observance of the Shabbat, all the laws… well, you know how serious such a sharp distinction can be."

I did know. Even at home, in Yavneh, which was mainly a Jewish town, we have had occasional clashes with the Greeks.

"But there is more: Jews in Egypt are perhaps a little better educated. Some of them have read the Prophets, and they are familiar with all the predictions about the coming of the Messiah. In Cyrenaica, we had to tell them about the Messiah, it was really revenge that drove them; but in Egypt, ever since the destruction of the Temple, they know, as we do, that the Messiah must come very soon and restore our country, our freedom and independence. And since they hear about our success, about our coming, they are getting more enthusiastic every day."

He thought a minute, then added:

"Of course, they are being taught by Zealots who come over from Eretz Yisrael."

"Perhaps people you know?"

He shrugged. "Perhaps."

I nodded. I knew some of Shimeon's friends. I actually liked them all, but I could see that trouble might develop if they were given a free hand to 'educate' the people. But then, why do I say trouble? They were doing what we were doing, getting the Jews everywhere to shake off their chains. That was the right thing, was it not?

Yet it could not be as simple as that. So I asked Shimeon:

"But what about the leadership?"

"Ah, that's a totally different situation," he replied. "The brothers had a long discussion with the Jewish leaders in Alexandria and came back quite discouraged on that account."

I knew there had to be something, some difficulty.

"Tell me about it."

"They say that the leaders don't want trouble. They feel that they are on good terms with the Romans. They trust the Roman occupiers. That judge that Trajan sent over, they think of him as a proof that the Romans are impartial and fair."

"Fair? My grandfather was telling me about their cruelty and injustice…"

"Of course. But the rich Jews are afraid of losing everything if a full-blown war starts. And they claim to have a reasonably good relationship not only with the Romans, but with the Greek city leaders as well."

"I can believe that. Rich Greeks would not mock them like the poor people do, at least not to their faces. They know how to get along."

"Yes. And the Jews have become very much like the Greeks themselves. They give Greek names to their children and send them to Greek schools."

"And so, they are afraid of us. I can understand that."

"Yes, and frankly, I don't blame them for it. They are wrong, of course, but yes, from their own viewpoint it is understandable."

"A selfish viewpoint, you mean."

"You know, I am not even certain of that. I think that they see themselves as the true representatives of all the Jews there, and they think that, slowly, the lot of their people will improve, if only they don't cause trouble. Behave nicely, quietly, respect your neighbor and especially the authorities, and everyone will learn to like you."

"But that's nonsense. The world does not work that way. If you are quiet and respectful, everyone learns to step on you." Strange, I thought, what's happening here, why was I arguing the stronger, perhaps Shammaite viewpoint, and Shimeon the weak, Hillelite view? But he was just explaining the other side's stand.

"I know that. We all know. But the Alexandria Jewish leaders don't. All I am saying is that they are honest, if misguided. We had a long debate about it in the council."

"Why, what about? This very question?"

"Yes. Lucuas and a few others argued as you did, but went further. They asserted that those leaders are traitors, that we must eliminate them as soon as possible, just as the Cyrenaican leaders were eliminated, or they will hold us back, create roadblocks in our war efforts, might even inform the Romans and so on."

"And you? What did you say?"

"I argued that those leaders are honest people, we should leave them alone. When the time comes, we shall talk to them again, and once they see that war is inevitable, they will join us. It will be better for everyone that way."

"Who won?"

"I think that I did. Pappus and Julianus were, for a while, in the middle. But when they heard my arguments, they came around, supported me, and then Lucuas gave in – somewhat reluctantly, I must say. He almost said that I shall be responsible if something goes wrong."

"Kind of him. Let's hope for the best."

*   *   *

So we entered Egypt, and it was again slow going. We were held up, no longer by rain, but by the fighting. Each day our soldiers had to ride forth and attack the local men, those that were still there. True, their number dwindled; after all, news of our coming had preceded us; many had escaped towards Alexandria. As a matter of fact, one thing that Pappus and Julianus had noticed during their trip there was that very many Greek refugees in the city were making themselves temporary shelters on the streets and in the temples, until the authorities chased them out of there.

Then, after we marched for some three weeks, marched and fought, a messenger rode out from Alexandria with awful news.

Again, Shimeon went to the council and told me about it afterwards.

It seemed that there were maybe a hundred thousand refugees in Alexandria, nearly half of them adult men, and they started to attack the Jews of the city. First, they ganged up on Jews walking in the Greek neighborhoods, killing some dozens of people.

In desperation, the city's Jews held meetings, among themselves and also with the Greek city elders. Many of the Jews demanded a counterattack. But the leaders did not want to fight.

Then the Greeks – not the refugees, but the Alexandrian Greeks – took advantage of the Jews' hesitation. They accused the Jews of disloyalty and at the same time set out on a horrendous carnage.

Now the Jews did have to fight back, but it was too late. Great numbers of them were killed. The Great Synagogue, the largest and proudest Jewish building outside the Temple in Jerusalem, was destroyed. Strangely, the Greeks also destroyed many of their own buildings. The Temple of Nemesis and the Sanctuary of Serapis lay in ruins simply because they were close to the Jewish quarter in the east of the city; they wanted to prevent the Jews from using the buldings as strategic locations in the fighting.

When the Jews were first attacked, word was sent to the Romans.

Perhaps some of our people were naive enough to hope that Rome would come running to their rescue.

Not all the Jews were massacred in the city, but perhaps as many as half of them. Alexandria's proud Jewish community, the most outstanding in the Diaspora, was finished.

*   *   *

We progressed slowly towards Alexandria, towards the center of Egypt. We got used to the slow progress of the march. We had a routine now: washing ourselves and eating in the morning, after which we marched till noon; then lunch, rest; march until it began to darken; then stop, put up the tents, prepare the evening meal; wash our clothes, do hundreds of other chores, and fall into bed.

Shimeon usually did not march with me. He rode a horse – there were a few dozen – up front with the leadership. Lucuas once sought me out and offered a horse-drawn cart for me to travel on, but I refused. I don't know if he realized my feelings, my opinion of him, but we hardly ever talked after that.

I made peace with my husband, but made him understand that I expected him to do his utmost to assure that this war would be conducted with as little unnecessary bloodshed as possible. Nevertheless, it was brutal.

Our troops plundered Egypt. All pagan temples were destroyed, all images were broken. So far, so good. But all dwelling places were also destroyed, and that I did not like. And then, the people. Any man they encountered, they simply killed, without even asking him what he thought of the Jews. Many women also perished, and quite a few children. Many others were left alone, to survive, if they could, or to die. Old people, too.

By now, there was less talk of revenge, though, and more discussion about the Messiah.

We, the women, talked, as we marched. I tried to listen, but not to express an opinion. I was afraid that they would think I am putting on superior airs because of my education, because of the position of my husband. So I just nodded, expressed interest in what they said, but seldom expressed a contrary opinion. Sometimes I had to, for example, when they explained to me how the Messiah was going to kill all gentiles.

"The King Messiah will now precede us into Eretz Yisrael, establish his kingdom and kill all Romans," said one.

"And not only Romans, but the Greeks, too," added a second, and a third woman chipped in:

"All gentiles, really. There will only be the Jews, all Jews from everywhere, going up to Jerusalem, but there will be no need for the gentiles."

I felt that I could not leave this without debate.

"But don't the Prophets say that all the nations shall go up to Jerusalem and bring offerings to God, our God?"

That confused them a little; not one of them had read the Prophets or much of anything else, for that matter. They did not argue with me, just shrugged.

But we had more serious conflicts. The soldiers attacked some small villages, killed the men, despite the protestation of those members of our army who joined us in Egypt. You see, many of the Egyptian natives were friendly with the Jews, we had no quarrel with them. But the Cyrenaican soldiers could not care less about such niceties. Again I talked with Shimeon, again I demanded that he get from Lucuas firm orders not to touch any gentiles who are not Greeks or Romans.

Again, Shimeon failed to secure such an order from Lucuas. It seems that a major exception like that would have interfered with the Grand Plan.

"What is this Grand Plan, after all?" I asked him.

"It is simply this: that in Cyrenaica, in Egypt and in Cyprus we shall leave scorched earth behind, with nobody to till the land, for many years."

"But these Egyptian natives sometimes helped the Jews!"

"Yes, and sometimes fought them. Lucuas is not interested in them."

"What about Pappus and Julianus?"

"They are on my side, but they don't have as much influence now as they used to..."

I am trying to explain to you, my nephew Yose, that I myself was a confused woman in those days. I knew – or thought I knew – that the days of the Messiah were almost upon us. I knew – or thought I knew – that we were going to liberate Eretz Yisrael, our land. I knew – or thought I knew – that my Shimeon was to be an important leader. Yet I did not like the way things were going. I did not understand why the Messiah demanded so much killing. I did not understand why my husband was not taking a stronger position, why he did not take over command from Lucuas, whom I detested. I thought that maybe, if Shimeon were at the head of the army, the entire plan could proceed in a more humane manner, and then the Messiah would make his appearance sooner.

Yes, I know, Yose, I was naive.

*   *   *

It was already early summer. There were a few days of *khamsin*, hot wind from the desert, even sandstorms. Yet we progressed faster, in generally pleasant weather, and were approaching Memphis when the first news came about Roman troops approaching. Shimeon told me.

"Well, should that be a surprise?" I asked him.

"Not exactly a surprise, no. But part of the plan was the assumption that we won't have to fight the Romans until all the Greek opponents are disposed of, that the Romans will be slow in realizing what is going on. While we marched through the countryside."

"Was that part of your strategy?"

"As modified by Lucuas," he said, without looking at me.

Was Shimeon a strong man, then?

He also admitted that he was a little worried at first about our men fighting the Romans whom they did not really hate, at least not as they hated the Greeks. But now he saw how they were full of Messianic fervor, and were willing to kill anybody who stood in the way.

There were a couple of minor skirmishes with Roman detachments. We won one, lost the second. I was told that they were not important. But we knew that the big battles were rapidly approaching.

The first major clash took place between Busiris and Leontopolis. Several Roman detachments, about eight thousand men, half of them on horses, attacked. Our soldiers were ready for them. We had only about five thousand in our cavalry, but they were better. Their spears were longer, they handled them faster, more strongly. We lost only about a hundred men, the Romans lost over a thousand and then turned and ran. Shimeon did very well on his horse, killed at least a dozen, I was told, and Lucuas then gave him command of the southern expedition, or the 'Nile Force.' A man named Isidorus, originally from Alexandria, was put in charge of the northern expedition, or the 'Alexandria Force.' Lucuas himself established his headquarters near Leontopolis.

For about two months nothing important happened. That gave Shimeon enough time to organize his troops. He frequently left for discussions at the headquarters but was usually back by the end of the day. I had not realized how he could ride a horse. So handsome, so manly!

But, meanwhile, things started to happen in Alexandria. When our people arrived there, they found the remainder of the local Jews well-armed, ready to fight. The leadership had melted away.

There was a series of battles involving not only the Greeks, but also Roman troops. During the late spring our men there killed about two hundred thousand of them, mainly Romans. But we also suffered losses there, very heavy losses, at least a hundred thousand men. Isidorus himself fell, as did some of his aides. The remainder of his troops made their way south and joined up with Shimeon's forces.

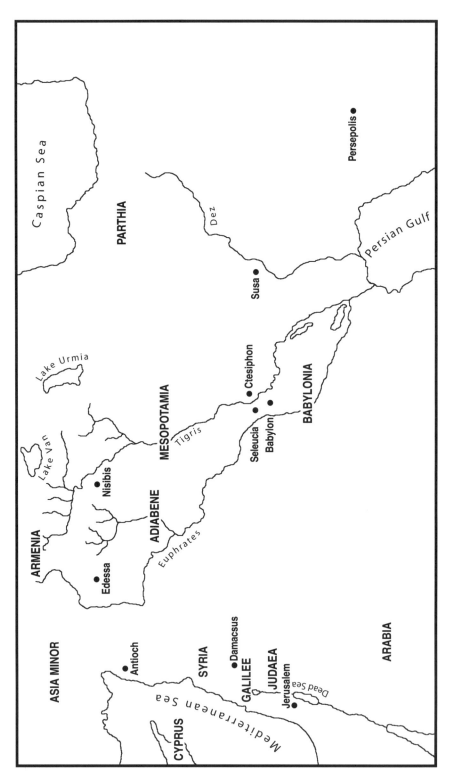

Parthian Empire (1st–2nd century C.E.)

THE NILE

Yes, Yose, by mid-summer it was real war. The Romans sent a messenger to Lucuas demanding that the Jews lay down their arms. Lucuas wanted to cut the messenger's head off, Shimeon prevented that. Eventually, Lucuas agreed that Shimeon was right.

But, again, I want to tell you, Yose, that I respected Lucuas as a leader. I did not like him at all, but I respected him. He came to our compound one day. They had a strategy meeting in our tent. I was, of course, not welcomed in, but neither was I forbidden to stay nearby and to come in occasionally to serve them food and drink. I heard the entire discussion.

In one of the main arguments, Shimeon asked Lucuas:

"Should we fight the Romans and keep fighting them, as they send in more and more troops?"

"Fight them to their last man!"

"But Lucuas, there are too many of them. There are millions of Roman soldiers, in Rome and everywhere else."

"They won't send all of them here. But if they do, so much the better. We shall kill them all, that will be the end of the Roman Empire."

Shimeon sounded doubtful.

"Would it not be sufficient if we handed them one crushing defeat, to send them a message that they cannot win over us, and then headed home, left here for Eretz Yisrael? We are not that far now."

"That won't be enough. They will come after us. This is the ideal fighting territory. We know this land now and we are ready for them. We have destroyed their pagan temples and statues, most of them, except some in Alexandria. We shall have to go back there, but that can wait. Remember, though, that this was not our only objective. Our main thrust is against the Greeks and their false gods. But we wanted to overthrow the Roman government, not just cause them some minor inconvenience."

"Don't misunderstand me, Lucuas, of course we shall fight. We shall fight and we shall win. But I don't know if you are realistic in expecting that we are strong enough to overthrow the entire Roman Empire."

"You don't have to overthrow them. Just make them realize that they are a small country, like we are, they should stay at home in their land and leave other people alone. We don't want to occupy them. They should not occupy us. Or the Parthians, for that matter."

Lucuas had a clear understanding of the Parthian events. I think that his genius lay in his ability to coordinate many distant events with wonderful precision.

"Things are going well in Cyprus," he told the others. "There are no Greeks left, all buildings have been demolished, and they are awaiting word from us in Eretz Yisrael, as well as for ships from there." He added with a smile: "Some are actually on the way to Eretz Yisrael now." That surprised me a little: I thought that they were supposed to wait in Cyprus until later.

"What about Parthia?" asked Shimeon.

"Now, that's a totally different matter. The Romans are very active there. That is the reason we can win against them here, fully half of their army is now in Parthia. Actually, most of their fighters from all over the world are there now. I hear that they are being attacked even in Britannia, because their defenses there have become very thin. But we do not attack the Greeks in Parthia."

"Are there as many Greeks there as here? As there were here, before we came?"

"No, but there are many. And everybody hates them. Not only the Jews, but all the other people. They fought against the Greeks for seven years in Seleucia. And now everybody is against the Romans. So they all fight together. More or less."

"What are the latest news from there?"

"Both good and not so good. The bad news first: It seems that the emperor Trajan is back in good health and is leading the advance personally. Last year, as you recall, he occupied all of Mesopotamia and Adiabene and Armenia."

"Yes, we knew about that. That is not good, Mesopotamia is full of Jewish cities."

"And Adiabene is a Jewish country, even if peopled by converted Jews. But most of our people live in Babylonia."

"So I assume he is heading that way now?"

"Yes, heading south. He's already taken Ctesiphon, their capital. The people there are really mad, for he ordered the golden throne of the Parthian kings to be carried off. Now they will finally understand how we felt when they sacked Jerusalem and carried off all the Temple treasures."

Lucuas was in his element. He liked to deal with world events. He was now walking up and down the tent.

"So now Trajan has taken Seleucia. Actually, much of Babylon is already his. And he hopes to reach the Gulf by the end of the summer."

"But you said that there was good news, too."

"Yes, I think that this whole campaign will collapse. Why? Look, the Parthian Empire was once huge and powerful, reaching from here all the way to China. But in the last fifty years or so it has been falling apart, into eighteen separate kingdoms. That's why Rome could advance as far as it did. But now they are uniting again, joining forces against Rome."

"There are clear signs?"

"Yes, there are. And meanwhile, in all the cities, the Jews are preparing to fight the occupiers, and the gentiles are also with them – you see, they live in harmony there, Jews and the others. Not like here."

He paced and continued.

"In Adiabene, the Romans have already suffered heavy losses. Adiabenian and Parthian cavalry attacked them. They have now retreated. And such attacks are beginning to take place all over Mesopotamia and Babylon. Take my word, they won't last there a year."

A little later, he admonished Shimeon.

"Learn this, my son, it's very important. Always have your messengers spread out. Always have twenty or thirty people coming and going to distant places. Always find out who is the strongest person, always make alliances. Always tie together the people of Judaea and the Diaspora. Always exchange views, always coordinate the timing of your attacks."

Shimeon did act like a good son, or student. He nodded and said, "I shall do so."

"Yes, and one other thing. Always probe the enemy. Always attack here and there, see how he reacts. There are times when he is weak. This is the essential thing for a military leader: He must know when the enemy is weak. That is the time to defeat him. Such an opportunity must not be missed!"

* * *

Shimeon was impressed by Lucuas, and so was I. Sometimes. But Shimeon did not need advice from anyone when it came to organizing his troops and preparing for battle.

That summer the Roman Third *Cyrenaica* Legion attacked us in full force. The battle was fierce, but we were better prepared and nearly as well armed. Our people were also more motivated.

The fighting took about a week. Each evening we had funerals, many funerals. By the end of the week we had lost about three thousand people, but the Romans lost many more, there was little left of their legion. They rebuilt it during the next few years.

The Romans also found more military forces to send against us, the auxiliary Cohort unit First *Lusitanorum*. We dealt with that, too; the few who remained alive ran like hares.

That summer and fall, victory followed victory. The Roman forces in Egypt were decimated. Lucuas was very proud of himself; I think he should have been particularly proud of naming Shimeon as the head of the Nile Force. Not that he withheld recognition from Shimeon, he praised him to everyone.

I was also told that our people were being careful not to harm innocent Egyptians. But in many places it was difficult to distinguish between Egyptian villages and Greek settlements, and quite a few of the Egyptian villages suffered. Sometimes they put up resistance; then they were wiped out by our troops. So, by the winter, there was some bad feeling there, pity.

Still, victory was sweet. Clearly the Romans underestimated our strength, our military potential. Of course, they were also occupied in Parthia – but that was the reason for the timing of our attack, Lucuas said; we found weakness there and took advantage.

*   *   *

Yet nothing lasts forever, it seems, except the Holy One, blessed be He. Our victories were so exhilarating that we gradually forgot that Rome could send a much larger force, with a much better commander than before.

The Emperor Trajan may have been preoccupied with his problems in Parthia, but he could not afford to lose the part of his empire that connected Parthia with the territories closer to Rome. So he sent a general, Marcius Turbo, with huge forces, innumerable cavalry and also a navy, of all things. Why a navy, you ask. Those ships could navigate the Nile, they surprised us and attacked our troops from several directions at once.

Lucuas' headquarters were relatively small, and one day they came under attack: half the people were killed. The rest abandoned the camp and moved out fast. They joined us near Memphis.

During the winter, the Romans killed tens of thousands of our people in many battles. The difference was that this time it was they who chose the time and place of the battle, not our commanders, not Shimeon.

The worst part was that we had to give up all hope of eventually attacking and taking Alexandria. Many of our people were supposed to enter Eretz Yisrael from there, by sea. That was no longer possible. Now we knew that it would have to be the land route for everyone.

But, in retrospect, there was one thing even more tragic than that:

Three of the main Jewish communities of the Diaspora, Cyrene, Alexandria, and Salamis in Cyprus, have ceased to exist. That may have been what our leaders wanted, hoping it would lead to a new, strong, independent Eretz Yisrael. Alas, it was not to be.

LAST STAND: PELUSIUM

You can imagine, Yose, that Shimeon's mood was getting darker. He was clearly worried. It was not difficult to understand why; but I would have liked to cheer him up, despite the military situation. A cheerful leader is a quicker-thinking, sharper one than a sad leader, I thought.

It occurred to me that one reason for his despondency might be that he did not have some of the people around him whom he liked most. I realized that we had not seen the brothers Pappus and Julianus for a long time.

I asked him about this.

"Shimeon, where are the two brothers?"

He thought about the answer. Finally, he said:

"I am not supposed to talk about them, but what harm can there be? They are in Judaea. Eretz Yisrael."

That really surprised me.

"What are they doing there? How did they get there?"

"I'll explain," he replied, "but wait here for me."

I waited, and he soon returned with a heavy leather pouch. From that, he pulled out a scroll and gave it to me.

"What is this?"

"A gift to you. From the two brothers. They asked me to hand it to you when you learn about their departure."

I looked at it. There were three pages. At the end, in smaller letters, it was explained that they were taken from the book of Philo, of Alexandria. I had read some of the writings of Philo, I knew that he lived at the time of my great-grandfather, Hanina ben Dosa. He died sixty or seventy years before the time I am telling you about.

I started to read aloud.

'For even though they dwell in the uttermost parts of the earth, in slavery to those who led them away captive, one signal, as it were, one day will bring liberty to all. This conversion in a body to virtue will strike awe into their masters, who will set them free, ashamed to rule over men who are better than themselves. When they gain this unexpected liberty, those who but now were scattered in Greece and the outside world over islands and continents will arise and post from every side with one impulse to the one appointed place, guided in their pilgrimage by a vision divine and superhuman unseen by

*others but manifest to them as they pass from exile to their home...
When they have arrived, the cities which now lay in ruins will be
cities once more; the desolate land will be inhabited; the barren will
change into fruitfulness...'*

I was touched.

"How did that man know all this so many years earlier?" I asked him.
He shrugged. "There are some who can see the future. They are the prophets. Maybe he was a prophet."

"And why did the brothers send this scroll to me?"

"They wanted you to understand what it is that's most important for
them. The ingathering of the exiles, that must be accomplished before
the Kingdom of the Messiah can arise. They were happy that all the Jews
from Cyrenaica and Egypt are progressing towards Eretz Yisrael, and they
decided to concern themselves with the Jews from Cyprus."

"They did not travel to Cyprus, first..."

"No, they sailed from Alexandria, while they still could, directly for
Jaffa. And I have already heard that they reached their destination safely
and have set up operations to arrange for ships that bring the Jews over
from Cyprus."

"Have any of them arrived already?"

"That I don't know. But Pappus and Julianus will be sitting in the ports,
waiting for them, guiding them to our camps, unless they want to go somewhere else, perhaps to relatives. I believe that they shall give them money,
if necessary. Give them from their own money."

"I am proud of them," I told him. "And I am looking forward to seeing
them in Eretz Yisrael."

"Perhaps that will not be too far in the future now," he answered, but
not too cheerfully.

* * *

We were in the middle of the cool season. The sky was very dark, rain
seemed imminent. Those downpours made life miserable in the camp,
because few people had proper tents. Many soldiers, and even families,
slept under coats and makeshift contraptions that did a poor job of keeping out the water and the wind.

We were more fortunate, we had a good tent. It was used for army pur-
poses, but at least we were allowed to sleep inside at night. That was one
privilege I accepted; I had to, if I wanted to be with my husband. During

the day, I entered only to serve food to the numerous people debating strategy and tactics inside.

Shimeon and Lucuas were having a strategy meeting. At least that's what they called it, but I thought a better term would have been a review of what went wrong. All right, let me be fair: what went right and what went wrong. Plans and achievements, successes and failures.

Lucuas was saying:

"I want to review our plan. We must see it clearly, for then we shall know what we have already achieved, and what remains to be done." I listened to that skeptically, outside the tent.

"Our main objective has always been to reach Eretz Yisrael," said Shimeon.

"And we are going to reach it, there is no question of that." Lucuas was confident. "But how did we plan to do that?"

"Well, to start with, we wanted to coordinate the movement of our people from several countries, establish good contacts with the strongest Jewish centers outside Judaea. We have done that. *You* have done that."

"Right. What next?"

"Next, we wanted to build up huge storehouses of arms, and food. We have done that. Again, mainly, you…"

"All right. Next, the training?"

"Yes, we wanted to train the people, make a strong army out of them. We have done that."

"That's all the preparation. Now what did we actually want to do?"

Shimeon continued:

"We wanted to eliminate the enemy first at his weakest points, in Cyrenaica and in Cyprus. We have done that."

No response from Lucuas; I suppose he nodded, but I could not see inside the tent.

"Then, we wanted to unite our forces with those of the Jews in Egypt; we did it. And then, with united forces, we wanted to take advantage of the absence of half of the Roman garrisons, and attack the weakened legions. Well, we did that, too."

"And then?"

"Then, we wanted to seize control of Alexandria, wipe out the remainder of the Roman forces and take control of the harbor."

"And what was our objective in doing that?"

"Two main objectives. We could then close the seaways completely. We have already destroyed much of the harbor at Apollonia. We shall soon have full control of Jaffa. If we had Alexandria, we would be able to put a rope around Rome's neck and twist it, especially because the grain ship-ments would not get through."

"Exactly. And have you not heard? There is actually a serious grain shortage now in Egypt."

"I know. That was the reason we had to slaughter so many of our ani-mals, mules and even horses. We could no longer feed them. Well, then, you could say that to some extent we have accomplished this aim, too, if not completely. The second reason for seizing the Alexandria harbor was to secure ships for the travel to Jaffa, to Eretz Yisrael."

"All right, we have not done that. But that was never an essential point, for we could always take the land route. We have come this far. It is not that much more to march there."

"No, that will be no problem," Shimeon agreed.

"Still, the Alexandria part of the plan has gone awry," commented Lucuas. "And why? Because of the local leaders, the rich Jews. They thought that they were sitting pretty, so why cause trouble? Stupid! Where are they now?"

"Dead, I suppose, all of them."

"Yes. They did not use the opportunity when it was ripe for the picking. That slowed our advances and gave more chance to the Romans to orga-nize their forces and attack us here. And we lost many people and now we are much weaker than we were half a year ago. The Romans were able to send many troops by sea, from Syria…"

Shimeon did not answer; I think I know why. Lucuas continued:

"You know, that was the one mistake we made. We should have elimi-nated the leadership, the rich Jews, in Alexandria, before we even got any-where near. It could have been done."

That was strong criticism of the person who advocated doing nothing of the sort. Shimeon, of course.

So again, Shimeon said nothing. Lucuas then resumed his review.

"More than once you objected to the scorched earth plan. It was nec-essary to assure that there would be no effective opposition from the rear. That's where Rome is making a mistake, that's why their Parthian campaign must fail. It is failing already. People are attacking them from behind. Soon they'll have to withdraw."

"Good."

"Yes. We were smarter than they. We made any such uprising impos-sible. Until we got to Alexandria."

Shimeon must have thought that some reply was wanted.

"I am sorry, Lucuas, if you think it was my advice…"

"It was not just you, others also thought that it would not be the right thing to eliminate the leadership. Who knows how things would have turned out. But the main thing is that we lost so many of our men. Yet we needed them, for the final fight against the Romans in Eretz Yisrael."

"We still have many men. We still have arms. We can fight them."

"We can and we shall. But there are fewer of us than we planned, and there are more of the enemy."

"That's true."

"And if we could have travelled by sea, our troops would have been in much better shape, less tired. But there, we cannot help that. We still have battles ahead of us here. We must win those."

"We shall, Lucuas."

"We better. And then, soon, we shall leave, probably at the end of the cool season."

*　*　*

Marcius Turbo had many ships, and they could quite comfortably sail up the Nile. Our soldiers shot fiery arrows at them, some ships actually caught fire, but those were put out soon enough, and our positions were revealed. If we only had some weapon against them, if we could sink them, but no, they sailed freely, and a large number of troops could suddenly land and attack us. During the next two months, there were many battles, small ones, we won some, but we also suffered defeats. We lost many brave fighters. Again, I attended funerals each evening, funerals of soldiers I knew, or whose families I was acquainted with.

There was fighting along the entire Nile valley. Our troops were spread too thin. If we could have concentrated against the Roman legions at a single point, perhaps we could have achieved a decisive victory, but we could not afford to leave any major section of the river valley undefended.

And meanwhile, there were ever more Roman troops. At one point, Shimeon suggested to Lucuas that perhaps it would be time to save what could be saved and leave.

Lucuas was very upset at the suggestion.

"Run and have a strong Roman army behind us? So that they can follow us to Judaea and finish us off there? No! No!"

And then came the battle of Memphis, not very far from our camp. It went on for three days, and we lost thirty-five thousand men.

There were still about two hundred thousand people left, but only about thirty thousand soldiers. The rest were women, children and old people.

We buried our dead.

Shimeon told Lucuas that now our people must leave. He may have used strong words, for Lucuas no longer objected. But he insisted that they head for Pelusium, at the easternmost branch of the Nile delta, on the seashore.

*   *   *

Lucuas knew history. He remembered that during the preceding few hundred years there was a strong Jewish military base at Pelusium. Any army wanting to move from Babylonia to Egypt or the Red Sea had to pass through there.

"We can still achieve our original purpose," he insisted. "We can stop all commerce there, even stop their armies, and slowly strangulate their forces."

Shimeon left comments like that without a response. But he ordered our troops and all others, all those able to march, to head to the northeast.

There were many, though, who said that they could not continue. They were mainly women and old people, but a number of soldiers asked to be permitted to remain with their families. After much consultation with Lucuas, Shimeon permitted about two thousand men to stay.

"Who knows, maybe they will surprise the Romans and win some key battles," he said without conviction.

An old woman had two sons, both still alive, thank the Lord. She asked if both young men could stay with her. Shimeon hesitated.

The younger one spoke up:

"Mother, I want to go with Shimeon. I want to go to Eretz Yisrael."

The mother wailed: "No, Hillel, no! You will never make it. Stay here with me and Yosef. Stay!"

I am not sure what Shimeon would have decided in the end, but Hillel insisted. He kissed his mother goodbye, grabbed his few possessions and ran to the other side. The mother continued crying, but we left her there, with Yosef to console her.

Our march took three weeks. We arrived at the edge of Pelusium. After two days' rest, our men attacked the harbor and seized the only ship there.

What to do with this vessel? Who should sail and who should continue marching? It was not large enough for all of us.

Soon it became obvious that Shimeon did not have any sailors among his men. Lucuas himself knew nothing about the sea. There was nobody among the local people who could be drafted to help us with the sails, for in the fighting they had all been killed or maimed.

Then more naval craft arrived, Roman ships – we could not attack them on water. We had to fight on land, and that was bad enough. We lost ten thousand more brave men.

Again, we buried our dead and continued on foot.

Long, long letter, Yose. Let me rest now, and I shall write to you again, soon, about what happened back home. Peace be with you.

BOOK II
Judaea

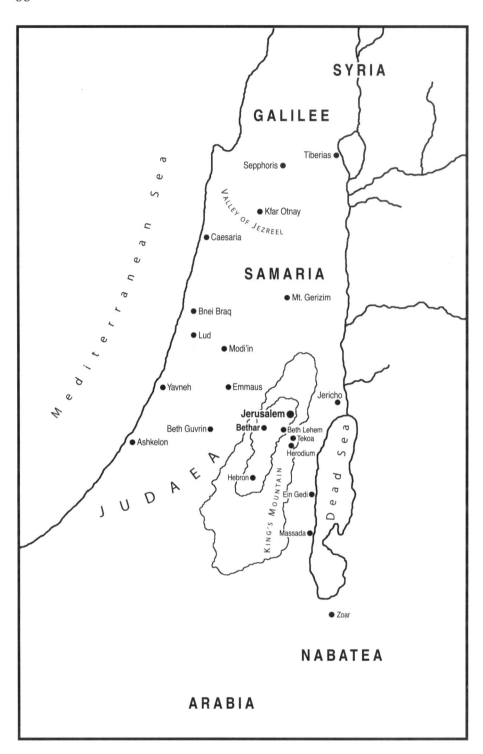

Judaea (2nd century C.E.)

Michal's letter to Yose

BREAKTHROUGH

From Michal bat Dosa – to my nephew –
Rabbi Yose ben Halafta, may your peace be great.

To continue my story, we marched another four weeks. There were few carts left, those were pulled by the stronger men. The animals had long been slaughtered. Most of the people were able to walk. We left the old and sick in Egypt. We did not fight with anybody along the way. In fact, we marched at night and hid during the day. It was early summer when we arrived at Jaffa.

Why Jaffa, you ask? Jaffa was the center of Cyrenean Jews in Eretz Yisrael. There were actually some disturbances there at the time of the Cyrenaican revolt. But those actions never came to anything. When a certain critical point had been reached, Trajan sent his nephew Hadrian to quiet down the rebelling Jews, which he did quite effectively and, fortunately, without too much bloodshed.

We were about ninety thousand people arriving in Jaffa. Another sixty thousand went to other places, to find refuge with their relatives. In Jaffa we all had to hide with the Cyrenean community. That was not easy, as the community itself was less numerous than the new arrivals. A family of four often had secretly to look after and feed eight more, at least for several weeks, until other places could be found for them in the country.

Shimeon and I hid with a family for a week, until we had a sense of the situation, when was it safe to go out and how to appear, what to wear and so on. Then we decided to head for Yavneh, to stay with our family.

The young man, Hillel, who did not want to remain behind with his mother, somehow attached himself to Shimeon. He was a clean-cut youngster, of medium height, with a very thin face, now beginning to be covered with a wispy beard. With a shy grin, he asked if he could come with us.

"Where are you from, Hillel?" Shimeon asked.

"From Cyrene."

"What did you do there? I suppose I should ask what your parents did, for you seem too young to have done anything on your own."

"No, I worked in my father's shop. He was a potter."

"Was? I suppose he is no longer alive, then?"

"No, he fell at Memphis."

"May his memory be blessed. Well, Hillel of Cyrene, come with us, I am sure that we'll find something useful for you to do."

We walked all night. Yavneh is not far from Jaffa, only one long night's journey. By early morning we knocked at my mother's house.

You can imagine the happiness, the crying and laughing, but then more crying, when we all suddenly felt the great emptiness left by my father's passing.

But Mother was there and Tzviyya, and Halafta soon joined us, and then Yonathan and Elisheva.

We introduced our young companion, Hillel of Cyrene; they found him a small room, and he volunteered to do any work around the house that might be needed. I sat down with Mother and Tzviyya and Elisheva, to tell them about the past two years, while Shimeon went with Yonathan to talk about the weighty matters occupying his mind.

Later that night, we all had our evening meal together. I had almost forgotten what it was like to have a good dinner. We ate all kinds of delicacies that I had not tasted for a long time – roasted eggs and many kinds of nuts and figs, and even a chicken or two and cakes. We talked about many things, about the situation and people we knew. I asked my brother-in-law Halafta how the sages were faring.

"Thank the Lord, most of them are in good health. Of course you know – no, perhaps you don't – that Rabban Gamaliel has passed away."

"No, I did not know. When?"

"About a month ago. It happened quite suddenly."

"That's sad. May his memory be blessed," we both said at the same time.

Shimeon asked: "And who is the new Nasi?"

"Nobody yet," answered Halafta. "There may not be a Nasi appointed for a long time, I think."

"Why is that?"

Yose, your father was a serious man. Not as serious, perhaps, as my Shimeon, but when you asked him a question, he took the trouble to explain it well, so that nobody would misunderstand his answers.

Halafta stood up and walked around the room, while he explained the situation to us.

"His son, Shimeon, is only thirty-seven years old. That's too young for such an important position. For the time being, our friend Eleazar ben Azariyah is *Av Bet Din*, really the person in charge, at least of all administrative matters. Then there is Tarfon, perhaps the strongest sage, not to mention Yehoshua ben Hananiyah, the father of the nation, and Ishmael ben Elisha."

"Are you not forgetting the man with the sharpest mind?" asked Yonathan.

"You mean Akiva. Of course, he is more clever than all of us put together. I almost said that he was also too young. He is sixty-seven! But somehow, everyone thinks of Akiva as a young man."

Shimeon had many other questions. He had to catch up with the news, had to understand the current circumstances.

"But has nobody suffered under the Romans? Has nobody had trouble because of his work?"

Halafta pondered the question.

"Yes, some have. I have been warned by the authorities to be more respectful of the Emperor in my teachings. My friend Yohanan ben Nuri was actually arrested for a few days after he taught that there is only one sovereign, the Lord."

"So is it not obvious that some sort of action is required? That we must do something?" Shimeon demanded an answer almost angrily.

Yonathan watched with a grin as Halafta was trying to phrase his answer.

"Some action will be required, certainly. But not necessarily violent action. That may achieve exactly the opposite of what we want."

"Ah, the Hillelite view," Yonathan commented.

"Yes, the Hillelite view." Halafta ignored Yonathan's smirk. "Have we not succeeded in keeping the nation, overall, out of trouble, for forty-seven years now?"

"Yes, nicely under the heel of Rome. As long as we are grateful to him for occupying us and oppressing us, he'll let us be."

"But at least nobody is forced to worship the pagan gods now. We don't have to bow down to their statues."

"But they do erect them, and build altars, too. Even in Jerusalem."

"Well, yes, they do," admitted Halafta.

I did not want them to start a major argument, so I switched the subject to more pleasurable matters. Shimeon was happy to switch, too. For him, these matters were too important to discuss at the dinner table.

But the next day, Yonathan invited Rabbi Akiva to have a long discussion with Shimeon and himself. Actually, there were four people there, for I simply sat in, and nobody objected. That was perhaps strange, for women seldom participated in serious discussions, what they called "men's talk."

But I had made it clear to Shimeon that I would not be left out, would not be just an ordinary housewife (I never was much of a housewife), and he did not object. Others, it seems, just had to get used to this.

We were sitting in Yonathan's working room. It was a large room, richly furnished, though not as elaborately as my father's room had been, with gold furniture. (I suppose that the gold furniture was still there. I never wanted to enter his old room.) No, Yonathan had an elaborately carved wooden table and comfortable stools for sitting on.

Akiva welcomed Shimeon with a hug and patted my head, too. Of course, he was used to my being present at discussions, even when I was much younger and they discussed things with my father, of blessed memory.

"Congratulations, my son, for work well done."

Shimeon protested: "Not that well done, Rabbi Akiva. I am not so proud of what we have achieved."

"But I am proud of you. You know that I am a man of peace, I don't like wars. But if we had to have a war, then it had to be fought well. And you fought well."

"May have fought well, sometimes, but we did not do everything well. In the end, we lost three quarters of our fighters."

"And how many did the Romans lose?"

"Oh, I don't know. Maybe a hundred and fifty thousand, two hundred thousand…"

"Far more than we lost, right?"

"Right, Akiva. But they have a lot more people than we have."

"Sure, that's why we could not win completely at this time. But we shall." I was surprised. Akiva was known for his peaceful views. Yet he was confidently talking about victory. His calm face had the self-assurance of a Roman emperor, or as I imagined a Roman emperor's face, for I certainly never set eyes on one. Well, yes, I saw the Emperor Trajan's face once, on a coin.

"I know we shall," nodded Shimeon. "With the help of the Messiah. But apparently the time was not yet ripe for the Messiah."

"No, my son, but I think it is near. Meanwhile, look what you have achieved. You have dealt blow after blow to the Roman Empire. You don't have to tell me, we have received the news here. And you have brought – how many – a hundred thousand Jews home?"

"Actually, a hundred and fifty thousand."

"And these are only from Africa. How many more from Cyprus?"

"I really don't know, I have not had a chance to find out what Pappus and Julianus have been doing."

"But I do know. They have already brought in fifty thousand, and there are ships plying the sea right now."

"That's good."

"Yes, but wait. You started the whole thing when Rome withdrew half of its legions from Africa. Now they were forced to send back several legions. So they have become that much weaker in Mesopotamia, and they are losing the war there. Your deeds have encouraged our people all over the Parthian Empire to revolt against Rome. A huge Roman Empire is in the process of changing into a small Roman Empire."

Rabbi Akiva had a smug expression on his wise old face. I knew that Shimeon was pleased by what he heard but pretended not to appreciate the praise.

"Not small enough: they are still here."

"Yes, but for how long? We shall talk about that later, when you have rested and organized your affairs."

"But tell me, Akiva, and you too, Yonathan, about the situation here. Is everyone happy under the Roman heel?"

Rabbi Akiva replied: "Nobody is happy. Most unhappy, of course, are the people who have lost their land."

"Just like in Cyrenaica."

"Yes, the Romans just love robbing people of their land."

"Except that in Africa it is the Greeks who do it."

"With the Romans behind them. Remember our *matzikim*, they act like Roman agents, but they are not necessarily Romans themselves. Some are Roman aristocrats who received the land after the last war. But they are, strangely enough, the best type, some of them allowed the original owner to live and work there, and they only extract a levy. And I am told that quite a few of them are thinking of converting to our faith. They are already paying the tithes!"

We all chuckled over this. Akiva continued.

"But there are all kinds of other *matzikim*. Any time the Romans want to reward someone, say a retiring soldier, they grab a piece of land. They give it to Greeks and Armenians and Moors. Look what happened to Agrippa's kingdom. The entire 'King's Mountain,' all the hills from here to Jerusalem, was part of it, yet when he died, the whole mountain was transferred to foreigners. Think of the situation of the Jewish farmer."

"Yes, I have thought that some of those people could be our best fighters, just like in Africa." Shimeon was beginning to assert himself.

"Some day. But there are some *matzikim* who are actually Jews, if you can believe that! They performed some disgusting service for the Romans, and were rewarded with somebody's land for that."

"Somehow, I don't predict a long life for people like that." This was Yonathan, with a wink to Shimeon.

"Well, at least the peasants have been left in place during the last forty years. It could have been worse. They could have been taken captive, as many of their fathers were after the war," commented Akiva.

"What about the Roman legions? What kind of forces do they have here these days?"

Akiva answered. He kept surprising me. A sage, a *tanna*, to be so knowledgeable about military matters.

"They have brought in heavy reinforcements recently, all from Mesopotamia. It seems that they are ready to withdraw from there, and at the same time they expect trouble here."

"Rightly so!"

"Yes, well, there is trouble already. The south was close to revolting already, and I understand that tens of thousands of your men stayed in that area after Pelusium." Shimeon nodded assent. "Also, there is some action at Gerassa and at Bethar, and in the region between Beth Guvrin and the Nabatean frontier, in the south. Even in Jaffa someone always provokes the Romans and there are local fights."

He continued:

"Do you know what the Romans are doing? They are building roads all over the country. Good, solid, paved roads. They need those to move their legions around."

"One day we may use those roads to our advantage."

"I hope so. But for now, they freely move detachments of the Tenth *Fretensis* Legion on those roads. The main legion is still in Jerusalem, some parts were sent to Parthia, but they are back now. And I hear that the Third *Cyrenaica* Legion is coming here, too, if they are not here already."

"But we know those. We have made mincemeat out of them in Egypt."

"I know you did, my son. But they are rebuilding them rapidly, as though they expected an immediate need."

"And how do the Jews feel about them?"

Akiva smiled.

"All the Jews hate them, of course. We encourage them to hate the Romans; mind you, not much encouragement is necessary. But more than that: the people all over the land are excited by what you have done, in Cyrenaica and Egypt and Cyprus, and by what our people are doing right now in Mesopotamia and Babylon – why, the entire Diaspora is on fire, and our people back home are ready to join in the fight."

"Akiva, you make me feel good about what happened. I am ready to continue the struggle."

"Good." Akiva stood up to go. He put his hand again over Shimeon's head. "But make sure, my son, that the time is ripe. Don't act prematurely."

"I shall not," promised Shimeon.

*   *   *

Next, Shimeon began to establish contact with his troops, most of them still in hiding. He wanted to make sure that he knew where they settled, how he could find them.

The most important contact was with Lucuas. Somehow, Shimeon assumed that he himself remained in charge of his army, and should remain so, but Lucuas was still the man who had the best knowledge about what the Jews and the Romans were doing everywhere. That was vital information, so Shimeon looked him up. I did not go with him; Shimeon told me about the meeting afterwards.

They embraced warmly. Lucuas was hiding among relatives from Cyrene. Shimeon was welcomed by a number of people in the house and offered refreshments. They then withdrew into a small room with no window, lighted by a lamp, and Lucuas related all the news to Shimeon.

"Mesopotamia. You surely want to know about Mesopotamia."

"Yes, of course, I do."

"Well, all my predictions are coming true." He had a triumphant smile on his face.

"Tell me."

"The Romans reached the Gulf without any difficulties. But then the trouble started in their rear. The Emperor Trajan was so eager to occupy all that land, all the way to the Gulf, I think he wanted to emulate Alexander so much, he never stopped to consolidate his new gains."

"Yes, that much I've heard."

"But listen. Our people led the battles against him. Nisibis and Edessa are practically Jewish cities. Seleucia, too. Nisibis is actually one of two or three fortified towns in Babylonia held by the Jews on their own military responsibility. And in Nisibis the Romans suffered the most. But at other places, too. And not only at the hands of the Jews. All the people rose up against them. All the conquered peoples of Parthia. In the Tigris-Euphrates valley, it was a general uprising, not just a Jewish one."

"That's fantastic!"

"Yes. And the result? The Romans decided to withdraw, to give up Parthia entirely."

"Excellent! And maybe we have contributed to that, to some extent."

"In Africa, right?" He really seemed proud.

"Yes."

"Sure we have, but in a different way, too. Listen to the bad news. The Jews were singled out for punishment. Trajan selected the most brutal of his generals, a man named Lusius Quietus, a Moorish prince. He gave that man responsibility for subduing Nisibis and Edessa. Seleucia was left to others."

Shimeon listened with apprehension.

"In those towns, the man Quietus negotiated with the Jews. He told them that he was a man of reason. He explained that he understood why they were fighting, but that the fight would be unnecessary now. The Emperor Trajan had decided to bow to the wishes of the people of Parthia and to withdraw his troops."

"Really? That's unprecedented."

"Wait. The people were happy. They shook the hand of Quietus and made a banquet in his honor, treated him royally. Then he rode back to his camp, got his soldiers ready, and in the middle of the night sneaked into the city – into the undefended city, where all the forces were happily celebrating their victory. Tens of thousands of Roman soldiers dispersed through the place and, upon a prearranged signal, attacked the inhabitants of the city and massacred them. They killed every last person they could find."

Shimeon was horrified.

"And did he repeat this at the second place?"

"Yes, before the Jews, the few surviving ones, had a chance to send word about what happened. That is how he operates, always through deception, fraud, trickery. Some people say that Trajan ordered him to arrange for the expulsion of the Jews, but he chose to murder them instead."

"What happened to the people in other cities? The non-Jews?"

"They were pacified somehow, but not murdered. The Jews all over Mesopotamia and Babylonia were massacred."

I don't know how Shimeon felt about that; remember, I was not there. But I was very upset when I heard these news later. I cried for our people, even though, by that time, I should have been used to tens of thousands being killed.

I think Shimeon was upset, too. He demanded from Lucuas, as if that man were to blame:

"What does he say, what kind of reason does he give for this?"

"He says that the Jews were rebelling in Africa and in Judaea, and now in Mesopotamia, and they had to be stopped."

"Stopped?"

"Well, he's probably heard of our actions in Cyrenaica."

"But that's not the same. Our enemies in Africa had a chance. They could fight and they did. We lost many of our best soldiers in battles. We did not make peace with them, only to attack later that night!"

"True, but I think that Trajan was really worried about the military power of the Jews. He heard about our decimating the Roman legions in Africa. He knows that our troops have arrived here. And then, the Jews attacked him all over Mesopotamia and Babylonia. I think that he was simply afraid of the Jews. And rightly so."

"Yes, so our poor relatives in Mesopotamia had to pay with their lives for our successes."

"But you have not heard the worst. Trajan is grateful to Lusius Quietus for his massacre of the Jews. So what reward does he offer the man? Can you guess?"

Shimeon shook his head.

"I have no idea, Lucuas."

"Well, I'll tell you. I've just heard this today. Lusius Quietus has been promoted to Governor."

"Governor of what?"

"Governor of Judaea!"

*   *   *

And now the era of terror began – mercifully, it was short.

The Romans announced that Judaea would become a consular province. What's that? A governor with the rank of consul has lots of power, and Quietus convinced Trajan that he would need it.

But a consular governor only headed provinces with at least two legions. They had the Tenth *Fretensis* in Jerusalem, but not yet the Sixth *Ferrata*. That came a little later. It seems that they were really worried about the potential situation here.

They doubled their forces, so that they could stop the revolt before it got out of hand. You know, Yose, those Romans were not stupid. They knew what they were doing.

The very first thing Quietus did in office was to issue orders for the arrest of Julianus and Pappus. As I told you, the brothers were working near the main harbors all the way to Antiochia, and they organized the return of our people from various places, but mainly from Cyprus.

By this time the forces of Marcius Turbo had gained the upper hand on that island and started murdering the Jews. It was imperative to bring as many Jews as possible to Eretz Yisrael. That was the two brothers' undertaking, and Quietus stopped it efficiently.

I felt very bad about that. Shimeon and I loved the two young men. We were hoping to look them up as soon as we dared to travel freely; now they had been thrown into jail. We were concerned about their fate.

The country was in a state of ferment. Shimeon had to be everywhere, organizing people: his own thirty thousand soldiers, or at least most of them (for quite a few disappeared, nobody knew where), as well as the young men of Judaea itself.

Jaffa was the first town to rise up. Almost all the men joined in hostile acts against the Romans, not fighting directly at first, because the Roman troops wisely held back, but sabotaging shipping and commerce.

Next, it was Beth Guvrin and Gerassa, and then most of the south was in revolt. The Romans finally pounced, they attacked with increasing forces. Our people were ready. They fought back. It was a real war, a *pulmus*. That's what it was called afterwards: 'Pulmus Quitos.' Bad Greek for the 'War of Quietus.'

Of course, our efforts were harshly crushed. Yet in the long run, who knows, that may have helped us.

How, you ask? The Romans nipped the revolt in the bud. They killed some of our people, but not too many. Most of our young fighters stayed alive, ready to fight another battle in the future.

One man they captured and killed was Lucuas.

*   *   *

The terrible events of that period affected my family and friends. Any sage

who had ever made an even slightly derogatory statement against the
Romans had to flee for his life. Your father, Rabbi Halafta, and his friend,
Rabbi Yohanan ben Nuri, both escaped to the Galilee and hid for nearly a
year at the house of Eleazar ben Azariyah.

Pappus and Julianus were tried and sentenced to death. We were hoping for a reprieve.

But the Emperor Trajan was heading back towards Syria with less
than half of the huge army he had started out with. He was a broken man,
and he must have had nightmares thinking about the reception he would
get in Rome.

He never made it there. He died along the way.

THE GOOD EMPEROR HADRIAN

Yose, listen to this: Two very strange years started then with two very strange weeks.

I already told you that Lucuas was killed by Lusius Quietus.

And also that Pappus and Julianus were captured and sentenced to death.

But then Julianus and Pappus were pardoned.

And then Lusius Quietus was demoted and ordered back to Rome.

And then Pappus and Julianus were executed.

And then Lusius Quietus was executed.

And then Julianus and Pappus prepared tables at the seashore.

And Shimeon was unusually quiet for a year.

*   *   *

You think, Yose, that I am not making much sense. But such were the times. Still, let me try to explain in detail what happened, at least as I remember those events.

After Lucuas was killed, it was natural that Shimeon would become the leader of the resistance, though I think that he was that already before. He was always away, visiting this community and that, organizing, organizing.

I stayed at home. There was so much to talk about with my mother and Tzviyya. My sister was happy to have me there, for her husband, Halafta, was already in hiding, at Sepphoris in the Galilee.

Even when Shimeon was at home, he rose very early, went over to the other wing of the house to pray with uncle Yonathan, and then to work. I stayed in bed until later.

Well, during those two weeks, Tzviyya woke me almost every day, with the latest news.

"Michal, wake up! Your friends Pappus and Julianus are pardoned!"

"Michal, listen! Lusius Quietus is no longer the governor! He was ordered back to Rome. He's left already."

"Michal, this is horrible. Pappus and Julianus were executed yesterday! Despite the pardon!"

"Michal! Lusius Quietus did not make it even to the ship! He was executed on the orders of the new emperor!"

Now, if you say, Yose, that it still does not make sense, you are right, but

I heard these things every morning from your own mother. Still, maybe I can explain some of the background.

You see, the nephew of Trajan, young Hadrian, became the new emperor. I have to tell you a little about that man, for he was so important to our fate. First we loved him, then we hated him.

I have to jump ahead in my story by about ten years. In the days before the war, the great war, Shimeon's war, we were very close to Rabbi Akiva. We met at his house many times; and there, a frequent visitor was a certain Aquila, a student of Akiva's. That young man was a convert to our faith just like several members of our family. He translated the Torah into Greek! Compared to that achievement, his further distinction, that of being the nephew of the Emperor Hadrian, was really insignificant. Still, it added to his being an interesting, unusual person. He was a very nice young man, tall, almost as tall as Shimeon, with a wide grin on his face most of the time. He was also blond, with a square jaw, and he wore no beard, imagine!

I recall Aquila talking to us about the emperor.

"My uncle just loves everything to do with the Greeks: their religion, their customs, their cities, their statues, their gymnasia, their public baths, but mainly their gods."

Somebody asked:

"So then he hates the Jewish religion?"

Aquila scratched where his beard should have been.

"You know, he does not exactly hate it. He has been around. He has seen many religions and cults. He finds all of them interesting. He even studies them, to some extent. You know that he is an intelligent man."

We all nodded, for that fact was known by then.

"But he wants to make the whole world Greek. He thinks that the only civilized lifestyle is the Greco-Roman culture, and he does not want you and others to remain barbarians."

"Barbarians! When compared to the Jewish religion, his is a primitive, pagan one!" My husband felt insulted.

"I know that." He spread his arms in a helpless gesture. "I know, but he does not, and it would not be possible to convince him. He wants to bring illumination to every country through the Greek culture."

"He can keep it."

"He can, but there is also politics in his approach."

"How does politics enter into religion?"

"You see, when he came to power ten years ago, the very first thing he had to do was to give up Parthia entirely."

"Did not his own uncle Trajan do that?"

"No, Trajan only withdrew as a strategic necessity. He pretended that he would return with a larger, better army. But Hadrian knew that he could never do that. So when he reported back to the Senate, he could blame Trajan to some extent for the loss of a third of the empire, but it was still a humiliating position. He had to build it up by promising that he would reinforce his hold on all the other territories under their control."

"Including our land."

"Yes, especially Judaea. And he thought that he could best achieve that result by making Romans out of all the people in all the occupied lands."

"That was not very likely."

"Well, in some places it worked. Some parts of Europe appear to have become parts of an enlarged Rome."

"For now."

"Yes, for now. Only time will tell how large the Roman Empire will be."

Shimeon wanted to say that if he has anything to do with it, the Roman Empire will be very small indeed, but he thought better of it.

Aquila added:

"And that is what was behind his promise to rebuild Jerusalem."

"He never meant it!"

"Yes, he did. Only you misunderstood him. He meant to rebuild it, and he made me responsible for that task. It would have been a beautiful Greek city."

"Greek city?!"

"Yes. A pagan city. Full of pagan statuary, temples to this god and that. He would have made it into the most beautiful city in the world."

Shimeon wanted to spit, but he realized in time where he was. Aquila smiled. "And it is fortunate that things turned out the way they did, for I could have been the builder of that city. I shudder at the thought."

Before becoming a Jew, Aquila was a Notzri, a follower of Yehoshua whom they thought the Messiah.

*   *   *

So let me then resume my story where I left off before.

When Hadrian became emperor, he was very familiar with our country and our people. Aquila said that Hadrian described the Jews as the most difficult people because they are all over the empire and elsewhere, their loyalty is only to their own nation and they will do anything they can to destroy Roman rule. Yet he thought that something should be done to try to win the favor of the Jews.

He wanted to consolidate his hold and that meant pacifying all regions, so he would not have to send large parts of his army to fight wars in every corner of the empire. He felt that he should make peace with the Jews.

The very first thing he did was to remove the Moorish troops from under Lusius Quietus' command. Quietus was a Moor himself, and these troops were loyal to him. Hadrian made them leave the country on the shortest notice.

A few days later, he sent two senior messengers to Quietus, relieving him of his post and ordering him to Rome immediately.

At the same time, he sent another messenger to wait for Quietus in the harbor, to arrest him and to execute him on the spot.

Did he do all that for our benefit? No, he had other reasons. Again, I quote Aquila.

"That part was very simple. Lusius Quietus was a big man, growing in power every day. He saw himself as the next emperor. Hadrian foresaw that Quietus could one day, soon, plot for his destruction, perhaps with certain members of the Senate. So he accused Quietus of treason and disposed of him."

I remember that Rabbi Akiva made a biting comment on that, to the effect that the civilized Romans had an awful lot to learn from the barbarian Jews about the system of justice. Not that he, or any of us, was particularly sad about the fate of Quietus.

But what about Pappus and Julianus, you ask.

Their execution was scheduled for a Thursday. The Sunday before, Quietus lost his loyal Moorish troops. Tuesday, he was relieved of his command. Of the two Roman emissaries, one asserted power until the emperor would appoint a new governor. He cancelled the death sentences of the two brothers and some other people.

Great was the rejoicing in the country. By then, everybody had heard of Pappus and Julianus (some called him Lulianus); they were much loved by all.

But there was a corrupt Roman, originally a Jew called Yaacov, who became a traitor, went over to the Romans, accepted their gods, and changed his name to Iago. He was an adjutant to Lusius Quietus, and some say that he led the man to his death by encouraging his ambition towards a grandiose career. Well, this man now convinced the new proconsul, or satrap, or whatever he was, that these two were dangerous criminals, intent on destroying the Roman structure. So the man reinstated their death sentence.

The rejoicing ceased, and there was wailing in the land as news of their execution spread.

*   *   *

Hadrian made it widely known that he wanted a new era of good relations with all his subjects, including the Jews. Especially including the Jews. He announced a new program of peaceful coexistence between the empire and all of its subjects. He called it Pax Iustitia Felicitas.

Our sages were quick to react. They sent a message to the emperor to find out if he was willing to receive a delegation of Jewish religious leaders. Word came back in the affirmative.

Who should go? Rabban Gamaliel had passed away not long before and there was no new Nasi. Eleazar ben Azariyah was the *Av Bet Din* and a rich and cultivated man. He was an obvious candidate for the trip.

In the old days Gamaliel used to travel to Rome with Rabbi Eliezer and Rabbi Yehoshua. Well, Eliezer was out of favor, but Yehoshua was still around and everybody loved and respected him. He was to become the second member of the delegation.

And as three members were traditionally required, there was no question that Rabbi Akiva would complete the mission. Off they went to Rome.

They returned four weeks later, and they brought great news. I heard the details in our own house, where Akiva visited us next day.

That was the day when Shimeon became quiet. For a year, he hardly uttered a word.

It was not unusual to see a cheerful look on Rabbi Akiva's face. He was a tall, powerful man, quite bald; wisdom glowed from his features and, more often than not, he displayed a confident, encouraging smile. But this time his face was radiant as he told us about the meeting with Hadrian.

"I have always believed in peace. Yet lately I allowed myself to be convinced" – here he looked at Shimeon – "that the Kingdom of the Messiah would not come until we fought for it. That was a mistake. It just shows how little I know of the ways of the Lord. For apparently He considers that we have suffered enough, and is willing to grant us our independence now without fighting. At least our religious independence. The rest shall come later."

Yonathan retorted:

"Religious independence is not enough. We must have our own country. We cannot be a province in the Roman Empire."

"That will come. It seems that Hadrian is a reasonable man. Let me tell you about our discussions."

We listened intently.

"We were prepared to wait for days for our audience, I am told that that's how it went in the past, when the others met Trajan. But no, we showed up one morning and let the authorities know that we are the delegation from Judaea; by the afternoon we received word that the emperor would see us next morning. So we went, and we had an excellent reception. We were welcomed like long-lost friends."

Akiva looked at the smirk on the faces of both Yonathan and Shimeon, and hastened to add:

"Now look, I am not new to this game. I know when to disregard appearances. But that young man was really earnest and emphasized, more than once, that he wanted to rehabilitate the eastern end of his empire, to bring real peace to that region. He explained that they have lost too many soldiers in ill-considered ventures, and they would prefer at least a hundred years of peace. I had no trouble believing him."

"So what does he want?"

"It is not a question of what he wants. He asked us, directly, what we wanted. He was very blunt about it. He said that if we really represented the Jews in Judaea, perhaps even elsewhere, then we should tell him what we wanted in exchange for peace. He said that if it was at all reasonable, he would agree."

"So what did you say?"

"Eleazar ben Azariyah was our spokesman. He said that we requested a full restoration of Jerusalem. But Yehoshua added that Jerusalem must be our religious and administrative capital. And I asked that our religious rights be respected and not tampered with."

"And what did he say?"

"He said: 'I can agree to almost all that you are requesting, my friends. One small matter: When you say religious and administrative capital, you must understand that the administration will have to remain the task of our representative in Judaea.' And Yehoshua asked if he thought that would be forever. Hadrian answered: 'Forever is a long time. No, I think that as the peace matures and the Jewish people demonstrate increasing responsibility, they shall take over more and more of the administrative functions, until, in the end, our role shall be no more than nominal.'"

Yonathan asked: "And you believed him?"

You see, Yose, Yonathan was old enough and sufficiently respected enough to put such a question to Rabbi Akiva. Shimeon probably felt the same way, but he could not be so impertinent as to imply naivety in the great man. Anyway, Akiva waved the comment away.

"Believe? No, I am not that simple-minded. But given the chance to establish ourselves in Jerusalem and to build up our strength and our entire nation, we shall be in a much better position to fight than we are now, should he then renege on his promises."

Shimeon made his first and last comment that day, indeed that year (excepting, of course, private conversations). He said:

"But we are in an excellent position to fight now."

"You are? I have some doubts, my son. No, you must be much stronger than the Romans to win and to scare them so badly that they don't dare to send reinforcements. You could not do that today."

Yonathan asked: "What about the Temple? Will they rebuild it?"

"No, they won't pay for it. I asked him who would pay for the reconstruction. Not specifically the Temple, for I did not want to draw his attention to that, just in general. I told him that Jerusalem was in ruins, and that funds must be found for the rebuilding. And he said that we must both contribute. They will pay for all buildings that they put up, and he assured us that Jerusalem will be more beautiful than ever. But if we wanted to put up buildings of our own, that will be our affair and we shall have to pay for them. It was hard to argue about that point, even though it was the Romans who destroyed our buildings fifty years ago. In any case, we thought it better not to emphasize the edifice we wanted to erect."

"But won't they object to our rebuilding the Temple?"

"Why should they? It will be our religious center, not administrative, remember, because they will handle the administrative functions. We promised them to coexist peacefully, so what difference will it make to them what kind of Temple we build?"

"I don't know," said Yonathan, "but I would feel more comfortable if a specific agreement had been reached about the Temple."

"Well, if they have a problem with it, that will become clear very soon, for we must start immediately. We must collect money and get ready for the construction."

* * *

News spread quickly and there was rejoicing in the land. Nobody worried about the little details, such as specifically what was agreed and what was assumed. The Emperor Hadrian had permitted the rebuilding of Jerusalem. Jerusalem was synonymous in the mind of every Jew with the Temple. Everybody happily celebrated the expectation that the Temple would now rise again.

There were a few hundred Jews already living in the western part of the ruins, and now thousands more began flocking to the city. They were putting up houses for themselves and claimed to be ready to build the House of the Lord when called upon to do so.

Meanwhile, the Sanhedrin started a major fundraising effort. They sent out emissaries to all Jewish settlements, in Judaea and also in the Diaspora, what remained of it, mainly in the Parthian Empire. Akiva himself went on numerous such trips and came back with huge sums of money and treasures, which were deposited in a special Temple fund.

And two brothers, named Shemayah and Ahiyah, appeared out of nowhere. They set up tables all along the seashore, near the major ports, welcoming returning Jews who came for the specific purpose of building the Temple, to direct them to Jerusalem and to supply them with sufficient funds for living expenses during the trip and afterwards.

Shemayah and Ahiyah. Need I tell you what their real names were?

Shimeon and I visited them, and they were our long-lost friends. They were so happy to see us, and we talked long into the night.

We asked them about their escape.

"Pappus, Julianus. Everybody thought that you are both dead. Your execution was announced long ago."

They grinned. Julianus spoke.

"There was a man there, a certain Yaacov. I think he was responsible for getting our death sentence reinstated. Ah, but that man liked money."

Pappus added:

"It was his wife who liked money even more, what was her name?"

"Emilia, I think."

"Yes, it may have been she who got Yaacov to arrange for our renewed death sentence, so that we would then bribe our way out of it."

"Thank the Lord for Emilia," I said.

"Amen," they responded.

Shimeon asked them:

"Do you really believe that everything will be good and beautiful now? That we shall be free?"

They looked at each other. Apparently, they had discussed the matter, more than once. Julianus answered.

"Free? No, not really free. But building our future, and once we have built the Temple, we hope that the Messiah will appear and *then* we shall be truly free."

Shimeon expected the coming of the Messiah as much as they did, so it was hard to argue with such a statement. All he said was: "Well, we could have tried for a peaceful solution in Cyrenaica. We could have negotiated and offered them no trouble in exchange for rights. But we thought that they would never really respect us if they did not learn about our strength through suffering from it."

Pappus answered: "We would have been right, if we were only strong enough. No, don't answer, Shimeon. I know what you want to say. We would have been strong enough, if it were not for the cowardly leadership in Alexandria…"

"We should have eliminated them, after all. I was wrong there."

"Perhaps. If so, we were all wrong. But surely it's better to get what we want peacefully than through blood and suffering."

"*If* we get what we want. But shall we?"

"We shall see. That's why we are here. One must always hope."

*   *   *

Still, those were good days. Everybody was relaxed and happy, all but Shimeon. He did not trust any Roman, be he an emperor, a procurator or a foot soldier.

All the same, there was less pressure on Shimeon than before. He could spend more time with me, perhaps more than any time during our marriage.

He was a good husband to me and I was a good wife. We loved each other very much and we were happy in those days. We finally had time for each other.

We could talk, and talk we did! I remember one night, we were together and I asked him why he always needed to fight. He was surprised at the question.

"I told you before, Michal. Our land is occupied and we must liberate it from the oppressors."

"Yes, you said that a long time ago. You think that the Romans are like the Greeks were in the past, they must be thrown out, just like the Maccabees threw out the Greeks."

"Exactly. You know that."

"Yes, I know. But it is different now. Different from the time you told me why you wanted to fight in Africa. Then you wanted to join the rebels. Now you want to lead the entire movement, the war. Shimeon, you want to be the leader of the nation! Is that not right?"

He had to think before he gave me an answer.

"Michal, I don't want to be the leader. Not just for the sake of being the leader. Believe me, I have no ambitions like that. But somebody must take a leading role, especially now that Lucuas is dead. I don't see anyone else, at least not a strong man, who could do it."

"And you think that you can do it?"

Shimeon swallowed before answering. I could see that it was no small statement that he was about to make.

"I can. If the Lord helps me, I shall be able to throw the Romans out of our land."

It was my turn to stop and take the measure of his statement.

"Shimeon, tell me. How important is this for you?"

"How important? What kind of question is that? Most important. All-important."

"That is the most important thing in your life, right?"

"Of course it is. To do the work of the Lord, to serve Him, to liberate my people, why, what could be more important than that?"

I did not say anything for a while. We were close and I moved even closer to him. Then I asked him.

"Shimeon, do you love me?"

Again he was surprised. Of course we loved each other, but we did not usually talk of such things.

"I love you very much, Michal."

"But not as much as the nation?"

"Now you are talking silly. How can you compare things like that?"

"But if you had to choose between me and the nation?"

He sighed, kissed me and held me tight.

"Look, my dear. I love you so much, I could not even tell you about it. But don't force me to make choices. So far, thank the Lord, I have not been in a situation where that choice had to be made. But if it ever happens, you should know that the nation comes first. The work of the Lord comes first."

I knew he would say that, but I cried a little. He kissed my face, and I turned to him.

"Shimeon, my dear, it would have been different if I had borne children, would it not?"

"No, Michal, no!" His face was so earnest, I had to believe him. "Not at all. I would still have to do my work. But I tell you something. It would have been more difficult with children. Maybe that is the reason we have not been given any. I have to thank the Lord for being so considerate, for blessing our marriage with that much less trouble."

That was a strange thing to say, I could not understand it at all.

"Should I then thank the Lord for not having given me children?"

"Perhaps it's different for you. I know how women feel about such things. They always want to have little children around them. It seems that you never got any because of me. I am sorry about that."

"Men also want children. They all want a boy to carry their name."

"That's not important for me. But I am truly sorry if I have caused such a lack in your life."

"There is no lack in my life. It is full because of you, my dear. But shall I always have you by my side?"

"Whatever the Lord decides, that's what will happen. We must be satisfied with that."

Nothing further was said. Shimeon stroked my face a couple of times, but was soon asleep. For a long time I lay awake, pondering his words. Mainly I was thinking about the political situation, about the hope for peace. Perhaps Shimeon would be wrong, perhaps everything would turn out as everyone expected, and there would be no need for him to fight again.

*   *   *

Messianic hope was in the air. Everybody (but Shimeon) thought that the long-awaited era was about to commence. I had never seen the country, the people so happy.

All the more bitter, therefore, was the disappointment when everything fell apart.

For those hopes did fall apart, as surely as Shimeon predicted that they would.

Hadrian intended to build a beautiful Greek city. He did not want a

Jewish city. He did not want our Temple. As Aquila told us later, he envisioned a 'polis' with statues and temples to Greek gods, Roman baths, gymnasia, sports events, theaters – everything he considered Greek culture, not resembling anything that we thought of as the City of the Lord.

And when he learned of the full extent of our effort, how the whole nation was struggling towards the rebuilding, and someone may even have explained to him that for us the Temple was the same thing as independence, he called a halt to the whole effort.

Alas, there shall be no Jewish city. There shall be no Greek city – at least not for now. He reneged on all of his promises.

He confiscated the money, all the funds we had collected!

Of course, he knew that we would not take such an affront lying down. So he prepared himself and his troops. He started to build roads everywhere. They paved new roads between Sepphoris and Kfar Otnay (they twisted that name into 'Caparcotna,' later changed it to 'Legio'). They built another road from Sepphoris to Acco.

Hadrian now brought the Sixth *Ferrata* Legion in from Arabia. That was the second legion, for the Tenth *Fretensis* was already in Jerusalem.

And he had Pappus and Julianus re-arrested, tried, sentenced to death and executed, this time with no corrupt Yaacov or Emilia to provide them an escape. May their memory be blessed.

I shall write to you more, the Lord willing.

Peace be with you.

Hadrian's letter to Plotina

I SHALL BRING THEM CIVILIZATION

The Emperor Caesar Trajan Hadrian August – to Plotina –
widow of the August Caesar Trajan, greetings.

My dear Plotina, my mother by adoption and my best friend, it has been three years since the gods have taken my Father, your husband Trajan, to become one of their members. As his unworthy heir, and thanking my position to you, I have been trying to fill the vast emptiness left by his exit from the leadership of the empire.

You had asked me about some of the decisions I have been making, some of the effort that stems from our discussions of yore. Let me assure you, my dear friend, that I have not forgotten any of our ideas, any of our great thoughts. Yes, admittedly I have ambition, but only for Rome, only for the well-being of the empire. I would hesitate making such a statement to a person less close to me than you are, for it might sound pretentious. Yet I know that you believe me, you know that what I have planned with you, what I have been trying to implement in these last three years, is really for the best of all citizens of our beloved Rome. I pray to the gods that I will succeed and thus, one day, I may be worthy of the mantle and name of my great predecessor, my Father, Trajan.

That is not to say, of course, that I am trying to follow exactly in his footsteps. You know that I have changed our expansion policy. Trajan thought that, in order to be successful, the empire must continually grow. I think he envied Alexander. He tried to absorb the entire Parthian Empire into Rome and nearly succeeded. If it were not for the rebellious Jews causing trouble in Africa and many other places, perhaps there would have been enough time to consolidate our rule in Mesopotamia and all the other kingdoms, all the way to the border of India. But he did not take those closer uprisings seriously at first, and later he was forced to bring back too many legions from the east. Had he lived, he might have tried to reinstate Roman rule over Parthia.

When I took over the reins, that was my first major decision: to abandon all territories east of Judaea and Syria and to make peace with our former enemies in such a way as to maintain our influence and security. I am proud to say that I have succeeded in achieving that peace.

So things are relatively stable now, and I must admit that I am proud of that achievement. Which takes me to your question: What am I trying to do with the empire? Perhaps you are the only one who will believe me: I would like to leave it exactly as it is now. Don't misunderstand me though, I will also want to make many changes. Let me explain. I was referring to the borders of the empire. I think that it is large enough. Perhaps some time in the future, when we shall be so strong, rich and happy as to be the envy of the whole world, some nations will, on their own, apply to join the Roman Empire. Perhaps we shall accept them, if they prove themselves worthy of the honor. But I don't see ourselves taking other lands, other kingdoms over by force. What we have is enough. But what we have, I intend to defend with all the force of our magnificent army.

You know that I have always been close to our legions. Some of my friends wondered if I should worry about the leaders of the army being unhappy with my decision to stop expansion. I don't think so. I travel constantly, visit one outpost after another, explain our policies to the consuls and tribunes. They will be busy enough putting down minor local skirmishes, rebellions; and in any case, I intend to increase their activities for the sake of improved military preparedness. If being a soldier was thought as a tough calling before, wait to see how tough I shall make it. But they will love it. No matter how difficult the tasks I devise, I will always be there to carry them out alongside the men, so they will say, "If the Caesar can do it, so can I." They must be able to throw a javelin while in full armor. The cavalrymen must be able to jump onto their horse while fully equipped with bronze helmet and breastplate, large sword, long pike, their oblong shield and their bow and quiver full of arrows. It is not easy, but it can be done. Too long have we had to rely on our foreign auxiliaries for the best horsemen; now I want our native Roman soldiers to become more expert than their foreign teachers.

Yes, a soldier's life is tough. They serve for twenty years, they are not even allowed to marry during that time, though they usually form some attachment with local women. But when they have fulfilled their obligation, we reward them richly, and I intend to make that reward even better. They get land, usually in the country where they last served. Up to now, that land was often of poor quality; I will make sure that theirs will always be the choicest field available. That was one reason your husband wanted to expand the empire, to find new lands for the soldiers; but there is enough, even if we need to take some away from local peasants, compensate them some other way, perhaps lower their taxes or, if they qualify, accept their children into our schools to get a Roman education.

Which takes me to the essence of my plan for the empire. I want to improve the lifestyle of every man and woman, every citizen, to unheard-of levels. I wish to make all citizens happy, healthy, well-educated, cultured. And listen to this: When I am talking about citizens, I mean not only those of Rome proper, but in all the lands of the empire. The Franks, Britons, Germans, and of course the Greeks and Spaniards; but also the now primitive people of far-away lands, those of Dacia and Pannonia, all of Northern Africa; and even those recalcitrant mischief-makers, the Jews of Judaea.

Yes, I have special plans for the Jews. I will forget their renegade actions, their disobedience, their rebellions. I will make peace with them, as with all other people in our realm. I will make them happy and satisfied, proud members of the empire. I will restore their once great city of Jerusalem! It will be a dazzling city again, with temples and sanctuaries, squares, public baths, markets, statuary, schools, theatres – it will compete with the most beautiful cities of the world, Athens and Alexandria. And they will thank me for that. They may re-name their city in my honor – not that I crave such honors, but it is always useful to remind the subjects of the source of their fortune. Lucius suggested that I should call Jerusalem Hadrianapolis. I thought about it, but I felt that perhaps, in some circles, there may be resentment of such an obvious appellation. My original name, as you know, is Publius Aelius Hadrianus. I shall call Jerusalem Aelia Capitolina. That will not be an insult to anyone. I will erect a huge statue there, to Jupiter. Let our Jewish subjects be proud and happy. That way, there will be no more rebellions, no more wars. They can even build a small sanctuary to their own god, I shall ask our priests to find the equivalence, which of our Roman or Greek deities would match theirs.

But I must be patient. There will always be difficulties, delays. Just a few days ago, they brought me news of potential new trouble from the Jews. They are a stubborn race! There are some people there, some of their religious leaders, who are still opposing us, still trying to stir up trouble. They apparently want to build a huge temple of their own, dedicated to their strange invisible god, and they don't want to allow – allow! – any other temples or sanctuaries. Also, my sources tell me that this temple of theirs would be something like the seat of a government, which is, of course, nonsense; there can only be one government, ours. I would have expected them to be more grateful for our generosity. If they don't want their great city rebuilt, they won't have it.

Yet that is not true. I must not allow a temporary pique to interfere with my overall plans for the empire. They will get their city, Aelia Capitolina, but not just yet. First, I shall have to pacify them more. That means, they must learn to respect our rule, our forces. I have ordered the strengthening of our army in Judaea. We shall build more roads, new camps. I shall order a second legion into Judaea, the VI *Ferrata*. The X *Fretensis* is doing well, but it will be useful to double our presence. Then, after a while, they will be ready to accept civilization.

So, my dear Plotina, you can see that I do have ambitious plans. They are very close to our ideas of old, the things we used to discuss in our small circle of friends. Making civilized men and women out of barbarians, creating a rich and happy empire – why, what could be a more noble, more lofty, yet at the same time more practical and more achievable design for the empire? Do write to me, let me have your thoughts, for I value them more than those of any of my advisors. Farewell.

Michal's letter to Yose

PREPARE FOR THE WAR OF REDEMPTION!

From Michal bat Dosa – to my nephew –
Rabbi Yose ben Halafta, may your peace be great.

Yose, we learned more about Hadrian's frightening decision later.

Aquila told us that the decision was brewing in his uncle's mind over several months. The Samaritans protested and warned him that, with a central command post in Jerusalem, we would be very strong and able to start a war against Rome.

His advisors warned of the same thing, told him that for us Jerusalem meant not just a religion, it meant independence.

He wanted to proceed and build his pagan city there, but Aquila at least managed to talk him out of it, for the time being. Eventually, he proceeded with that plan, but only much later.

Pappus and Julianus protested the confiscation of the funds. That's why they were arrested. I am not sure why they had to be sentenced to death, it may have been the doing of some overeager Roman official; but of course, they may have seen through the 'Shemayah and Ahiyah' disguise and realized that these people were supposed to have been executed a couple of years earlier.

Needless to say, these events changed our personal lives completely. I should have known that something like that would happen, sooner or later, but somehow I fooled myself, along with everyone else, that there would be peace and tranquillity. But Shimeon never fooled himself, he never expected real peace, let alone freedom. He was quietly biding his time.

I advised him, during those two years, before Hadrian's abominable edict banning us from building the Temple, to avoid any revolutionary activity. He was willing to accept at least part of my counsel: He went back to Torah studies with Rabbi Akiva. How much he studied Torah there and how much he argued with his master, I cannot say.

One event I particularly recall during those good months. Rabbi Halafta, your father, Yose, came back from hiding in his hometown, Sepphoris. There was no longer any need to hide, and he was very pleased.

The very first evening, when we all had our meal together, even drank a little wine, your father was gloating about the beauty of the Hillelite position.

"Now you have to admit, Yonathan, that in the long run the School of Hillel is always proven right."

"I admit no such thing." His beautiful old face was very red. Uncle Yonathan was angry. "In the long run, the School of Hillel is a disaster."

"But look! You and Shimeon here would have fought them, and we would have suffered more and lost many more people. We counselled peace and cooperation, making compromises, coexistence. Well, we won. Is that not proof enough for you?"

"But wait until the end. Don't be naive, Halafta. They will take advantage of us. I don't know how they'll do it, but this whole beautiful dream will collapse. Remember that I said so."

"Yonathan, you are a painfully pessimistic person, you don't see further than the tip of your nose. Why can't you accept that these Romans are reasonable people, looking for peace and a way to live together without trouble?"

That was when Shimeon could no longer endure listening politely. I saw that he was ready to say something rude. I squeezed his hand strongly. He hesitated, then he jumped up and stormed out of the room.

*   *   *

I am sorry to tell you that uncle Yonathan passed away shortly after the debate I've just described. May his memory be blessed. At least he did not live to see the Roman perfidy, although, perhaps, he would have liked to see it, if only to feel justified.

In any case, the Romans tricked us, and for some time nobody espoused the Hillelite position. We all felt betrayed, and Shimeon was moving fast.

He had many contacts. Eventually he managed to get in touch with all of his Cyrenaican men, began organizing them, promoting certain individuals to sub-command posts. He often took young Hillel with him, trusted the fellow; Shimeon had a good sense for choosing the right people.

With the death of Lucuas, nobody doubted anymore that Shimeon bar Kosiva, as he preferred to be called, was the leader of the resistance. That gave me plenty of causes for worry, we never knew when the Roman authorities would appear at our door, dragging him away. Not that Shimeon spent much time at home.

He also knew many young men throughout the land, especially in the hill country, what they call 'King's Mountain,' going up all the way to Jerusalem. Those young fighters were the sons of dispossessed peasants, bitter about the Romans, waiting for a liberator. They were ready to follow Shimeon into any battle.

Shimeon did not want to start a war yet. He wanted to be very well prepared. So he asked Rabbi Akiva to try to calm the people. Akiva, in turn, suggested that his master and friend, Yehoshua ben Hananiyah, talk to the angry masses. Yehoshua addressed them, and gave them the allegory of a stork who extracted a bone from the throat of a lion and then, when asking for the promised reward, was told that having his beak in the lion's mouth and being allowed to live was reward enough. Apparently, the people accepted this, they had such respect and love for Yehoshua. The old man also visited Ishmael ben Elisha at his village of Azziz and asked that sage to exert his influence in calming the people. Ishmael had never been very sympathetic to the Romans, perhaps now he felt that his constant arguments with Rabbi Akiva would come to a satisfactory conclusion. He recognized that Akiva had received a horrible shock and would not be able to take up full leadership of the nation soon. He himself was not very surprised by the turn of events. But he did not know about Shimeon's work.

Eventually, Shimeon got his young men to dig underground fortifications. There were many of these already prepared, from his earlier days, but now Shimeon wanted the land, especially the Judaean foothills, full of these fortified hiding places, so that any Roman advance could be frustrated before it could even approach the hills.

He started with twenty or thirty thousand fighters, and in five years he had two hundred thousand. It is not easy to hide two hundred thousand soldiers. Of course, these people went about their normal occupation most of the time: They were peasants, shepherds, bakers, tailors, weavers, masons, potters and so on. There were even some musicians amongst them and barbers and surgeons. But when Shimeon sent out a message that it was training time in a certain area, they all came to the valley or forest, with sentries posted carefully; or else, they met in the underground complexes.

Shimeon tried to avoid clashes with the Romans until he was certain of being ready for them; this was Rabbi Akiva's counsel. But at a certain time, fifty-five years after the destruction of the Temple, they were meeting in a valley at the lower hills, and a Roman cavalry detachment happened to enter the valley. I don't know if our sentry was asleep, or if they managed to kill him before he could raise the alarm, but suddenly three hundred Roman soldiers were charging at our people. They were mounted, while our people, though far more numerous, were on foot. It was a bloodbath. Shimeon managed to direct his people so as to avoid unnecessary losses, but even so we lost five hundred. The Romans lost all but one or two, those managed to escape and report the battle to their superiors. Pity; or as Shimeon put it afterwards, that was highly undesirable.

There were also two smaller skirmishes. The Romans came in to the valley later, with large forces, to wipe out what they considered 'banditry.' Needless to say, they did not find one person there or any evidence of trouble. They may have doubted the words of their own people, but the term 'banditry' spread, it was used by the Romans to describe any of our activities. That did not bother us at all.

Some bandits may not have been Shimeon's men. It was very confusing sometimes to know who commanded whom. But even the most unruly bandits respected the leadership and especially the great sages.

Hillel of Cyrene, by then an important lieutenant in Shimeon's army, and married, sometimes attended Rabbi Akiva's house, even though he was no scholar or even student. Yet he helped out with the chores and was now and then allowed to sit in on study sessions. In the evenings, though, he returned to our house, helped the servants with various tasks, then joined us at the dinner table. I remember that once he told us an interesting story.

"One day, several disciples of Rabbi Akiva returned from a mission in the north. On their way back, before they reached Acco, they were harassed by bandits. They kept going, but when they stopped at Achziv, the bandits, who could see that they were young scholars, questioned them as to whose disciples they were.

"They told the bandits truthfully that they studied under Rabbi Akiva.

"'You should have seen the change on their faces' they told me. 'Happy are Rabbi Akiva and his disciples, for no evil person has ever done them harm.'" Thus Hillel's report.

The Romans kept increasing the number of their troops, though. I don't think that this worried Shimeon unduly. When I mentioned that I heard the Romans had thirty thousand soldiers in the country, he told me that he had two hundred thousand and would soon have twice as many.

In jest, I began to call him 'bandit.' He smiled. Generally, Shimeon was a lot happier during those years than he had been for a long time previously.

*   *   *

And so, Yose, ten years went by. Ten years of preparation for the inevitable war.

The Romans reinforced the Tenth *Fretensis* legion in Jerusalem with a detachment of the Third *Cyrenaica*, our old enemies. They also appointed a new governor, a most cruel and unjust man, a certain Q. Tinneius Rufus. I think he really called himself a consul, not that it made any difference to us. He made more troop movements, it was under his rule that the Sixth *Ferrata* Legion was moved to its new base at Kfar Otnay, I told you they now called it Caparcotna, or Legio.

And they kept building roads. Now it was a new road from Jerusalem to Beth Guvrin. They had this thing about building roads, they always did that, but now the action became frenetic. Shimeon thought that perhaps they expected trouble, or were getting ready to suppress all hostile activities.

But in the end it turned out that they were preparing for an imperial visit. Hadrian himself was to honor this remote province of his with his glorious presence; I almost said divine presence, he would have liked that.

The emperor arrived in Judaea – he would not call it Eretz Yisrael – exactly sixty years after they destroyed the Temple. He came from Syria and eventually left for Egypt. While he was here, he visited Gaza, Petra, Caesarea, Tiberias and other places. They loved him! They celebrated his imperial presence in those cities full of Greeks and Romans and other pagans. He went to Sepphoris, our town, and that was when they renamed the place Diocaesaria, of all silly names.

We debated why Hadrian had come here. But after a few weeks, the answer became clear.

By then Shimeon had established his headquarters in the Judaean foothills, in one of the largest underground complexes, called Amatzia. I did not live there with him, there would not have been much point, as he was away most of the time. But I visited often, it was not that far from Yavneh.

I remember one occasion when Hillel came back to report to Shimeon about the emperor's movement.

"He is trying to re-create Cyrene here," Hillel told him. "He is putting up fancy buildings everywhere. Statues, temples."

"So what, Hillel?" Shimeon shrugged. "That does not matter much, does it? The country is full of them, anyway. We shall demolish them all in good time."

"Yes, Shimeon. But the sages have been meeting at Rabbi Akiva's house. What they find annoying is that Hadrian wants to civilize us. He has established something they call the Pan-Hellenic League. They arrange Greek festivities all over the land. Theaters and sporting events. He is spending more money on these things than he collects in taxes here. Everything must be Greek here."

"Yes, I know," said Shimeon. "We shall soon put a stop to all that nonsense."

"But let me tell you more. Everywhere he goes, he is adulated as a god. It seems that he encourages his people to call him a god, to pretend that he is one."

"Does he believe that himself?" Shimeon smiled.

"Hard to know. He could not be that stupid. But perhaps he thinks that his subjects are stupid, and they will respect a divine being more than a mere mortal."

My husband made an impolite comment that I shall not report.

"And meanwhile he encourages immoral behaviour among the young. I suppose he favors young men himself."

Shimeon did not even bother responding to that.

*   *   *

But Hadrian did worse than that during the coming months. He was in our land for about a year, and before he finally left for Egypt, he decided to put his old plans for Jerusalem into effect.

You remember that I wrote to you about his plans for building a Greek city there, full of temples to their weird gods. Well, he thought that the Jews were peaceful enough by then, he could proceed with that plan.

He decreed that henceforth our holy Jerusalem should be called Aelia Capitolina for his own name, Aelius.

And he gave orders to build a huge temple there to Jupiter. Now that really upset our people, and Shimeon sensed that the country was getting ready to support him, that there would be a war very soon now.

At Shimeon's request I invited Rabbi Akiva to our house. Shimeon himself came at night.

After greetings were exchanged and we sat down, Shimeon asked:

"Now tell me, my master, is the Hillelite approach of compromises and appeasement finally discredited? Can we start acting as proud, independent people?"

Akiva shook his head angrily.

"Don't talk Hillelism and Shammaism to me, my son. We are all united now. I admit that I was wrong when I trusted Hadrian. He stopped the rebuilding of the Temple; that's one thing. But now he is putting up his pagan city in Jerusalem. That is too much. That we cannot allow."

"I am glad to hear you say that, Akiva. It means so much to me. I shall be ready quite soon."

"Don't start anything while Hadrian is still in the country, for he has lots of extra troops with him. No, not only in the country, even in the vicinity. It does not take long for those troops to get here from Egypt. Wait until he is far away."

Shimeon nodded. That's how he planned things, too. Then he asked:

"But what I don't understand is, how can he be so shortsighted? How come he does not understand what his actions will provoke?"

Akiva nodded.

"I think that he has misinterpreted the past ten years of peace. He thinks that we forgot how to wage war."

"Hah!"

"Yes, and he is just unable to understand how we Jews hate his Hellenistic dreams. He loves those ideas so much, he thinks that sooner or later everybody will accept them."

"But there is one more thing that puzzles me. How is it possible that they have not yet tried to arrest me? Or any of our fighters? They have never discovered any of our storehouses, any of our hiding places. I expected problems there, but none have materialized."

"Yes, that comes from being overconfident. Either they don't think it necessary to employ spies from among our people, or they find it too difficult, or impossible, to get such spies."

"I hope it's the latter. I don't want to think that there is any Jew who would betray his country."

"There will be, my son, believe me. There will be."

Hadrian's letter to Lucius Ceionius Commodus

OH, FOR THE CULTURE OF GREECE!

*The Emperor Caesar Trajan Hadrian August,
from the great city of Aelia Capitolina –
to Lucius Ceionius Commodus – greetings.*

My dear Lucius, the gods willing, soon we can embrace again in Egypt. We have spent over a year in the East, in Syria and then in Judaea, and it has been one of my best sojourns.

Everything is going very well now, the gods have been kind to me. I am grateful to them and never miss an opportunity to build new temples to one or the other. You recall that, ten years ago, I intended to build a beautiful new city on the ruins of Jerusalem, but the recalcitrant Jews prevented me from realizing my plans. They wanted to build a large temple of their own, which would have been the center of their government, and they would not allow any other temple there. I was patient; I thought, let us wait, let us pacify them, they will be ready for my city eventually. Well, that time has now arrived. The land is relatively peaceful. There is some banditry, true, but our two strong legions can handle it without too much difficulty. I think that by now those Jews understand that they cannot trifle with the might of the Roman Empire.

Still, I must be careful. I don't want to cause trouble, so must pay heed to Jewish sensibilities. Also, I must always remind myself that I have made the idea of justice coupled with human kindness a cornerstone of my reign. So if they object to a statue here, a temple there, I told Aquila that he can be a little flexible, I don't mind. He had suggested this, and he caught me in a good mood. (Although sometimes I worry about that young relative of mine, he is too easily influenced by these eastern rites. Rufus Tinneius tells me that his spies saw Aquila enter their houses of prayer, at first those of the new type of Jews that call themselves Christians, and lately even those of the ordinary Jews. I will have to have a talk with him soon.)

I've received several delegations of the religious leadership of the Jews. We had some pleasant discussions, we talked about the advantages of Greek philosophy – they prefer their own, if you can call their strange ideas about an invisible god philosophy – but I must say that they are very convincing in their own way. A few years earlier I met one of their religious leaders, a very reasonable old man, Rabbi Yehoshua ben Hananiyah, very witty and with a quick answer to any question I asked or comment I made. I was hoping that he would be a member of their delegation, but it seems that old man died recently. There was another old man, Rabbi Akiva, he seems to be their current leader (one can never be sure of that, another member of their deputation, a Rabbi Eleazar ben Azariyah, may have been the real head of the group; there was also somebody called Tarfon). I have actually met this Akiva on an earlier occasion. I am told he is eighty years old; that is hard to believe, he behaves like a sprightly fifty-year-old man. But he seems to be the least flexible of all. He insists that they must always revere their own god and seems to have no interest in any of our Greek or Roman deities. Well, he is old, the new generation will see things differently.

Yes, they must come into the modern world. They must accept the glories of Greek culture. They are barbarians, and it is time that they become civilized people, for they certainly have the mind, the intelligence to understand the beauty of everything that Greece has produced. The sculptures. The architecture. The music. The sports, the games. And yes, the veneration of the gods. They must be assimilated into the higher levels of Hellenism, even if they must be dragged into civilization by thousands of horses.

You know me, Lucius. You know how I have always loved things Greek. Now I love one thing Greek even more than any other. You may have heard that I found a boy, a young man (he will soon be twenty), a Greek from Bythinia; his name is Antinous. He is everything to me. I adore him. His smile makes me melt, his sadness breaks my heart. When he is not with me – which happens rarely – I think of his face, his body, his grace, his movements, his surprised look when I give him a present, his caress – yes, I love him dearly. I can hardly wait for you to meet him, see what you think. You will love him, too, but be careful, don't love him too much. No, don't worry, I am not jealous. It is only that my thoughts are full of Antinous. I think that he already shows signs of being divine. If he is not yet a god, he surely will be before long. I myself certainly feel divine by now; the gods are acting through me, that is why everything is going so well these days. They have accepted me into their ranks. I hope that you will also achieve that distinction one day. Farewell.

Hadrian's letter to Rufus Tinneius

LET THEM PAY FOR MY LOSS!

The Emperor Caesar Trajan Hadrian August,
from the shores of the Nile in Egypt – to Rufus Tinneius –
Consul of the Imperial province of Judaea, greetings.

Rufus, my friend, you have done well as Governor of Syria, the empire is grateful to you for that. More recently, you have taken over as Governor of the province of Judaea, an incomparably more difficult job. Be strong and determined at your task. You have all the forces of the empire available to you. Spare them not. The Jewish people are a recalcitrant race. They must be taught a lesson.

As I came down here, to Egypt, I viewed the destruction that the Jews caused fourteen, fifteen years ago. So many lovely temples ruined, so many statues torn down. I saw the tomb of Pompey at Pelusium, ordered it restored. Yes, they must be punished for everything they did to us.

You may have heard of my loss. Yes, my lovely Antinous is dead. Drowned in the Nile. I almost expected something like that to happen. There were portents. I consulted the astrologers, the Egyptian priests and magicians. They counselled me to be heedful to the gods, Isis and Horus, but particularly to Osiris. As you know, he is the god of death. That worried me a lot. I tried to put the thought out of my head. I occupied myself with affairs of the empire.

A delegation came from Judaea, they brought that letter from you, recommending that I receive them. Did you find them too difficult to appease? I tried to do so myself, but it proved to be an impossible task. There were three of them, again, but the only one I knew was Rabbi Akiva, they say that he is over eighty years old. Frankly, I don't care how old he is, except that the sooner he goes to his god, the better.

They tried to convince me not to build temples to any god in Aelia Capitolina except to their own god, and they offered to undertake that task themselves, pay for it themselves, if only we let them. How they could afford that, I don't know. Maybe we don't tax them enough. I tried to explain to them that we were giving them a beautiful city, one they would be very proud of, which would compete with Alexandria, not only aesthetically but also commercially. They would all become wealthy, being at the hub of all the caravan routes, from Egypt and Damascus to the sea and all the way to Asia. But, increasingly, it appeared as though we were talking about totally different things. I talked commerce to them and they talked god to me. I explained about culture and they tried to tell me about their commandments. I attempted to familiarize them with the beauty of Greek physical activities, sports, baths and hygiene; they talked about learning their Torah, some holy book they have. And they had the temerity to assume that they would be able to convince me of these things.

At the end, I felt the need to make them understand the futility of their effort. I told them that while I was willing to listen to their arguments, they should not dream about halting Greek and Roman civilization in their part of the world, that is something that Rome will never accept. I impressed on them that this was my final word, expecting them to bow and leave. What do you think they did? They tore their clothes, moved over to a corner, cried and then prayed and chanted something. It was very strange, very disturbing. I asked one of my interpreters what they were chanting, what kind of ritual it was. He told me that they were turning to their god for consolation, were repeating some ancient formula for praising that god; that they must praise him even when he rejects them. They even asked their god to understand *me*, to forgive *me*, to bring enlightenment to *me*! I refused to believe any of that.

Let me tell you, Rufus, what I really thought they were doing. They were simply cursing me! That's what they did in that corner, and I could feel shivers running down my back. I don't accept their god, but he may have some power we don't understand. I felt apprehensive for several weeks afterwards, even more so than before. I consulted more priests and magicians, but they could bring no relief to my worries.

And then it happened, that horrible day, when Antinous disappeared and we later found him at the bottom of the Nile. Throughout my shock and pain I felt, I knew, that this must come from the curse of Akiva and his colleagues. Maybe you should arrest them and make them admit their crime. But I want you to do more than that. The time has come for you to show these Jews, unmercifully, who has the power, who is the ruler and who is the subordinate. Mind you, that is not a petty personal revenge; it is something that Rome needs, something that I should probably have ordered long before, but I have been trying to be considerate, just, kind. What futility. But no more!

They want to destroy the Pax Romana? I shall show them that it is their peace that will be destroyed. I shall settle this Jewish question once and for all. Start with their religious edicts. Forbid them to practice the most important aspects of their religion. One thing in particular I know is important to them: mutilating their newborn sons. Forbid circumcision! Make them pay with their lives if they ever do it again. It is a barbarous practice, anyway.

Tell Aquila to go ahead with putting up our buildings, our temples and sanctuaries, our baths and markets, everything that I planned. But especially, build the temple to Jupiter and Zeus at the site of their holy of holies. Put up a huge statue to Jupiter right at that spot.

Should they object in words, ignore them. But should they do anything more than that, harm even one of our soldiers, or the foreigners who will work at the construction, put their rebellion down with full force, brutally if necessary.

Rufus, I know that you are an extremely capable commander. But should you find that the Jews employ more force than you can handle, an unlikely eventuality, I shall send Gaius Publius Marcellus, who has taken over from you as Governor of Syria, to Judaea. Things are quiet there, and he will be happy to come to your assistance at any time. Farewell.

Michal's letter to Yose

WAITING FOR THE RIGHT TIME

From Michal bat Dosa – to my nephew –
Rabbi Yose ben Halafta, may your peace be great.

Yose, by the end of that year Hadrian left, went to Egypt with his latest love, some boy called Antinous, but the boy drowned, and Hadrian returned the following year. He stayed in Judaea only briefly, on his way to Syria and then Asia Minor. But while here, he made things much worse (perhaps you would say much better for Shimeon). He enacted new, draconian laws. Actually, it could be that it was Tinneius Rufus who dreamed them up, just got Hadrian to agree to them. Incidentally, Tinneius Rufus has now been promoted to legatee.

What new laws, you ask?

They decreed that anybody who castrates a man or child shall be punished by death.

So what, you ask, we don't castrate.

No, but we circumcise.

To Tinneius Rufus, and maybe to Hadrian, that was the same as castration!

And Tinneius Rufus enforced that law. They checked all small boys, and if any of them was found circumcised, his father was simply executed.

What were we to do? We could not ignore the divine commandment. Yet we could not have all fathers simply forfeit their lives either.

Older boys and men tried to do things that I don't fully understand, tried to hide their being Jewish. They pulled their skins and some of them underwent surgery. I know they did such things because, when the sages met, they ruled that such men must undergo circumcision again.

But that was not all. They now came out with all kinds of rules against our practicing our faith. Public assemblies were not permitted, which meant that the Torah could no longer be taught in public.

We could no longer declare that the Lord is One. We are required to do that at least twice a day, but they forbade it. You can ask Meir, he was but a child, sitting at the feet of Rabbi Akiva. He related that they were saying the *Shema* silently, while a *quaestor* was standing just outside the door, listening.

New rabbis could no longer be ordained. Jewish legal documents, such as a *get* or a *prosbul*, could no longer be issued.

The years could not be intercalated, at least not in the Land. Yet we needed to know which year shall have an extra month. Of course it could have been done in secret, but Rabbi Akiva went outside Judaea to do it.

In fact, Rabbi Akiva went abroad a lot in those days. He travelled to Mesopotamia, to Media and Phoenicia. He visited Cilicia and Cappadocia and every other place where Jews lived.

Why did he go there? To intercalate the year, over and over again?

You know better than that, Yose. He went to get everyone ready for war. And to collect money. Shimeon was ready, but he needed lots of money for arms and food supply, and to pay people when they had to be away from their work for a long time.

So we suffered. Akiva organized support, Shimeon organized people. We were getting ready for the big event. But why did the Romans treat us like that? They did not know then what was going to hit them and how. It was awful, the laws and the persecution. Apparently they did not understand what it meant to our people, when circumcision was proscribed, when we could not say the *Shema*.

It seems that, during his trip to Egypt, Hadrian decided he did not want to compromise with the Jews, did not want to be thought of as the 'good emperor.' He wanted a Hellenistic empire, and Judaea would be incorporated into that. It is rumored that the emperor announced, when declaring his plans for Aelia Capitolina, that the cult of Jupiter there would eclipse the God of the Jews.

And the ban on circumcision? Did he really think that circumcision was barbaric, close to castration? Or did he only view it as one measure by which the Jews made themselves different, and he did not want them to be different?

He wanted not only the land but also its people Hellenized. He never achieved that. And therefore, whatever the eventual outcome, our fight was not in vain.

*   *   *

One thing is certain, Hadrian may have been slightly apprehensive about the reaction of the Jews to his repressive measures, but he was not truly concerned, for he did not reinforce his troops in Judaea. It seems that the two legions were not warned of what to expect. Perhaps the adulation of the people in the cities – but not many Jewish people, did he not notice? – blinded him.

He was totally unaware of the organization, the preparation taking place all over the land, especially in the hills and under the foothills. Why, even the sages were collaborating.

Rabbi Akiva invited the three other leading sages, Eleazar ben Azariyah, Ishmael ben Elisha and Tarfon to his house to discuss the ferment with them. Ishmael could not come, perhaps the Romans would not let him leave his village in the Negev. The other two came, but they were both very old and weak, one was troubled by his heart, the other had something inside him that gave him constant pain and discomfort. Still, these were the only leaders left, leaders of the nation. Akiva wanted their support, or firm opposition, because a decision was now absolutely necessary. The situation was increasingly tense, and the people, especially the young, were ready to act with or without the leadership. Akiva wanted to explain that the Sanhedrin had to lead or disappear. In the end both gave him their support. Would Yehoshua ben Hananiyah, had he lived, also have supported the revolution? I would like to think that he would, although the old man always counselled peace and compromise. He passed away about a year before the big trouble started. May his memory be blessed.

Eventually, the matter was taken up, without any formal meeting, with most members of the Sanhedrin; this time they gathered at Lod, all those members that could be reached. With the exception of two men, they all gave Akiva their support. The two were Rabbi Yohanan ben Torta and Rabbi Eleazar of Modi`in. Yes, Shimeon bar Kosiva's uncle!

Akiva wanted to bring the old rabbi (old! He was younger than Akiva himself) around to our view, invited him, Shimeon and me to his house. It was to be a family get-together. We exchanged greetings politely, but the argument gradually became more heated. Eleazar had a full head of white hair, a pinkish face; he reminded me of a big baby – a baby full of righteousness and bitterness. Indeed, he was very bitter, and it appeared that all the troubles of the world were due to Shimeon's wrongdoings, now and always.

He accused Shimeon of many things.

"Shimeon, my boy, you are just a troublemaker. Always have been. I remember way back, when I taught you, you were my most difficult student. Asking questions that you were not supposed to ask, putting silly ideas in the heads of the other students."

"You mean about the Maccabees? Fighting for our freedom?"

"Yes, about how such things were more important than devotion to the All-Powerful, more important than the study of Torah."

"And now, Uncle, when the study of Torah is not even permitted by the occupiers, do you still counsel compromise and being nice to the forces of Edom?"

Our people often used Edom as an allegorical reference to Rome.

"But they have not banned the study of Torah. They only oppose our public teaching of it."

"And circumcision? Are you happy to allow newborn boys remain uncircumcised, like heathens?"

Clearly, that made Eleazar uncomfortable. I could see Akiva looking at him intently.

"We have to work closely with the Romans. We must assure them of our good intentions. They must be convinced that we don't mean trouble, don't intend to start anything, any action against them. And then they will rescind those intolerable edicts."

"And they will resurrect Pappus and Julianus and the other martyrs, I suppose. You are talking nonsense, Eleazar," responded Shimeon angrily.

"I am talking nonsense? What is it that you are doing? Getting all the young men in the country impassioned and ready to fight! Does that make sense? That they should wage a war which they cannot win, that they should all be killed?"

"If they listened to you, they would go to war convinced that they could not win, and then we would surely lose the war. Fortunately, they won't listen to an old…"

"That's enough," Akiva interrupted. "If you start accusing us of being old, don't be surprised if you are called a young whippersnapper."

Shimeon was contrite. "I am sorry, Akiva. I am sorry, Eleazar. I did not mean it that way. It's just…"

"I know. But enough said. Clearly, our friend Eleazar sees the current situation differently than you do, Shimeon. People must be allowed to have different opinions. I wanted you to talk about this matter, to exchange views, because you are relatives and because one day, soon, you may have to rely on each other more closely."

"That would be a calamitous day," murmured Shimeon and, simultaneously, Eleazar declared: "May the Lord protect us from that day."

*   *   *

By the time Hadrian passed through the area again, there were many actions against the Romans. They still thought of it as banditry, did not realize that there was a strong central organization ready to pounce on them as soon as the emperor was safely away from the area – we heard that he was heading for Athens. But they were forced to use their troops more. The legions became quite active, they were moving up and down the country. I am not sure if Shimeon welcomed that, but he claimed that this was part of the plan. In any case, it was time for him to move. For him and for me, and eventually for everyone in Yavneh and Lod, where many of the sages lived in that last decade.

We were heading for Bethar, up in the King's Mountain, not very far from Jerusalem.

It was a lovely town, with many schools. Young Shimeon ben Gamaliel, the son of the Nasi, spent some time studying in one of them. It was located among the hills, on a small plateau, directly next to an oval hill that held a fort. The area was surrounded by higher hills and mountains. It had two or three springs, providing plenty of water, enough even later, when many people lived on that hill, around the fortress.

It seems that Shimeon had his people reinforce the fort and store a huge amount of supplies there, everything from food to arms and even scrolls, the Torah in the synagogue and all other permissible books.

We had a house there, inside the fortress. There were a few thousand people living in the town, below the hill.

"Michal, make your home here," Shimeon told me. "We shall be here for a long time."

"And where shall we go from here?" I asked him, half in jest.

"To Jerusalem, I hope. Or, to the World-to-Come."

My preference was, for the time being, the former place.

THE WAR BEGINS

Yose, Shimeon was troubled by his uncle Eleazar's blindness. He had lived with the idea of revolution and war so long, he found it hard to understand how anyone, let alone a so-called sage ('so-called' was his sneering term) could still talk about making peace, treating them with respect, hoping for a retraction of those edicts.

Nevertheless, Eleazar was a man of great importance in the Sanhedrin and could not be just ignored. When Rabban Gamaliel was still alive, he called Eleazar his pupil and friend and often asked him to come to Yavneh, even when the Sanhedrin was not in session. He used to say, before deciding on a difficult issue: "We must still hear from the man from Modi`in." Even after Gamaliel's death, Eleazar had lots of influence in Yavneh and Lod, because of his friendship with Eleazar ben Azariyah, who respected him greatly. (Did I tell you that Eleazar ben Azariyah, our great friend, died in that year, just before the war? And that Rabbi Tarfon also lost his life at about the same time? Both died within a few weeks of their last meeting with Akiva at his house. May their memory be blessed. A little earlier, they both accompanied Rabbi Akiva on the last, useless trip to Egypt, one more attempt to talk sense into Emperor Hadrian.) And he was considered an outstanding preacher, whose listeners were always entranced by the beauty of his words.

Not all the sages were so impressed by him, though. He annoyed some of them. More than once, they asked him: "Oh man of Modi`in, how long will you continue to heap words upon us?"

Still, he was much respected. His importance actually increased after the death of Eleazar ben Azariyah. Even Akiva, who strongly disagreed with him politically, liked his approach to Torah exposition; unlike Yehoshua ben Hananiyah, who explained the Torah in a common-sense manner, Eleazar, like Akiva, preferred to find hidden meaning in the texts.

Shimeon decided to write his uncle a letter. Eleazar kept the letter and later, during the early days of the siege, showed it to me. I asked him to give it to me, and somewhat reluctantly he did. I have it still.

Here, I am copying it for you, Yose. I would like to know what you think of it. Would you have agreed with Shimeon's arguments fully? Your father was a Hillelite scholar, yet in those days he agreed that war was necessary. Was he wrong? Were we all wrong? I value your opinion. Tell me what you think.

"To my respected Uncle, Eleazar haKohen, of Modi`in, from Shimeon bar Kosiva, in Bethar. Uncle, may your peace be great. We had some words recently about the upcoming war, and to my great regret I was not respectful enough and polite enough and calm enough to explain to you why I thought war inevitable. Please read my reasons with patience, for I am certain that in the end you will agree with me.

"These are the reasons: The peasants are desperately unhappy because their land was expropriated; they became tenants on their own land, and the conditions of tenure are often unbearable. Next: Hadrian's determination to Hellenize this part of his empire is unacceptable to all Jews. Next: He promised to rebuild Jerusalem, and then he went back on his promise, I am told because of Samaritan complaints. Next: He not only broke his promise to rebuild, but he confiscated all the funds we collected, and killed Pappus and Julianus. Next: Many thought that he would liberate our lands just as he liberated the countries in the Parthian Empire; we were disappointed. Next: The new governor, Tinneius Rufus, whom many call Tyrannus Rufus, rules with an iron hand, cruelly and mercilessly. Next: Their new rule forbidding circumcision. Hadrian calls it 'genital mutilation' and equates it with castration. Next: His building his pagan city, 'Aelia Capitolina' in Jerusalem and especially his temple to Jupiter, in place of our holy Temple. Next: Our unavoidable opposition to the emperor-worship that he demands.

"Let me tell you, Uncle, what this war is not. It is not a Shammaite affair. Believe me, Hillelites and Shammaites are now together in this, both seeing the inevitability of action. It is not a sudden eruption, but a slow buildup of unhappiness, which cannot but culminate in revolution. Our people once had independence and want to have it restored. Remember, all the sages at Yavneh have said, repeatedly: 'May the Temple be built speedily.' You cannot continually repeat such statements in every synagogue throughout the land, without people taking it seriously.

"I could summarize all this by saying that our people demand freedom and salvation. We lost the war, our Temple was destroyed, but we have always known that this will be reversed. We have sinned, we were punished for our sins. But the days of the Messiah are upon us, and we must act. The Romans may not believe that we shall dare to do this, but we must, for we cannot do otherwise. We expect to win, with the help of the Holy One, blessed be His Name."

*   *   *

The isolated incidents, attacking Romans troops here and there, eventually came to an end. Now it was full war, under one general only: Shimeon bar Kosiva, the leader of the nation. How did that make me feel? I was quite used to being close to the center of power, but this was still a new, frightening role for my husband and, by extension, for me. I could still visit Yavneh now and then, but people treated me differently, I cannot tell you how, it may have been respect, more like – what? pity? fear? – it was strange, not pleasant.

But I don't want to talk about myself. I am telling you the story of my husband, he was important, I was not. I have to resist any tendency to make myself the central character of this story.

It was good to know, as Shimeon explained to me, that for the first time in many years, all the Jews were united. There used to be 'minim,' sects of many kinds that Rabban Yohanan ben Zakkai used to rail against. They were gone now. Whoever remained Jewish was behind us, while those who could no longer be counted on, such as the Notzrim, were finally expelled.

Our people – I should say our army – were well organized by Shimeon. They gave up their jobs now and gathered in fortified camps and hiding places, many in the underground complexes in the foothills, but most of them in the hills. That we could build such fortifications, under the eyes of the Romans, that we could assemble such an army, without their knowing anything about it at all, shows how united our people were. There was not one traitor amongst us.

The Romans remained ignorant of our efforts to the last minute. We were ready to attack powerfully, awaiting only word from the commander, Shimeon bar Kosiva.

And Shimeon bar Kosiva became something else.

An increasing number of sages came to Bethar, some to visit, others to stay. And they all supported the revolution, all but Rabbi Eleazar of Modi'in. He still had not replied to Shimeon's letter.

But the others were enthusiastic about the war. They quoted Balaam: "There shall step forth a star from Yaacov, and a scepter shall rise out of Israel, and shall smite through the corners of Moab, and break down all the sons of Seth…" You see, the 'star,' *kokhav*, was my husband, Shimeon! They began to call him Shimeon bar Kokhba now, the son of a star.

Yose, I still tremble and cry when I think of those days. For they loved Shimeon, the man who brought us all together, towards the greatest war of the nation. I say this because I want to remind you of what your colleague Shimeon bar Yohai said, much later, when it was all over. He said "There shall step forth a star from Yaacov? Lies, *koziva*, stepped forth out of Yaacov." And I heard some people sniggering afterwards about 'Shimeon bar Koziva.' That hurt me very much.

But back to Bethar: We have finally received the letter from Eleazar haKohen, the man of Modi`in. Here is what he wrote:

"To Shimeon bar Kosiva, at Bethar, from Eleazar haKohen, in Modi`in, may your peace be great. My nephew, I read your letter carefully, and this is what I have to say. If the Romans attack you, defend yourself and our people with all your strength, But do not attack directly. Why? Because we shall only be liberated by the Messiah. You shall know when the messianic era starts, for it shall start with many miracles. Do not try to hasten the days of the Messiah, especially not with violence, for you shall cause grievous harm to yourself and to our people."

*   *   *

That was the sixty-second year after the destruction of the Temple.

We received word that the Emperor Hadrian was safely ensconced in Athens, probably occupied with another boy lover. That was the last piece of information that Shimeon needed. He issued orders.

We attacked. We attacked everywhere at once. In the foothills and in the hills. Even in the cities. In Jerusalem!

We were all as one nation then. The city people did not actually fight with weapons, they were too soft for that, too Hellenized perhaps; but they were not against us. On the other hand, quite a few Samaritans joined our forces. We accepted them, although Shimeon told me that they were always viewed with a certain measure of suspicion.

We won our battles! Not just one, but many. All of them! One after the other, we fought against the Roman legions, and we won.

The Romans rushed to reinforce their Tenth *Fretensis* Legion in Jerusalem; they had lost so many people, they had to recruit in haste in all neighboring countries.

Shimeon was even considering using the trading vessels of our family and some friends to attack the Romans at sea.

He was victorious! I cannot tell you how proud I was of him.

There was one thought I would have liked to share with him, if we could have just spent one quiet night together.

This is what I wanted to tell him: "Shimeon, my dear, do you remember when on that ship to Cyrene we talked about that nymph, how she fought with the lion? You told me that one should never fight against a lion, one should fight only those battles that one is confident of winning. Shimeon, my love, you have fought against the lion now! And you have won your fight!"

THE MESSIAH – SAYS RABBI AKIVA

Now Yose, I have to tell you about a strange thing, and in an unusual way: first, I shall tell you what happened, and then I shall have to go back and try to explain why it happened. I hope you won't mind. In any case, the 'why' of it comes from your father.

You see, what happened was that, after the death of Yehoshua ben Hananiyah, Eleazar ben Azariyah and Tarfon, all within a year or so, there was nobody left to lead the nation but Akiva. Even before that time, many considered him the man with the best mind, but now he was the undisputed leader.

I told you already how he supported Shimeon's efforts, how he travelled all over the world to get money and support for the war. In fact, he went to some places few had even heard of: to Mazaca-Caesarea in Cappadocia, to Ecbatana in Parthia, and so many more.

He saw the situation in the same way as Shimeon: The Messiah was needed to liberate our nation, but the Messiah would not come until we proved that we were willing to fight.

There were one or two sages who did not approve. I told you already about Shimeon's uncle, Eleazar haKohen, and also Yohanan ben Torta. Then there was Rabbi Onya, who did not like what Akiva did. He said that Akiva was 'forcing the end,' because he is of insufficient faith! Rabbi Akiva having insufficient faith! Onya also said something like "this shows what kind of background he had, what kind of family he comes from" or words to that effect.

But Onya was the exception. Everybody else respected Akiva. So when Akiva made his famous pronouncement, soon after the first series of victories, people were surprised, but few openly disagreed.

What Akiva announced was simply this: He saw Shimeon bar Kokhba in all his glory, and said: 'This is the King, the Messiah!'

My world just about collapsed when I heard that. For a wild moment, I thought about how to keep this from reaching Shimeon's ears. Impossible, of course.

As it happens, Shimeon was not in Bethar, he was commanding a battle around Beth Guvrin. I always worried when he was in battle. At this time, though, my mind was taken up with other matters: My sister Tzviyya and her husband, your father, Rabbi Halafta, had arrived at Bethar. They were finally convinced that it was no longer safe to stay in Yavneh. (As I recall, Yose, you were no longer living with them in Yavneh. You were a budding young scholar by then, just past your bar-mitzvah, the student of such luminaries, while they lived, as Yehoshua ben Hananiyah, Tarfon, Akiva, Ishmael ben Elisha and, of course, your father's best friend, Yohanan ben Nuri. They all considered you a most promising future scholar, and they sent you to Babylonia.)

I showed them around the house. It was clean, but very simple and quite a bit smaller than our family house in Yavneh. They would have two rooms, and a small area for the servants that they brought with them.

I was waiting for them to settle in, for I was anxious to talk and to find out what was said and by whom and why.

Finally they came around. I asked them how they were satisfied with their accommodation, and they assured me that it would do just fine. In the circumstances, there was not much else that they could have said, nor was there much they could have asked for, and of course they were not the demanding type. Your parents were lovely people, Yose, I am not saying this because your mother was my sister, but there were not many people around as lovable as they were.

I asked my brother-in-law Halafta what had happened, had Akiva gone mad? Why did he say what he said, and what was the reaction of various people? Halafta thought about the matter for a minute and then, in his usual, quiet and patient manner, began to explain to me.

"You recall, Michal, that ever since the death of Rabban Gamaliel, may his memory be blessed, we've had no Nasi."

"Yes, of course. Everyone knows that."

"Right. That has been so for nearly fifteen years now. The *Av Bet Din* was Eleazar ben Azariyah, later Tarfon took over. We actually met a number of times at his town, in Lod. But the Sanhedrin has been getting weaker. It's been hard to bring together more than thirty-five sages. To function smoothly, we had to appoint a standing committee, called 'council of five,' to deal with the issues of the day."

"I've heard about that. But who was really in charge? Who *is* in charge?"

"I am coming to that. First, Yehoshua ben Hananiyah was in charge in everything but name. Then, when he died, it was Eleazar ben Azariyah, then Tarfon. Actually, I think Akiva was really running things in the background. But when these sages all passed away, there was nobody left but Akiva. That created a problem."

I looked at him expectantly. He explained it like a teacher explains things to small children.

"What distinguished both Eleazar ben Azariyah and Tarfon? I mean apart from their being the most outstanding scholars and the most noble human beings? They were both rich and they were both priests. Priesthood is useful for prestige, while money is necessary to support the poor scholars, such as Yehoshua used to be. There are many scholars, sages even, who live in abject poverty today. Akiva is not poor himself, but he does not have the wealth required for the position of Nasi, formal or informal."

I still did not see where he was heading, but he bade me to be patient.

"Because of that situation, Akiva does not feel that he is fully in control. He thinks that there are quite a few sages and other scholars who question his authority."

"I think he is wrong there."

"So do I, but he told me himself that he would like to pass the leadership over to somebody else. And lately, he has come to realize that the days of a sage leading the country are over."

"Why would they be over?"

"Because, for now, we live in war. And when you have war, then the head of the war effort has to be the leader of the nation."

"Do you mean Shimeon?"

"Exactly. So Akiva was toying with the idea of announcing that henceforth Shimeon should be the Nasi."

I did not know what to say. He continued.

"But then he thought that this would not be enough. He could announce it, but people would not necessarily accept it. He thought that something stronger was needed. He wanted a king."

"King?!"

"Yes. A war king. A king must be anointed. That's what the word 'Messiah' means, anointed. When there is no prophet, the liberation of Israel may be accomplished by a king. Akiva in effect anointed Shimeon as King of Israel on the authority of all Israel and the leading sages."

"But... a king?"

"Don't be scared, Michal. That may mean no more than Nasi."

"Well, that's enough! Even to be Nasi..."

"What do you want? He is the leader of the nation now, is he not?"

I had to admit that he was.

"And there is another thing. There are two kinds of Messiahs. Or there could be two kinds."

"I've heard something about that. You mean the Messiah ben Yosef, who is kind of a junior Messiah, and then the Messiah ben David..."

"No, not at all. That's all silly. Your father, of blessed memory, started that whole nonsense, they misunderstood him completely. No, Akiva was thinking that there was the old Messianic idea, the man who would liberate Israel, the national redeemer leading this nation to victory and freedom. And then, there is this new idea, the Messiah as the universal redeemer, who would resurrect the dead and bring about the World-to-Come. Certainly Akiva did not propose that Shimeon should be this second kind of Messiah. No, he was thinking of the earlier idea, the national redeemer, the liberator. That's what Shimeon must be."

"But what will people say? What *do* they say? Can they accept Shimeon as the Messiah, even as the first kind of Messiah?"

Halafta hesitated.

"Many can, especially when they listen to Akiva. I admit, there are others who reject the idea. But the prevalent view seems to be, at least among the sages, that we shall have to watch, we shall soon find out."

"I suppose." I was worried.

"Interesting, what Rabbi Yohanan ben Torta said to him: 'Akiva, grass will grow out of your cheekbones and the Son of David will still not have arrived.'"

"Yes, I see. So there are the skeptics."

"Of course, there always are some. It does not matter. But look what Akiva has done. He has moved heaven and earth to bring everyone together, all people, all resources, here and abroad, to achieve the redemption of Israel. As part of that effort, he has named a new national leader, a commander, a King Messiah. And now, he is working to assure that the majority of Israel shall accept the appointment of this new king, so he can rule with full legitimacy. You can see, can't you, that all this has been necessary?"

"Yes, now that you explain it like that."

"And Shimeon alone could never have achieved that. He would have been a military commander, but not the official leader of the nation. He needed Akiva for that, and it was Akiva's brilliant mind that has secured the necessary full appointment for him."

"I understand. And I'll try to explain it to Shimeon. So that he won't get confused about the matter."

"Or conceited?" he smiled.

"Or conceited," I acknowledged.

✶   ✶   ✶

He learned about his new designation when he returned, victorious, from the latest battle. By the time he got to the house, shock had set in.

I explained to him everything that Halafta said. I emphasized that this was only to assure the full support of the whole nation, that it was not like being the Messiah who would resurrect the dead; it was more like being a king, only for the purpose of national redemption, but that he should not think of himself as a king, either, rather a Nasi. But he was still dazed.

He told me that he wanted to think about it.

He was very busy for the next two days, meeting with people, issuing orders, planning the next attacks. On the third day he came home earlier and said that he wanted to talk to me.

"This Messiah thing."

I looked at him curiously.

"Have you thought it over?"

"I have thought about it. I'll have to think more. But there is one thing. That term 'national redemption.' I think that I must take that seriously."

I waited.

"Look, our nation was great under the Maccabees. But for two hundred years now, we have had nothing but military losses. We have been humiliated, again and again. Our nation has suffered, sometimes less, usually more. Is it not clear to you that what we must now achieve is national redemption?"

"Yes, of course. With the help of the Holy One, blessed be He."

"Exactly. And somehow, it has become my lot to lead the nation in this particular fight, the war of national redemption. I think that I can do that."

"Let us hope so. With the help of the Holy One, blessed be He," I repeated emphatically.

"Look, I am not trying to diminish the role of the Lord. Of course we could not do this without His help. But what I am trying to tell you is that the leadership of the nation, towards that particular objective, national redemption, has been given to me. Perhaps that justifies Akiva in according me that title."

I was not sure that I liked that statement. I wanted to temper his conceit.

"Shimeon. I have read a little about the qualifications of the Messiah. I am not sure that you meet them fully."

He was slightly taken aback.

"What qualifications are you talking about?"

"First, that he must be a descendant of King David. Right there, you are in trouble. As far as I know, your family are descendants of proselytes, like my family, not kings."

"On my father's side, true. But my mother comes from a true Jewish family, there may have been kings amongst my ancestors, even King David. Who knows?"

"May have been, that's too vague. But let me continue. This Messiah shall free Israel from foreign oppression and establish a Jewish monarchy."

"I intend to free Israel from foreign oppression."

"But you cannot establish a monarchy, because you have no sons. No children. That is my fault, I know. I offered to you, many times, to leave me for another woman, but you have always refused. Thank you, I am happy for that. But now you cannot establish a monarchy."

"Yes, I can. Not a dynasty, but why not a monarchy? I can be the monarch, and I can provide for a successor. I have no brothers or sisters, but we could use someone else's children. Perhaps your sister's son…"

(Yose, do you see how close you came to being King of Israel?)

I continued.

"Then, he will have to fight wars with all the great nations."

"That's what I am doing. I am fighting a war with the greatest nation of all, the Roman Empire. What other great nations are there? The Parthian Empire? Why should I fight them? They are not our enemies. They may become our friends. I have already sent messages to them…"

I shrugged and continued.

"He has to gather in all the exiles."

"Exiles. Well, you have to admit that we have brought in just about everybody from Cyrenaica and from Egypt and many even from Cyprus."

"Yes, you have. Not all, but most. There are also exiles in Asia Minor, in Mesopotamia and Babylonia, and in Europe, but you cannot be perfect, I suppose. Now, to the last item: When the Messiah appears, there will have to be heavenly portents."

"Like what?"

"Like natural upheavals, disasters."

He thought for a moment, then grinned.

"Do you recall what happened when we started our work in Cyrene? There was a whole series of such upheavals. Antioch was destroyed, also Rhodes, nearly, and many cities in Asia Minor. Yes, that happened seventeen years ago, but could we not assume that it was then our work really started?"

What could I say?

"Shimeon, I ask you not to be conceited. You have a role, yes. It is an important role. You may even think of yourself as the leader of the nation, in some sense, though not in all. You will never be a spiritual leader. You will never be like Rabbi Akiva, or any of the sages. I love you and respect you, and I am proud of you. But don't let this Messiah thing go to your head."

He smiled then.

"Don't worry, my little Michal, I am not crazy. Any time I shall feel like the Son of David, the real Messiah, I shall come to you to set my thinking right."

"And promise me that you shall not call yourself king."

"I promise. I shall call myself Nasi."

*   *   *

Did he believe that he was the Messiah? The real Messiah?

I don't think so, at least not at that time.

During the second year, he said a few things that made me wonder if by then he felt convinced of his divine appointment. But he never stated outright that he was the Messiah.

He would not dare to say it, he was afraid that I would ridicule him if he did – and he was right in that!

But did *I* believe, deep down, that *he* was the Messiah?

I think that there was a time, for perhaps two years or more, when, secretly, I did believe it.

JERUSALEM

Try to imagine, Yose, the strategy sessions. Most of them were held at our house. Unlike Lucuas of old, Shimeon had no objection to my participating, but somehow I did not think it seemly. I was in and out, serving refreshments, so I heard most of the discussions. On one particular occasion Shimeon was talking about the Roman structures and how to destroy them.

"They have many kinds of structures. We have to familiarize ourselves with each type. There are forts and mini-forts, blockhouses, signal-towers. Most of their troops are in fortified camps. Large, square areas, with streets running from one end to the other. An armed city, a tent city. The tents are surrounded by an open area and then the fence, the palisades. It has a wall, watch towers, and in that open area they keep their military machines, rock throwers, catapults and the like. Those machines are usually made of wood…"

"One flaming arrow may be enough to start a fire," said one of his men.

"Of course. But we need many more arrows to keep the Romans from putting out that fire. In any case, most of those structures are located in the valleys, or nearby, not on distant hillsides. That is good."

Somebody asked: "Don't we need to take the valleys as well as the hills?"

"Of course we'll take them. One by one. Their strategy is to maintain a continuous line, all the way from Jerusalem to the sea. If we fracture that line, they are lost. What we must do is find one or more weak spots between any two stations, move through quietly, eliminate whatever Roman soldiers there might be posted there, then strengthen our position in every direction from that point. Thus each of those stations will be isolated. We surround them and wipe them out."

I was serving food then, and saw the general satisfaction on the faces of the men. They knew that now they had a real leader. Shimeon continued.

"Then we establish our own fortification around that site, so the Romans can never recapture it. Now think of the Tenth *Fretensis* in Jerusalem. They will know what's happening. They will see their line to the port disappearing. They will have to act."

"What can they do?"

"They will have to decide whether to fight a losing battle, or try to escape to the sea before it's too late. And when they do, we can take them out, one-by-one. Not many will make it to the foothills. And if they do, we have people there, too."

And we did indeed. Action followed strategy accurately, and in a few months the supply line to the sea was broken. Shimeon's forces caused serious damage to the Roman garrison town of Emmaus, at the bottom of the hills, where some detachments of the Fifth *Macedonica* Legion were located at the time. They could no longer help the Tenth *Fretensis*, which was increasingly in trouble. Even the Sixth *Ferrata* suffered in the plains. Those were the two legions under the command of the tyrant Tinneius Rufus, and they were beaten badly by our forces.

We did not actually destroy most of the Roman garrisons on the plains, the strongly fortified ones, but they were totally isolated. The Roman forces could not count on them. Our troops were always active, always every-where, or so it must have seemed to the Romans. They were immobilized and wondered if their provisions would hold out.

Soon, Shimeon's forces controlled all of the mountains and large parts of the surrounding foothills. We had dealt a crushing blow to the Romans, the Tenth *Fretensis* was finally forced to abandon Jerusalem, just as Shimeon had predicted.

Jerusalem – or what they had made of it, what they now called Aelia Capitolina – was a sizable city, and some troops allied with the Romans were still there. We did not take full possession in a day, it was more like several weeks, even months. But inevitably it would happen. Jerusalem was to be ours again!

*   *   *

Meanwhile, Shimeon was getting ready to declare formal independence for our land. He was already talking of the characteristics of the new Jew-ish nation.

You don't just declare independence and hope that everything falls neatly into place. You have to decide what kind of country you want. Fortu-nately, Shimeon was well prepared on that score. He had a firm idea about such a state. It was based on his heroes, the Maccabees, on the independent Jewish state they established two hundred and eighty years earlier.

Shimeon explained his ideas to me.

"They did not establish a kingdom. They wanted a principate, a *nesiut*. They had a reigning princeps, a *nasi* in charge. That's what I want. You asked me not to call myself a king, and I won't. I shall be a Nasi. Not the sort of Nasi that was in charge of the Sanhedrin, the head of the sages, but a Maccabean Nasi."

I was impressed by this. He knew how to rule, without appearing to presume honors that some might consider he was not entitled to claim.

"Now, there will have to be a popular council, so everybody will have a say in how the country is run."

I was a little confused.

"But then, who will make the decisions?"

"The Nasi will, of course, But he will have to listen to the people, or they can put him down. And one more thing. Unlike the Sanhedrin, this Nasi will have no religious authority at all."

"But then, who will make the religious decisions? I suppose the Sanhedrin will continue to operate as before?"

"Not as before. Yes, there will be a Sanhedrin, but there will also be a priesthood."

"Priesthood!" I was impressed. There has not been such a thing for sixty-two years. There are many priests, of course, but they are simply individuals. I asked him: "Do you propose to reestablish the entire priestly structure?"

"Indeed I am. We always had priesthood, why should we not have it again, when our country is rebuilt? But that may come a little later. First, sovereignty will have to be declared."

"How do you want to declare it?"

"I will make sure that everybody in Eretz Yisrael knows ours is now an independent country, free of foreign occupation. How? What is it that reaches every household, every man and woman in the country, yet you can write a message on it?"

I had no idea what that would be.

"I tell you what. It is money. Coins. Everybody uses coins. I shall strike coins, the official money of the independent state of the Jews. On those coins, we shall declare that Israel is redeemed and free."

I must have looked at him admiringly, for he smiled and patted my head. I asked him: "Is this kind of thing done? Have other people issued coins?"

"Not at all," he answered. "Nobody but our ancestors. The Maccabees issued coins when they became independent. Also, our grandparents, in the great war, issued coins. We shall be more successful."

"The Romans will not be too pleased," I commented.

"Let them go to the devil. It is time they learn that the Jewish nation is reborn in its land. This will teach them."

*   *   *

But Shimeon needed another thing before he was ready to mint his coins. He mentioned to me that, for a proper state, he needed the priesthood. There was no immediate requirement for the whole priestly structure, but he wanted the name of the high priest on the coins, along with his own name, as Nasi.

Rabbi Akiva had to be consulted. He still travelled, still sought support for our cause abroad, but we saw him often in Bethar. Shimeon cautioned him to be careful, his travels were getting dangerous, and Akiva knew this well. But he just did not see himself sitting in relative comfort while the younger people risked their lives every day.

So, during his next visit to Bethar, Shimeon asked him who should be named High Priest. Akiva was taken aback.

"No, Shimeon, it is too early. When we have peace, when it is time to rededicate the rebuilt Temple, that's when we shall have a High Priest."

"But we need somebody to stand beside me, as representative of the priesthood. I may be called Nasi these days, but I am not a religious authority. I think that even the most senior sage, such as yourself, is not what's needed. I must have a name on the coins." He explained to Akiva about his plans to strike coins.

"Fine. That's a good plan. You shall have a priest on the coins. But not a High Priest. Let's get you somebody else. Do you not have priests amongst your men?"

"Well, yes, but just any priest won't do. It would have to be somebody widely known and respected."

"Yes, I see. Somebody like Rabbi Tarfon. Or Eleazar ben Azariyah."

"Exactly."

"It is a pity those two great men are gone now. But I tell you what. There is one respected priest among the sages, your uncle, Eleazar of Modi`in. Why not ask him?"

"I was afraid that you would say that, Akiva. You know that he does not support the war. He would have preferred finding some accommodation with the Romans."

"He would have, but it's too late for that. He knows that we are now in the middle of the war. He is with us. He has to be."

"But will he support me personally? I don't think so. He's never liked me."

"I shall talk with him. I think he understands that the interest of the nation comes first, before any personal feelings."

Akiva did talk with Rabbi Eleazar and brought word from him that he wouldn't object to being the nominal priest representing the priesthood of the new nation. Shimeon was reasonably satisfied: He had his priest, if not High Priest, so his sovereignty had now gained additional legitimacy.

Events were moving fast. Full control of Jerusalem was now in sight, and Shimeon said that he wanted his coins to be struck there, even if this meant a delay of a few weeks.

It was autumn, the New Year was approaching, and Shimeon was hoping to celebrate the festivals in Jerusalem. The western part of the city was already in our hands, but there were still troops in the center and the eastern end, no longer the Tenth *Fretensis*, but allied attachments. They put up strong resistance here and there, but they were steadily being eliminated.

Yose, a week before the New Year all of Jerusalem was ours!

And now came the next question: How should we proceed?

Shimeon wanted to rebuild the Temple. Akiva wanted him to wait.

"Shimeon, there is still a war. There are Roman troops all over the land. You must concentrate your efforts on fighting the war. The Temple can wait."

"I know, Akiva, but what's Jerusalem without the Temple?"

"Jerusalem is our Holy City. It will remain that forever. The House will be built, but not just yet. It will require lots of planning, years of planning, thinking about all of the details. I will tell you, Shimeon, I shall not live to see the Temple in all its glory."

"I don't believe you, Akiva. You shall bring sacrifices in Jerusalem yet."

Akiva sighed but smiled.

"No, my son, there you are wrong. But I tell you what. Build a small Temple in Jerusalem. Just a small building that will look a little like the Holy of Holies used to look. And there, we can perform certain services."

"Sacrifices?"

"No, no that. That will have to wait until the full Temple is built, until a High Priest is chosen and consecrated. But more simple ceremonies. We shall discuss them with your priest."

"You mean Eleazar?"

"Yes, Eleazar haKohen, your uncle. He shall preside over the small Temple in Jerusalem, and everybody shall know that this is a temporary structure, and these are temporary services, until the time comes for the Third House of the Lord to be built."

And that's what happened. Shimeon, in full consultation with his uncle Eleazar, built the small Temple. It was completed in a week and was dedicated on the second day of Sukkoth, with all the sages in attendance. Services were performed, conducted by Eleazar the Priest.

*　*　*

The Sanhedrin moved to Jerusalem. Most of the sages did not actually live there, since it was thought to be still a somewhat dangerous place. Some of them lived at Bethar, most stayed on their own properties, in various places in the country.

Shimeon and I also stayed in Bethar, along with Halafta and Tzviyya. Shimeon had his organization set up, his commanders reported to him there, and his assistants were usually nearby. His most trusted assistant was still Hillel of Cyrene.

The administration of the country – well, those parts of the country that were in our hands, which was most of Judaea – became very efficient. Shimeon was recognized by all as the Nasi. People paid taxes and approached Shimeon's emissaries on official business, seeking justice or resolution of their local problems, disputes, marital difficulties and so on. We had a local administration set up at an increasing number of places now.

And finally, we had our own money. The coins were struck in Jerusalem. There were large and small silver coins, and bronzes in three sizes. We issued – Shimeon issued – bronze dinars and silver selahs, which were the tetradrachma, worth four silver dinars or zuzim. And on all coins were images of the Temple, and things related to the Temple, and each had an important message, such as 'Year One of the Redemption of Israel' on it's face. On the other side was written: 'Shimeon, Nasi of Israel', or 'Eleazar the Priest.'

And Shimeon insisted that the writing be in the old Hebrew script, not the modern Aramaic letters.

Hadrian's letter to Julius Severus

GET HERE, AND FAST!

*The Emperor Caesar Trajan Hadrian August,
in the Imperial province of Judaea – to Julius Severus –
Consul of the Imperial province of Britannia, greetings.*

You have done well in Britannia, suppressing the revolts in the south-west and especially in the north. You have acted with valor, strength and courage. For that, I praise you. The barbarians in Caledonia no longer pose a threat to the security of the empire. Rome is grateful to you.

But there is another part of the world where the peace and security of the empire is threatened. It is here, in this troublesome province of Judaea. The empire needs you here. The situation is as follows:

We have been fighting the insurgents here for more than a year. It started with a series of local actions: a sentry attacked here, a small detachment there, an outpost overrun. We have seen banditry before and thought that we should be able to handle it without too much trouble. There were atrocities committed against our units. We have a very able commander of our forces here, the Consul for the province of Judaea, Rufus Tinneius. He acted mercilessly, had a number of rebels arrested and executed. But rather than disappearing from the scene, the insurgency suddenly got out of control. Before we noticed, there were tens of thousands of rebel troops all over the land. First they just attacked any of our smaller formations, but very soon they became bolder and ran over our camps and fortifications.

They have concentrated their activities over a large hilly area called the 'King's Mountain.' The area includes the city of Aelia Capitolina, what used to be Jerusalem, as well as a handful of other towns and nearly a thousand villages. Our intelligence was inadequate. Our people failed to appreciate two things: first, that the rebels had been preparing for this war – yes, war, not just insurgency – for years, building underground fortifications and collecting arms systematically, maybe for as long as ten years. We did not know that, and the person responsible for the failure has received his just punishment. The other thing that we had not realized was the extent of popular support these rebels had. We have known Jewish leaders of all sorts, in Judaea, Alexandria, Greece, Rome and everywhere else; they seemed to be, on the whole, rational men, willing to compromise, valuing their lives and possessions. But here, among the ordinary people, village dwellers, tradesmen, small landowners and lessors, apparently rationality is non-existent. What they do have, instead, is fanaticism. That is expressed in three related ways. First, they seem to trust their invisible god explicitly, they are convinced that this god will come to their help. Second, they expect some strange being, somebody called "the Messiah," to come and help them. This Messiah, apparently, would be a man, not a god, but he would lead them to unheard-of victories. He would be strong enough to defeat the might of Rome! If I believed in their god, I would almost be concerned. And third, they believe in their leader, one Shimeon bar Kokhba, a large, strong brigand who seems to have been the main organizer of the insurrection for a number of years. Some of them apparently connect the last two, believe that this Bar Kokhba himself is their expected Messiah. I happen to know one of their religious leaders, a very old man named Akiva, who may be responsible for promulgating that stupid, but dangerous idea.

All of these things have added up to a well-organized and committed mob that has, at least for now, succeeded in taking the upper hand in this war. They fully control the hilly areas I mentioned and quite a sizable territory beyond, too. At the moment, the area they have occupied is about sixteen leagues in the north-south direction and ten leagues east-west. You might think that this is not so large, facing the Roman army; but the area, as I said, is very mountainous; they know every hill, every valley, every crag, every cave. Our detachments cannot enter a valley without suffering horrible losses, usually total elimination.

As I have noted, they have taken over Aelia Capitolina and, as I understand it, they have rebuilt their temple there, or at least put up some building that they call their temple. Who cares, you would ask. But that kind of thing is very important to them, it gives them extra strength, extra conviction that they are being supported by their god and that they are on their way to victory over Rome.

Now, as to our forces here: At the leadership level, we have Rufus Tinneius, the local Consul, as well as Gaius Publius Marcellus, Governor of Syria. He brought with him eighteen thousand men, including a whole legion, the *III Gallica*, but also many foreign soldiers, including a sizable cavalry. Despite my efforts during the last ten or twelve years, cavalry is still one of our weaknesses. Fortunately, the enemy is not as strong on horseback as our auxiliaries from Asia are. But the mountains do not always lend themselves to mounted operations.

In addition, we have by now six legions in the area: The *III Cyrenaic*, the x *Fretensic*, the *iii Gallic* of Publius Marcellus, the x *Gemina*, the vi *Ferrata* and the xvi *Flavia Firma*. Two of these, the *Fretensic* and the *Ferrata*, have been here for many years, the others I ordered in more recently. They are all under the overall command of Rufus Tinneius and Publius Marcellus. But all of these legions have suffered terrible losses. Their fighting spirit is not, I think, compromised; but their numbers are diminished by as much as a third. We can bring in more legions, if we must.

I am sorry to tell you that one more legion, the xxii *Deiotariana*, has encountered a worse fate: They met the enemy in fierce battle; they were overrun, they panicked, turned around and ran, despite the very thorough training that all Roman soldiers receive. They were surrounded in a hilly area, the rebels were all over them. They had nowhere to run. In the end, only a handful of our soldiers survived. The once noble legion *Deiotariana*, with eight thousand foot soldiers, hundreds of cavalry and thousands of auxiliaries, is no more.

As to arms, the enemy is well equipped. They don't have as many machines as we have and their machines are not nearly as advanced as ours. But their men know how to throw javelins, how to aim their arrows. They are good with swords when they get close enough to our troops. We have also improved our fighting methods. We have taught our men to sharpen the end of their javelins so fine that they bend when they enter the body. This way, they cannot be quickly pulled out and thrown back at our soldiers. We also use iron-tipped javelins and now, more and more, the double-edged Spanish swords. The *triiari* have spears, instead of javelins. As you know, each of our soldiers carries a breastplate or, if they can afford it, chain mail. The enemy don't have these protective devices, not even helmets. So they are easy targets for our arrows, our javelins, if we can see them, but usually we cannot.

Yes, they are good at fighting. They have already lost many of their men, their severed heads decorate the stakes of the palisades around our camps. But we have lost at least as many, thousands, tens of thousands. And that must stop! I am not afraid of losing the war, of Rome suffering a humiliating defeat at the hand of the Jews; at least they could not contemplate waging a war against us elsewhere, in other provinces or in Rome proper. For one thing, they are a small tribe, their numbers are only a million or two, an anthill when compared to our mighty empire. For another thing, they know next to nothing about the sea, about fighting ships; so how could they even contemplate attacking us in Rome? No, that is not the danger. What worries me is that we may have to give up this province, withdraw from here, as we withdrew from Parthia. If that were to happen, we would have lost the land connecting Syria to Egypt, and that would be intolerable. More than that, other tribes, other nations would be encouraged to declare their independence, we might find ourselves facing not one or two rebellions, but dozens, all over our world. That we cannot allow to happen.

And that is the reason I want you to come here, now; immediately, as soon as you receive my letter. If you feel that the Caledonians are quiet enough, then bring troops with you, as many as Britannia can spare without compromising security. I have also ordered additional troops from Pannonia, they should arrive here by the time you will.

Julius, I am appointing you the chief commander of all our forces in Judaea. I must travel to Rome soon, expect to spend a few months there, but then I intend to be back here myself. I want to observe the action directly, but I shall not interfere with your decisions. At most, I shall mingle among the troops, as I always have, my presence may instill them with even more courage, more steadfastness, more perseverance than they possess naturally or have acquired through our rigorous training. I am confident of victory. I have confidence in you. Farewell.

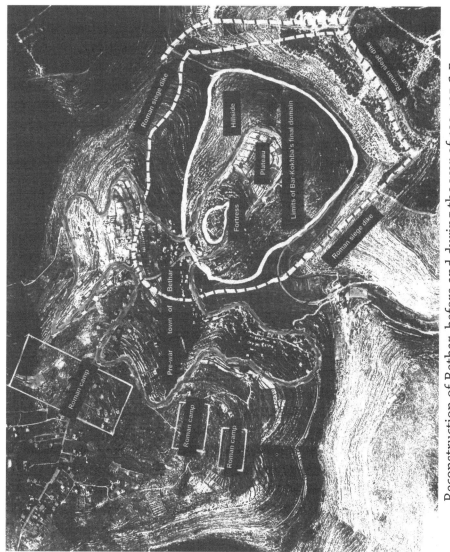

Reconstruction of Bethar, before and during the war of 132–135 C.E.

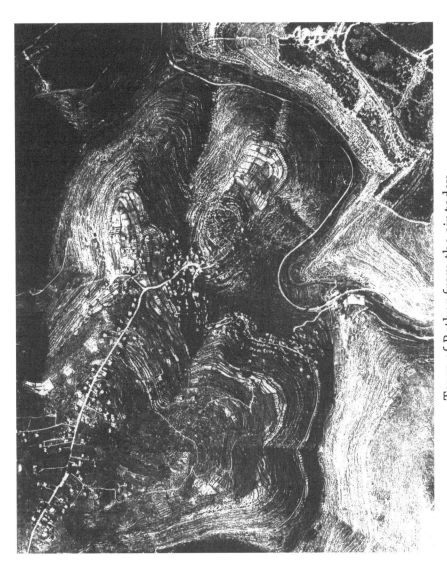

Town of Bethar from the air today
Photograph taken on 25 December 1986 by Pantomap, Jerusalem, No. 7463/86

Michal's letter to Yose

THE TOWN OF BETHAR

> *From Michal bat Dosa – to my nephew –*
> *Rabbi Yose ben Halafta, may your peace be great.*

Yose, not only was Shimeon often away from the town but also your father, Halafta.

We were in the middle of war, but we still had to live close to normal lives. We still had a household to manage, get food on the table, especially when the men were at home. It was not difficult, there were two of us, your mother Tzviyya and myself, and there were two servant girls.

I want to tell you about some of our conversations with those girls. We had a lot of time to talk during the second year of the war. The men were usually away.

I had a local Bethar girl working for me almost from the beginning. Her name was Sarah, a small, dark girl with a ready smile. We often talked. She knew everything about the town, its history and its people. It was completely destroyed during the war more than sixty years ago and rebuilt soon after. Now it was a successful commercial center; for a while, it was the most important place around the central hills, taking the place of Jerusalem.

Early one summer evening, while we waited for the men to return, Sarah was telling me about her grandparents who lived right here, in Bethar, before the war.

"My grandfather did not like those Jerusalem city people at all. They cheated him out of his money all the time."

"How did they do that?" I asked.

She hesitated.

"I think that perhaps he was not very good with numbers. So when he went into the city, selling his vegetables, there was always somebody who played tricks with the change. Later, it was my grandmother who sold the produce, for she understood money better."

"That's awful, people who treat honest townsfolk that way."

"I know of some people who were treated worse. There were some city councillors who talked fast, and in a way that our people did not really understand. Quite often, as a result, some man from Bethar found that he had sold his land to somebody for a pittance."

"Who were those people in Jerusalem? Surely not Jews?"

Sarah did not know. But she said:

"I should not tell you this, but when we first heard that Jerusalem was destroyed, there were those here that cheered. Of course that was before they knew that Bethar would also be destroyed."

What could I say to that? We were working in the kitchen in quiet.

After a while I asked Sarah about her parents.

"My father is a schoolteacher. My mother also works. She is a weaver."

"Where does your father teach, in what kind of school?"

"It is a school for small children. I have a brother, before the war he taught in a school for bigger ones, up to age thirteen."

"Yes, I have heard that there are many schools in Bethar."

"More than a hundred. There are schools for all kinds of people. There are even Torah schools."

"Yes, the son of the last Nasi, Rabban Gamaliel, studied here."

"They all live here, not in town, but nearby. His family."

"And what did your brother teach to those youngsters?"

The question surprised her.

"What? Why, everything they needed to know. How to read and write and how to count and what is what and where everything is."

She thought a bit, then her eyes lit up as she added:

"I once knew a man who taught Greek."

"Do they teach Greek in the schools in Bethar?" I was surprised.

"No, they don't now. On account of that emperor that wanted everybody to become Greek. But before he came, many young people studied Greek here."

"Does your father also teach reading and writing to the little ones?"

"He sure does. These kids come from all the neighboring towns and villages. Their parents say that if the children learn to write, they can become scribes and earn good money; they won't have to till the land like their fathers did before them."

I like it when people have ambition. It should always be encouraged.

"I am glad to hear that. When the Temple is rebuilt, there will be a need for many scribes."

"They will be ready. The children understand what it means to rebuild the Temple. They hate the Romans."

"Good, so they are also taught things like who we are and who our enemies are?"

Sarah nodded enthusiastically.

"They are indeed. They are playing war all the time. They shout that if the Romans come here, they will attack them with their styluses and poke their eyes out." We laughed.

"So, then, all the people in Bethar are ready to fight if they must? People like your brother?"

"My brother is in the army now. So are many others. But not everybody wants to fight, some would like to work and earn money."

"Is money a problem? Are people poor?"

"No, not now. There is enough money, for so many foreigners have come here with money… I mean outsiders, no, I mean city people like you…" she was turning red.

"I know what you mean. Don't worry."

"Excuse me, my lady, I just wanted to say that there is work for everybody now, because new people have moved into the town. People with money."

"Is everybody happy about that?"

She did not quite know how to answer. I prodded.

"For instance, the friends of your parents. Are they all satisfied with the situation?"

"Well, not all. There are those whose houses were requisitioned by the army."

"Were they not paid for them?"

"They were paid, but they think not enough. They could not buy a similar house for that money, not in the middle of town, where they lived before."

"I suppose they had to move to the outskirts, where all the new houses are."

"Yes, and those are not the best houses. They are cold in the winter. Those houses were supposed to be built for the Nabateans."

"Nabateans? I did not know that there were any Nabateans here."

"There are all kinds of folks here, people from everywhere. Jews had to escape from wherever they lived. They are all coming here."

"But Nabateans are not Jews!"

"No, but their fathers may be, or mothers, or somebody. I know one woman, lives down by the salty sea. She escaped from the Zoar, now she lives at Ein Gedi. Smart woman, makes lots of money."

"Do these people, the men I mean, also join the army?"

"Many do, if your husband takes them. He is very finicky."

I knew that.

"But he did take your brother?"

"He did that. It was not easy for my brother. He had to prove how strong he was and how brave. He is a brave man, my brother."

"Good, you can be proud of him."

She thought a little and then spoke again.

"You don't have to be a Jew to join the army."

"No?"

"No, I know people who have come here from all over, foreign countries, they are not Jews, and they are now fighting."

"What are they then? Nabateans?"

"Those, too, and Parthians. Samaritans. They say there are even some Romans on our side."

"I have not heard that. Very interesting. Tell me, are there any Notzrim in the army? Do you know any Notzrim?"

"I don't know any, but I have heard of them." Her face took on a disdainful look.

"What have you heard?" I remembered that my father supported their cause at some time.

"They kept saying that they were real Jews. But when it was time to fight, none came. They are packing up now and escaping to the other side of the Jordan, further up."

Later I heard even uglier things about them. I wished my father was still around, so I could tell him.

*　*　*

At another time Tzviyya and I were assisting at the camp, repairing torn clothes for the fighters. Halafta was away, I think he may have been visiting you, Yose, in Babylonia. He also travelled up to Sepphoris several times.

It was in the summer, the weather was very pleasant. If we had not had to worry about our husbands, we could have been almost happy.

The man in charge of the camp where we worked was our old friend Hillel of Cyrene. We talked with him while sewing. He was so full of admiration for Shimeon, it was almost embarrassing.

"It is really wonderful what a strong army he's created. And how he manages to control it. Decisively. Powerfully. Some say harshly, but that's good. You have to be harsh, so people respect you."

"They respect Shimeon, then?" I asked him.

"Respect? They fear him and adore him, almost as if he were a – a Messiah. But that's what he is!"

That's what I mean when I say embarrassing. How could I respond to a comment like that? Should I agree that, yes, he is the Messiah? Should I protest that, no, surely my husband is no such thing?

I had to remain quiet, and Tzviyya also looked down to the floor and said nothing. Hillel took no notice.

"Even his senior officers fear him. But they also love him. If he tells them to jump off a cliff, they will jump without any question."

"Tell me, Hillel, where is my husband now?" Shimeon just went, without telling me where. This time, he was away for almost a week.

"I think he is at Herodium." That did not surprise me. While the overall administration was at Bethar, many of the details were handled from Herodium; Bethar was not sizable enough to hold a large army headquarters. But then, Shimeon would not let control out of his hand for long.

"Last week, he was at Ein Gedi," Hillel added. "He set up the administrative center there. All kinds of lands to look after, they used to belong to the Romans, now they are the property of the House of Israel. That's how he puts it."

"Why, what does Shimeon do with the lands? Surely he does not work them." We all laughed at the idea.

"No, but he leases them to the local people. Lots of money comes in that way. You know, Ein Gedi was once called 'the village of the Lord Caesar.' So now it's 'the village of the Nasi of Israel.'"

"Wonderful."

Tzviyya asked: "How much money comes in from leasing a good plot of land?"

"Well, one with a house on it, a large one and some smaller buildings, and irrigation rights, it can bring in 650 dinars a year."

"That's a lot. That would be, let me see, over 160 tetradrachmas." Your mother was always quick with numbers.

"Yes, lots of money. The treasury is full. The economy is well managed. Shimeon bar Kokhba understands those things, too."

Hillel kept talking to us about the wonderful deeds of Shimeon. How he organized people in 'brotherhoods,' where everybody was responsible for everybody else. How he ran an army that observed all the laws of the Torah, including the oral Torah, the *Mishnah*, whenever that was possible (for sometimes you had to break the Shabbat, when there was fighting to be done, or preparation for fighting next day, but they were told that the sages approved). He even insisted that every Jew who had not undergone circumcision for fear of Tinneius Rufus do so now, even those who had tried to reverse the process to hide their Jewishness.

But what impressed Hillel most was how Shimeon kept control of his army commanders, how they all feared and respected him. He kept coming back to that issue, what a disciplined army Shimeon ran. I think he was right, that was what made the difference between a rebel force and a real army that could stand up to the Roman legions.

*   *   *

Shimeon came home after a while, and for once he was willing to tell me how things were going.

"This war must be a horrible shock to the Romans," he told me. "They must do something quickly. Tinneius Rufus must act, he cannot just go back to Rome and tell the Senate there 'I've just lost Judaea.'"

"So what can he do?"

"He can attack us, of course."

"I don't like that."

"Why not? That's part of our plan. He attacks and we counterattack. And we win." He smiled.

"When do you think he'll do that?"

"Oh, he has started already. That's what we had to deal with last week. He got it into his head that the best place to attack us would be in the hills."

"That does not make sense to me."

"Neither to me. But that's what he's done. He sent some troops into the hills, infantry without supporting units, they did not last long. We took out every last one of them."

"Really?"

"Yes. Of course, he has sent more. But he is at a great disadvantage. Among the trees, on the hills, we can hide and attack them very efficiently. Fifty of our fighters are enough to stop two or three hundred of theirs. We can watch their movement, we can move around ourselves without their noticing us, we can suddenly deal a devastating attack and, if necessary, we can easily escape. And there are plenty of rocks for our slingers. There are all those terraces to use, perfect for aiming, yet they cannot hit us there."

Still, I was worried. He had accused me before of hearing only the bad parts, never the good ones. That was not fair, I was proud of the great things he did. But can a wife not worry about her husband? Not to mention the country!

"So he has sent more troops now?"

"More troops? He's sent a whole legion."

"Legion? No! Why, a legion has – what – eight thousand people?"

"Twelve thousand, this one. It is the Twelfth *Deiotariana*, They were in Egypt until recently, apparently Hadrian ordered them here. Tinneius sent them into the hills, and you know what?"

"What?"

"There is no Twelfth *Deiotariana* any more."

I had to sit down.

"Don't tell me you've eliminated a whole Roman Legion?"

"That's what we have done, Michal. We did not kill every one of them, but we effectively destroyed the legion. My guess is that the world shall never hear of that particular legion again."

"Has such a thing ever been done?"

"Not for a long time, if ever. They have suffered losses in Parthia, and we did some serious damage to the Third *Cyrenaica*, but I believe this is the first time an entire legion has been wiped out."

Shimeon was grinning, I have seldom seen him so pleased with himself. Well, he had every right to be pleased. I was proud of him.

* * *

Halafta came back. We were a little worried about him, because we thought, how could he make his way back through all that fighting? Will he know when to lie low and when to travel safely? But he did know; your father may not have been a military man, but he had a sharp mind.

He told us about the situation in the countryside.

"As far west as Emmaus and as far south as Beth Guvrin, there are no Roman troops, it's all Shimeon's country. But it goes farther than that. I would say that even Yavneh and Bnei Braq are ours, up to Mount Gerizim and down to Ashkelon. People everywhere are in full support and very happy to see our troops. They are a little worried about the Romans, because, of course, they are more exposed down there, on the plains."

Tzviyya was so happy to see her husband; it was good to see her this way, with that glowing, happy smile. She did not say much, leaving the questioning to me.

"What about the north?" I asked. "What about the Galilee?"

"The Galilee is another matter. There has been some action there, but there is a lack of communication between us and them. I could get through, but there are Roman troops everywhere in the lower Galilee. Especially in the Valley of Jezreel. There are so many of them there, practically no action is possible in the Galilee."

"And Sepphoris?" We were always concerned about our hometown. We had relatives there and, of course, property.

"Nothing in Sepphoris. The town prides itself on being 'loyal' to the Roman empire. Jews and all."

I thought this over.

"I should say that's not very good news, but personally we have to be grateful. Our relatives and friends there seem to be safe."

* * *

Before long, the second wave of Roman attacks started. There were all kinds of activities, everybody was busy. While I had a general idea about what was happening, I was anxiously waiting for Shimeon to explain it all to me (and I admit, I was anxiously waiting for Shimeon).

When he came, he told me about the actions of one Publius Marcellus.

"This guy is the Syrian legatee. Hadrian sent him over here, to help poor little Tinneius Rufus. I would not like to be in Rufus' shoes. Marcellus came from Syria with a whole legion, the Third *Gallica*."

"Another legion."

"Not the only one. He has brought still another, or part of one, from there. Also, there is talk of more legions being brought here from Egypt and Arabia."

All right, so I was a worrier and did not like that.

"Is that still good? Is it still within your plans?"

"Well, we have already battled with some of the new unit, with Marcellus' people."

"And?"

"Oh, we won, of course," said he nonchalantly. I looked at him. I knew him well. Something was not quite right.

"Good. I am still proud of you. But…?"

"Why do you say 'but'?"

"You look worried."

"No, I am not worried. Well, this was a more serious battle. We have lost many people. But we won."

He looked tired.

And I began to attend funerals again.

Peace be with you.

THE THIRD STAGE BEGINS

Yose, it was now early fall of the second year. The coins recently struck proclaimed "Year Two of the Freedom of Israel." "Shimeon the Nasi" was also imprinted on them. There were also coins struck with "Eleazar the Priest" on them, but not very many, I don't know why.

Shimeon had one meeting at our house with his commanders; they discussed the entire military situation, which gave me an insight into how things were going.

One commander – I did not know the names of all, for Shimeon changed them often – reported on the action between the foothills and the sea.

"We used horses. Rode through the entire length, from Beth Guvrin to Yavneh and then back to Emmaus."

"Any encounters?" Shimeon asked him.

"Just two Roman companies. They caused no trouble. We lost eight men. They lost maybe fifty."

Shimeon asked the man for the names of the men lost. All the commanders said, "May their memory be blessed."

Shimeon then turned to the next man about his assignment.

"Yes, we managed to borrow eight ships. Had some trouble with the oarsmen, had to do some of the work ourselves. But that did not go so well."

"What happened?"

"There were many more Roman ships. Their crews knew better how to throw rocks and other things at us, heavy things. They also threw lighted torches, started some fires. One way or another, we lost half the ships and many of our men."

Shimeon just looked at him, kept looking, said nothing. He did not ask for the names of the men lost. The commander spoke again.

"I just followed orders. I never wanted a sea battle. They are better at such things than we are."

Shimeon still did not answer, slowly turned to the third commander. That man reported on the size of the attacking force from Emmaus.

"It was mainly infantry, but they had some cavalry and archers."

"Mounted archers?"

"Yes, many on horses, many others without. Non-Romans."

"Where are they from?"

"From the Orient and from Thrace. Those people have lived with their bows and arrows all their lives."

"Are we getting any better at it?"

"I would say we are getting much better. We still have a long way to go. Remember, very few Jews knew how to use a bow before. There was no point. If we killed an animal with an arrow, we could not eat it, anyway."

"Don't tell me things that you learned from me in the first place! Have we not been training for years now?" The man looked scared, but nodded.

"Yes, and we are improving. And in other areas we are better than they are."

"I hope so. But tell me." Not that he did not know; perhaps that was for my benefit.

"We can throw javelins better than they can. We are better slingers, even though they recruit slingers, too, from the countries around here. And we are really good at throwing rocks from catapults. We throw them much farther than they can, and much more accurately."

Shimeon nodded impatiently. The man, thinking that he was being encouraged, continued to report.

"This gives us a great advantage. We occupy the best positions in the hills, and hit them with huge rocks. Our people know the terrain well. Most of them are from around here, the mountain. And we are really good with scimitars and spears and sickle-swords, to finish them off after we hit them with rocks."

Shimeon was angry.

"I know all that. We have discussed it many times. Tell me what's been happening. Or are you afraid to report on that?"

"Sorry, sir, I have not realized that all you…"

"The outcome?!"

"Well, at first, when they brought in those foreign archers, we suffered some losses, that's true, but during the last few weeks we've learned how to protect ourselves with shields and by hiding behind trees, and hitting them with slings. We have some mounted archers, too. All in all, I would say, we are ahead of them and getting better."

Shimeon did not reply. We all hoped that the man's report was based on facts, not hopes.

*   *   *

In the fall there was some bad news about the fighting down on the plains. Apparently, our troops were trying to extend the area under our control all the way to the sea and were badly beaten by the Romans who could move up and down the roads with their cavalry more easily than we could. They were used to that kind of terrain. Shimeon was not there, I thanked the Lord, although perhaps he would have made a difference.

We also had some intelligence reports. A man came to Shimeon at our house with information gathered at Caesarea.

"Publius Marcellus is the governor now. Nobody knows what happened to Tinneius Rufus."

Shimeon shrugged, the news did not impress him.

"But he is not going to be responsible for the legions."

"No? So who is?"

"A man, a Roman general, called Julius Severus."

"Never heard of him."

"He has been Roman governor in Britannia. There was lots of resistance there against the Roman rule, first in a province called Wales and later at lots of other places, mainly in the north of the land. This man put the rebellion down mercilessly, wiped out the rebels. So Hadrian sent a message to him, ordering him to come here as soon as possible and take over."

"Do they know when he'll come?"

"They expect him by early winter."

"It will take him a few months to learn about the situation. That should give us enough time to consolidate our positions," Shimeon mused.

But he did not have as much time as he hoped. By the beginning of winter, probably before the new man could take over, there were lots of new Roman troops in the country, and they attacked us more and more frequently, with fewer mistakes than before.

One of the new attacking forces was a legion from the Danube river, somewhere in Europe. They were fierce fighters and we suffered heavy losses. There was some talk of their trying to break through to Jerusalem from the north.

Shimeon rode off to Bnei Braq. The town was still in our hands, and he needed to talk to Rabbi Akiva. When he came back, I asked him about the old man, how he was and what he suggested.

"Akiva is well, thank the Lord. He will visit us here, soon. We had a long discussion."

"About the situation?"

"Of course. About the new Roman advances. About Jerusalem and other places."

"What does he say?"

"You see, the question is where we should concentrate our forces: In the hills, where we can fight well, on the plains where the Romans have the upper hand – but perhaps we could change that – or in the cities. We don't have enough people to fight everywhere."

"And Akiva suggests…?"

"He suggests that, first of all, we should not defend towns, even cities that have a large non-Jewish population. He thinks that when the Roman presence is heavy there, the non-Jews would switch sides, turn against us."

"That makes sense."

"Yes, but one such city is Jerusalem!"

I looked at him. I thought that I could detect pain in his eyes.

"He says that you should not defend Jerusalem?!"

Shimeon nodded. "He does. He argues that the important thing is to maintain our forces, strengthen them if possible. We can retake Jerusalem later, if things go well."

"Is that what you are going to do?"

"I think so." A big sigh. "Of course, after evacuating our troops and all the Jews from there."

That was a blow. Shimeon was very proud of Jerusalem. If he was ready to give it up, that was cause for worry.

*　*　*

One problem was the Sanhedrin. It would have to move from Jerusalem, probably to Bethar. Shimeon made arrangements.

But the sages in Jerusalem did not like his arrangements. Eventually, there was a meeting in Jerusalem between Shimeon and many members of the Sanhedrin.

I heard of that meeting a little later from Halafta. He was there, tried to say little; after all, everybody knew that he was the brother-in-law of Shimeon.

"There were some sharp words. They accused Shimeon of all kinds of things. Not nice things. Akiva tried to defend him, actually many people did. But some people said that he was weak. Others accused him of faulty strategy. Again there were those who said that he was a tyrant himself, not listening to the advice of wiser men, or even to his own military commanders."

"I suppose Shimeon defended himself."

"Oh, very well, indeed. It was hard to disagree with his arguments, put in direct, military terms. He was talking about the number of troops, ours and the Romans. But they reminded him of some earlier promises."

"I see." I did not quite like the sound of that.

"One of the problems was," continued Halafta, "that they did not want to move to Bethar. Many insisted on staying in Jerusalem. But most of them don't actually live there, and if the city should be taken over by the Romans, there is no way the Sanhedrin could operate there."

"So they'll come here, after all?" I was thinking where we would house nearly seventy men, presumably with their families, servants and households.

"They will set up a so-called 'small Sanhedrin' here, just twenty-one members. I am not sure if all twenty-one want to live here, or just meet occasionally."

"Well, that's their business." I was perhaps relieved. "I would think that it was safer here than elsewhere in Judaea. Or perhaps they all want to go to the Galilee?"

"Many do. But there was another point raised in the meeting that was rather awkward."

Apprehension again.

"What point?"

Halafta saw that I was concerned. He smiled a little, waving the matter away as something not very important.

"It's just that they started a debate on whether Shimeon was the Messiah, after all."

That shocked me.

"But he was not supposed to be *that* kind of Messiah, anyway. Just a king. A Nasi. Not the redeemer promised by the prophets."

"Well," he said apologetically, as if he were responsible, "they reminded the others that, earlier on, expressions such as 'the spirit of the Lord shall rest upon him' and 'the spirit of wisdom and understanding, the spirit of counsel and might, the spirit of knowledge and the fear of the Lord' had been used, quoting from the prophet Isaiah. They questioned those qualities now."

"I suppose that Eleazar of Modi'in was the most vocal, most critical?"

"Surprisingly, no. He was there, but said nothing at all during the whole time."

"I wonder why. But then, who made the strongest attack?"

"The most outspoken was Yohanan ben Torta. He raised a point that, eventually, most agreed with. And that point was that the Messiah must be able to judge by smell."

"Smell?!" I must have made a funny face, for he grinned, too.

"Yes, what that means is that when he meets with people, with contestants, say, he must be able to make the right decision based not only on the dry facts, which could be written down on paper, but just by looking at people, listening to the tone of their voices, the way the talk, the way they move their faces and their bodies, whether they are self-confident or fearful, oh, many, many things that cannot be defined; but all of those things together, should tell the person what the truth is."

"The smell."

"Yes, probably that, too. How each person smells. One cannot actually smell them, but somehow a perceptive leader, a Messiah, should have a certain awareness."

"And they think that Shimeon cannot do that?"

"Yes, that's what they say. That he is too crude, not sensitive enough to understand each person, whether friend or enemy, and make decisions accordingly. They think that this proves he is no Messiah, and is therefore not fit to lead the nation."

"And what did Shimeon have to say to that?"

"Nothing. He just sat there and looked bored."

Of course, I thought, what should he have said? Nothing, if he did not wish to be impolite.

"Do they have an alternative?"

"No, they don't. That's why they agreed, in the end, to set up the small Sanhedrin here and to move out of Jerusalem. But there was much bitterness."

SETBACKS

Let me tell you, Yose, about another situation meeting between Shimeon and his top commanders. I came to dislike those meetings. I was not pleased about the way Shimeon treated his senior officers; but perhaps you have to be brusque and impolite in war.

One of the issues was intelligence gathering, and the man in charge seemed to have been up to the task, he had lots of important information for Shimeon.

"Sir, first of all, we have found out that the Emperor Hadrian has returned here. He is staying at Caesarea."

"Pity, but I don't think it matters. I would have preferred him in Greece with his little friends."

"Yes, sir. Now to the matter of the legions. There is a total of twelve Roman legions in the country."

"What!" Shimeon stood up and glared at the man. "How many?!"

The fellow was a little scared, but he repeated.

"Twelve. The manpower is about one hundred and fifty thousand men in arms."

"But that's more than twice as much as the last number you provided."

"Yes, sir, but that was four months ago. Troops are pouring in, by land and by sea."

Shimeon grunted and started to walk around the room. The commander continued.

"Most of the legions are still in training. The active ones are the *Fretensis*, as always, the *Ferrata* and the Second *Trajana*."

Shimeon stopped pacing. He nodded a few times.

"Well, we are familiar with the first two. So we shall get to know the Trajana. They'll get a taste of our weapons. They shall remember that." He was covering up his shock about the size of the enemy troops.

The commanders, too, nodded their heads. What else could they do?

"Now, what about our own forces?" Shimeon turned to another man.

"We continue to be strong," he reported. "We have lost many, but there are plenty of new fighters waiting to join in."

"Yes, let's estimate how many. What is the total population of the King's Mountain?"

"Well, there are something like four hundred villages, some smaller, some larger. A village may have a thousand people. But there are some larger towns, too. About 550,000 I would say."

"Well, if every healthy man were to fight, that would give us – let me see – half are men, that's 280,000. We leave out the old, say forty thousand, the small children, another fifty thousand, and the sick – so there could be as many as 180,000 men under arms."

"Yes, sir, but many of them are already fighting."

"How many?"

"Hard to say. We have about two hundred thousand fighters, but at least half came from outside the hills. Could be that one hundred thousand of our men are from around here. Maybe a little less," he added with hope.

"So we can count on another hundred thousand, nearly," said Shimeon.

"Yes, I suppose." Pause. "If we take everybody."

That was an allusion to Shimeon's early insistence of being extremely selective, taking only the strongest and the bravest.

Shimeon was not fazed, though.

"We'll take everybody who can take up a spear or sword. Any weapon at all."

He looked around for approval, and slowly everybody nodded. Then he added:

"All mortals will have to join the struggle."

Another man said:

"Yes, well, we have actually started drafting people."

"Good. Going well?"

"Ye…es, reasonably well. We have no problem with the Jews. But the Samaritans are causing lots of trouble. Few want to join and I don't trust even those."

"Don't take them. I don't trust them either. Any other problem groups?"

"Only the Notzrim. The ones who have not yet escaped. They don't want to fight. We had to treat some of them really roughly, to get them to the camp."

Another man spoke up.

"Perhaps too roughly? They are complaining all over the land that we are killing them, persecuting them, if they refuse to join."

Shimeon grunted: "Let them complain."

The man scratched his head: "Yes, but they go around blaming the Nasi."

"Do they now?"

"Yes, sir. They say things like 'Bar Kokhba is a false Messiah, a murderer.'"

Shimeon shrugged. "Of course they'll say that. They have their own Messiah, they have been expecting him back for a hundred years now, and still he has not come. So they won't accept another. Let them complain."

"They do more than complain. They run. Most of them are escaping to the other side of the Jordan."

"Rats leaving the sinking ship?" murmured Shimeon. Perhaps he should not have said that.

*   *   *

I did not feel very good about the situation. And I was not the only one with concerns. During the same week – it was already winter – I had a long discussion with your mother, Tzviyya. More than a discussion perhaps, you could have called it a clash.

It started with Tzviyya beginning to talk about leaving Bethar, moving up to Sepphoris in the Galilee. I was not very polite, I admit. Upon reflection, I feel bad about the incident.

"Are you also one of the rats?" I asked her. "The ones who leave the sinking ship?"

She was quick to respond. I can still see her face, she had such a small, sweet face, not like my stronger face at all, most of the time with a pleasant smile, but now she turned furious.

"Rats, eh? Well, the rats are smart. Should they go down with the ship? So you admit that the ship is sinking."

"I admit nothing of the kind," I returned, angry, probably with myself for starting this. "We are strong. We have lots of people, more than ever. We await the dry weather, then we'll attack them with all we have."

"And you think that will be enough?"

"It will be. I have heard the numbers. We'll have twice the number of their troops."

"But they have highly trained, professional soldiers, not peasant boys like we have. And we all thought that Shimeon was oh, so selective." She could actually sneer, Do you recall her doing that?

"He was," I responded. What could I say? "But when he has to take everybody, he will take everybody. Nothing wrong with that."

"Yes, there is. The local boys can stop the Romans here in the hills, perhaps, because they know the hills. But there is no way they are a match to the legions on the plains."

"So we'll concentrate on defending the hills."

"Yes, but are the hills getting smaller?"

"What do you mean?"

"Look, I hear things, too. We have lost Jericho and Lod and Modi'in. Emmaus was never really ours, but now it's a Roman stronghold. We no longer have Hebron, or Beth Guvrin."

I did not reply. I knew that she was correct.

"What we have is about a third of the free and independent nation that Shimeon declared last year. Just these hills, and not all of them, either."

"Yes, but Jerusalem is still ours. Shimeon has just ordered new coins struck, with the words 'Third Year of the Freedom of Jerusalem,'" I insisted.

Her face now softened, she was no longer angry, rather sad.

"I am told that we are no longer defending Jerusalem, and in a few weeks it will be gone."

I could see that she was close to crying, and so was I. That must not be allowed. So I made a brave statement.

"We shall regain all of those places quite soon, you shall see."

And with that, I left the room quickly.

*　　*　　*

We had been expecting the great Roman attack, but when it came, it was a surprise. They did not come in with massive forces. Small, powerful groups attacked, well equipped with bows and arrows, and with slings, even catapults. And they attacked the weakest links, our connections from one stronghold to another. I thought – Shimeon said the same later – that they had learned from us how to fight in the hills, they had copied our fighting methods, and very well, indeed. We lost many good young men and our position in the hill became weaker as a result.

These were the crack soldiers from the Danube river, from Pannonia. It was hard to fight against them. Our soldiers held out, but they were exhausted. We were no longer in a position to surprise them with major attacks. Rather, we had to concentrate on self-defense.

As Shimeon explained afterwards, it was to be our subsequent strategy to attack them in a small way, at many places, just to maintain the pressure and, at the same time, keep our men in fighting spirit. But the main activity, from now on, was to be defensive.

Yet I was heartbroken to see that the areas under our control got steadily smaller.

One day, Shimeon spent enough time at home to talk to me about the next phases.

"The key is Bethar," he told me that day. "This is a major stronghold. Look, it is very well fortified, and this is a strategic location; here we control the Beth Guvrin to Jerusalem road. We can defend Bethar indefinitely."

"But what if they surround us? What shall we eat?"

"Don't worry, we have a plentiful supply of food stored here. It's well hidden in the city walls. Also arms, an almost inexhaustible quantity."

"But Shimeon, you say Bethar is well fortified. Yet I can see walls only around the fortress, here, on this hill. Not on the plateau behind the fortress, and certainly not around the main town."

"Yes, that's true. If necessary, we'll have to move everybody from the town inside the fortress."

"Inside? There is not that much room here. This is a small area. There is no room here for more than a few hundred people, at the most."

"Yes, there is. We can put a lot more in here, if we must. And also the plateau, behind the hill, that is quite easily defendable. You have seen how it's surrounded by deep chasms on every side."

"They can still climb up there, can't they?"

"Not with our men watching on top."

I was not very happy with that prospect.

* * *

Then Rabbi Akiva came to visit one day. It was not easy by then to arrange his trip, Shimeon had to send special guides and guards for him. Apparently, Shimeon needed his mentor's advice.

Akiva spent three days at our house, and there were discussions about many things. I have never seen the old man so sad, so dejected.

He told us one cause:

"I have just heard that Rabbi Ishmael has been killed. Killed in his own home town of 'Azziz, in the Negev. By the troops of this new commander, Julius Severus."

He sat quietly for some minutes, then added: "Bad news is in store for the nation." And I knew that the news he had in mind was worse than bad.

The next day, they discussed the Sanhedrin. The small one that was set up in Bethar. Now it seemed that they might not stay there.

Akiva expressed a strong opinion on that:

"I am not going to recommend one place or another for the Sanhedrin. There is no suitable place now. We shall have to wait and see. For now, everybody, all the sages, should just go home."

Shimeon was very unhappy about that, and said so.

"Akiva, this place here, Bethar, is going to be the center of our nation for a long time. Should there not be some religious presence here?"

Akiva thought.

"Yes, Shimeon, you are right. There should be. But not a small Sanhedrin, not even a very small one, not nine, not five, not even three. Just one man, one strong sage who is not afraid."

"Yourself?"

"I wish I could. I am too old. I am tired and sick. No, it will have to be someone else. Also, I feel that it should be a Hillelite scholar. No, don't protest. The sages feel that you need someone to stress the approach of Bet Hillel. You are too far gone in the other direction. And I think I know just the right person."

"Don't tell me it's..." Shimeon protested.

"Yes, my son, it will indeed have to be Rabbi Eleazar. Your uncle. I know that you have had your differences, but he will help you. It will be good for you to have a wise old man like him around."

Shimeon did not answer immediately. He walked around the room, quite unhappy, deep in thought. Then he asked Akiva:

"Would you mind very much, my master, if I considered this until tomorrow? It is an important thing for me. I don't want to make a mistake."

"Sure, think about it, Shimeon."

And he thought. He also talked to me, a lot. He did not like Eleazar. He had even taken his name off the coins in the third year. But it was difficult to oppose Akiva. I told him that something good might come out of it. Eleazar's devotion certainly should be an asset. So in the morning he told Akiva that if Eleazar was willing to stay, he would accept him.

"I knew you would say that, my son," nodded Akiva. "Now listen to me, and listen well. I shall not be able to advise you anymore. Rabbi Eleazar will be here. He is very different from me. But what you will need now, during the next months or years, is the help of the Lord. Don't interrupt now. The situation is not good. You know that and I know that. What we don't know is the reason. Maybe the Lord is just testing us. If you remain devoted, do good deeds as far as possible during a war, study the Torah when you can spare the time, you and all your men, observe the commandments, maybe He will then reverse the fortunes and you will be victorious again. I shall pray for that, but more important, Rabbi Eleazar will pray for that, here, with you. Listen to him, respect him, for he is as learned in Torah as anybody I know."

He paused. All the talk tired him.

"And one more thing. If you receive news about me, bad news, accept it. Don't try anything foolish, for now your people and yourself are more valuable than I am."

"But Akiva, why would you talk like that? You must be careful, and nothing will happen to you. And you are valuable, the most valuable man in Israel."

"No, my son, no. I don't even want an escort when I leave here. We shall leave that to the will of the Lord. Watch your men, my son, watch your people. Watch our land. The Lord be with you, my son."

He kissed Shimeon, bade me goodbye and left the house.

Shimeon ran after him, and I after Shimeon, but the old man sent us back with a very firm, strong movement of his arms, and especially with an expression on his face that made us understand that his visit was over. Perhaps that his life was over. It was very clear that we were to do nothing about that.

I was heartbroken.

"Shimeon, why did he not want any escort?"

"He thought that we needed every man here. And he thought that where he was going, right through Roman territory, the escorts would be vulnerable."

"And he himself?"

"You know him. He thinks that they may not harm him; if they do, so be it. It's the will of the Lord."

I thought for a while. There was another thing that kept bothering me:

"The way he talked to you, called you 'my son' many times. I was thinking, perhaps you are really his son? Is there something I should know, that you've kept a secret?"

He hesitated.

"No, Michal, I am not his son. No, definitely not."

I accepted that.

*　*　*

And soon word came that Akiva had been arrested by the Romans.

We knew that it was only a question of time before they would kill him.

Then, Shimeon told me:

"Michal, when you asked me why he said 'my son' so much? If he might be my father?"

"Yes?"

"No, he is not my father. But he is my uncle."

"Uncle? How? I thought Rabbi Eleazar…"

"No, not through marriage. He is my father's brother."

I just stared at him. He explained.

"They were the children of a proselyte, Yosef. He had some other name before becoming a Jew. They were poor, and each worked hard to make something of himself. Or herself, even. They had a sister, Tzippora; she married well, to the famous Hillelite scholar, the priest Rabbi Eleazar. My father worked at trades, but he studied at nights, and became a scholar himself, a Shammaite one. When Akiva became famous, joined the Sanhedrin, my father thought that having a Shammaite brother would be a great disadvantage for Akiva. That was the time when Rabbi Eliezer and all the Shammaites were expelled. So we decided to keep quiet about it."

"Did Akiva agree to that?"

"At first he did not want to. But when his wife Rachel also insisted that they should not talk about the matter, he reluctantly consented. Remember, nobody lied about anything. If you had asked Akiva at any time about his brother, he would not have said 'I have no brother.' He would not have denied his family. But of course, nobody ever asked him that question."

"Does Rabbi Eleazar know this?"

"Of course he does. He is a member of the family. But he was also embarrassed by us. He strongly disliked my father and me, too, I suppose. He certainly does not like me now."

"That's because he did not want this war."

"Well, maybe in the end he will turn out to be right."

"Don't say that, Shimeon. Things will only improve from now on. You shall be victorious again."

THE NASI STRUGGLES

Do not think, Yose, that Shimeon's words indicated he feared he might be losing the war. No, he was certain that he was going to win. Despite the setbacks, he was convinced that somehow he would defeat the Romans, that he would be victorious. Is that not what a Messiah is supposed to do? One does not worry about the fine distinction between various kinds of Messiahs.

One day he sent for Hillel, his Cyrenean aide.

"Hillel, have we received the spices and balsam from Ein Gedi?"

"No, Shimeon, we have not."

"Well, have you done anything about it?"

"I've sent two letters so far."

"Obviously, that's not enough. Write a letter in my name, immediately ordering the local military governor to come here. What is his name again?"

"Yehonathan bar Ba'ayan. Well, that's the trouble, there are two of them, they always expect the other to do what you order. Masabala bar Shimeon, that's the other one."

"Order both of them here. While we are at it, order a couple of other local governors here, too, we shall have a meeting. Let me see: from Kiryat Arabaya, that will be…"

"Yehuda bar Manasse."

"Yes, and from Beth Mashko?"

"Yehoshua ben Galgula."

"Make sure they are all here by the evening of the second day next week. Does that give them enough time to travel after the Shabbat?"

"Yes, they can make it. I shall send the letters with the fastest riders, so they'll get them tomorrow. They'll have plenty of time to prepare."

Shimeon was concerned about the supply lines. He explained to me that evening that he just could not allow some of those local governors to use the presence of Roman troops in the area as an excuse for not delivering the requisitioned supply.

"You see, the land they use belongs to the nation. I am leasing it to them, on condition that they shall provide whatever is required of them for our people."

"And if there are difficulties on the way?"

"Then they should use better people to make the delivery. Ride at night, find the place and the time when the Romans are not around. They cannot be always everywhere."

Sometimes I was not sure if Shimeon was simply authoritative, or perhaps naive in his inflexible demands. I worried that the summoned local governors might even be bold enough to ignore his orders. But no, I was the naive one, for on the second day of the following week, the governors arrived. They were full of excuses for being slow in delivering the requisitioned food and supply.

"Not everyone cultivates the leased land," complained Masabala bar Shimeon. "Some people just want to have the lease for future use."

"Give me the names of people who have not planted anything."

Somewhat reluctantly, Masabala and his colleague Yehonathan gave him six names.

"When you go back to Ein Gedi, you call in those six people and tell them that they have lost the lease. Not just the uncultivated fields but everything they lease from us. Then you can lease those lands to others, people who are ready to work the fields."

"But Nasi, they have paid for the lease."

"They were supposed to produce food. The lease is void!"

The two looked at each other, but said nothing. They understood that there was to be no further argument on that matter.

But after some talk on other topics, Shimeon came back to the question of uncultivated fields.

"The problem, I think, is that a few smart peasants grabbed as much land as they could, whether or not they wanted to cultivate the fields. If the lessees were simple people, peasants who needed the land to make a living, we would have plenty of food."

They all agreed on that, but Yehonathan bar Ba'ayan dared to qualify his agreement.

"Yes, Nasi, but many of those people are now here, in the army. They like it here, call each other 'brothers.' That is good, but then they cannot work the fields."

Shimeon would not buy that argument.

"What about their wives, or parents? We don't have any old people among the brothers. There is always someone to work on the fields. The land is rich. There is good irrigation. It does not require that much effort to plant and gather the produce."

He then asked Yehoshua ben Galgula about the wheat produced at Beth Mashko, heard the man make some excuses about poor harvest results, and ordered him to have the requisitioned wheat delivered within a week.

After some further discussion of local matters, Shimeon asked the

Ein Gedi governors about the Tekoans. Theirs was a village east of Beth Lehem.

"I hear that those people refused to join the army when I issued mobilization orders. Have you heard that, too?"

The two governors admitted that they had.

"And I have also heard that they escaped from Tekoa and have sought refuge at Ein Gedi. Is that true?"

Neither of them replied.

"Is that true?!" Shimeon thundered.

Masabala could not stand Shimeon's piercing eyes, and said:

"Nasi, all kinds of people have come to Ein Gedi. We don't know from where they hail. There is upheaval all over the land, many come to our district."

"Well, my friend, you better find out where everyone comes from, and fast! For if I were to hear that anyone gave shelter to the Tekoans, that man's house shall be burnt down and he will be punished severely. And that includes the governors of the place. Is that understood?"

They all murmured, "yes, Sir."

"Look. Your job is to promote the war effort. Is that clear?"

"Yes, yes," they all said.

"And that means to have as many fighters in the army as possible. We have volunteers from all over the world, not just Jews, but Parthians, Thracians, Nabateans, even Greeks, all kinds. Well, I just won't stand for a Jew shirking his national duty, and I don't care what excuse he uses. Is that fully understood?!"

"Yes, Nasi," they all said.

*　　*　　*

I write down that particular discussion only to show you the type of problems Shimeon had to deal with, and also, because that was one of the few discussions held at our house, and therefore I could hear what was said. But, of course, that meeting did not solve the problem of supply. Shimeon had to write many letters to his local governors. Sometimes Hillel did the letter-writing for Shimeon, others were sent from one of the camps closer to the area where they were expecting deliveries. Once Shimeon came back from Herodium and was annoyed that they were almost completely out of salt; he had to write to Masabala and Yehonathan demanding salt, well packed, so they would not lose half on the way.

When the summer was past and the fall holidays were approaching,

Shimeon wrote to Kiryat Arabaya for the "four species," needed for Sukkoth. I remember that, because he asked Hillel to write the letter in his name, ordering *lulav* and *etrog* from Ein Gedi and *hadas* and *arava* from Kiryat Arabaya. He demanded that they send a sizable quantity, for the army was very large.

One day Yehonathan bar Ba'ayan's people, at Ein Gedi, captured a Roman soldier. They dragged him to the fortress and were ready to kill him, cruelly, but Bar Ba'ayan did not permit it. He ordered his men to tie the Roman properly, give him food and water. He explained patiently that the information they were going to extract from their captive would be much more valuable than a dead body.

He sent a message to Shimeon, who ordered the man brought over to Bethar. He wanted the Roman to be questioned under his own supervision.

The interrogation went on for hours. The man did not want to say anything at first, only his name – as I recall, it was Tyrsus, the son of Theodorus – but thought better of it later. I am certain that our methods were very effective.

That evening Rabbi Eleazar came to our house.

"Shimeon, what will happen to Tyrsus, the captured Roman?" he demanded to know.

Shimeon shrugged. "He will tell us everything he knows. That may not be much, but at least we shall know what unit he comes from, how many men they have, what weapons they possess, what their immediate plans are, who their commander is, their weakest point, and so on."

"You will continue to torture him, then?"

"Only if he does not talk."

"And after he has talked? What will happen to him then?"

Shimeon looked bored. He did not answer at first. Eleazar insisted.

"What will you do to him afterwards? Tell me!"

"It's up to the commander of the men who are interrogating him. I suppose they'll kill him. We don't have enough food to keep every captured enemy alive."

"You will do nothing of the sort! You don't have to feed him. Send him back."

"Back where?"

"Back to his people. To the Romans."

Shimeon did not want to believe his ears.

"Are you crazy? He would tell them everything he saw here."

"What did he see? Nothing. A square in the town and people who tortured him. Feed him well, give him new clothes, and send him back. But wait, there is more than that. Tell him to go directly to the commander of the Roman forces. Send a gift to that man. Something beautiful, something made of gold. And send a letter suggesting that the two sides sit down to talk. If you like, I'll write the letter. I can write in Greek, I could even try Latin…"

Shimeon had been staring at him, still not believing what he heard. Now he started to scream.

"Uncle Eleazar, you are mad! Shame on you! You want to talk to the enemy? Next thing, you will give him the country."

Eleazar shouted back.

"Shame on you, Shimeon. Would you rather kill all of our own people, along with the Romans? Of course one should talk to the enemy. You might find that he is willing to listen to reason. I won't give him the country, he might not even want it, or not all of it. There is always room for compromise."

"And how much are you willing to give him? Jerusalem? Most of Judaea? The Galilee? Will you accept the generous gift of Bethar from him? So we can live in this small town until he changes his mind? Give him our arms? Send him our soldiers as hostages? What?!"

"You are being unreasonable, my nephew. We shall first have to find out what he demands. Then we'll make a counteroffer. We'll negotiate like civilized people and, at the end, with the help of the Lord, we shall have a compromise that we can live with. It won't be the all that we would like, but we shall be alive."

"Alive, and Roman slaves."

"Live another day. We shall find solutions to all our problems."

Shimeon was livid with rage.

"Is that why they sent you here? Is that what the Sanhedrin wanted? To have somebody here who frustrates all of our efforts? Somebody who represents the weak Hillelite stand? Cowardly, spineless, timid people, who would lick the enemy's…"

It was time for me to step into the fray. I stopped him, put a restraining hand on his arm.

"Enough said, Shimeon. You have your opinion and your uncle has his. There is no need to insult him." I turned to Eleazar. "Rabbi Eleazar, please leave these matters to Shimeon. You are right to advise him, that's why you are here. But the final decision must be made by him. He is the Nasi."

Eleazar looked at me, said nothing, then turned and left the room. I patted Shimeon's arm again. He did not say anything either. Finally, he shook his head and strode out of the house.

* * *

The fighting continued. I was not privy to all the details, sometimes Shimeon preferred to keep things from me. He never told me what happened to the captured Roman soldier, and I did not ask him. Why irritate him needlessly? But I noticed it was not the good news he kept from me. I had to attend many funerals and pay visits to mourners. I did not fool myself with the idea that things were going well.

My sister Tzviyya was even more concerned. She talked to me about the possibility of leaving earlier, but now she approached her husband, your father Rabbi Halafta, to talk to Shimeon.

Halafta suggested that we have our evening meal together, the four of us, one day when Shimeon was at home. While we ate, we made small talk about people we all knew. But after the final blessing, Halafta confronted Shimeon directly:

"How is the military situation? Are we gaining ground or losing it?"

Shimeon took his time answering the question.

"Many people think that we are losing. The sages, in particular. I am surprised that you are still here. According to the reports I receive, most of the others have already gone into hiding, or left for Babylonia."

"Is that what you think? That we are losing the war?"

"I did not say that, did I?"

"Well, what *do* you say?"

"I say that the Romans are building up their camps around Bethar. I think that they want to bring very large forces to this place. That is not surprising. This is the center of operations. They have amassed a siege force of some ten thousand soldiers from two legions, the Fifth *Macedonica* and the Eleventh *Claudia*. Those are strong legions."

"And so you expect a full siege against Bethar to start soon?"

"Yes, I do. I think they are waiting for some more troops from Jerusalem; we have given Jerusalem up, as you know."

I did not know. Neither did Tzviyya. She looked at me, saw how I felt and held my hand.

Shimeon added:

"In a few weeks, they will attack."

We all waited for him to continue. We knew that this was no ordinary discussion. It was leading somewhere.

"We can defend Bethar, that is not the problem. What I mean is, we can defend the fortress here, and the plateau. Not the town down there. When the siege starts, we shall have to bring everybody from the town inside here, or onto the plateau. The problem is that we may be surrounded."

We were still quiet.

"Not completely surrounded, I suppose. Not around the ravines. They cannot position their troops at the bottom of the ravines, for we can easily get them with catapults. They would have to take positions on the surrounding hillsides, and that would require too many troops. I think we shall still be able to get through when we must. But it will be more and more difficult."

"So what do you suggest?" Halafta finally asked him. We knew what was coming.

"You must leave. You must go to the Galilee, while you still can. Take Tzviyya and take Michal also. You shall be safe at Sepphoris."

"No, Shimeon, no! I don't want to go! I won't go!" I shouted.

"Yes, Michal, you'll go. It is time. There is nothing useful for you to do here. We need the room for fighters."

"I don't need much room. One small room is enough for the two of us. We could even share that room with others."

"You would have to. But that is not the point. We want as few women and children here as possible. And frankly, I can operate more freely if you are not here, if I don't have to think of coming home at night. I don't want to worry about you. I have thought about this, and I was ready to talk to you, Halafta, but you spoke first."

"When should we go?" Halafta asked him.

"Within two days. You need time to prepare things, so leave the day after tomorrow, in the evening."

After Halafta and Tzviyya had gone to their room, I argued with Shimeon again, but it was no use. His mind was made up. I had to leave.

And so the time came for us to get ready. I asked Shimeon to come with me into the inner room.

"Shimeon, my dear, my love, shall I ever see you again?"

He saw that my eyes were full of tears, and he cried a little as he kissed me.

"I hope so, Michal. The Lord may help us yet. One never knows what

He has planned." He tried to smile. "I may just show up at the house in Sepphoris one day."

"Yes, my dear, you shall come to me soon. Every morning I shall hope that this will be the day."

* * *

Shimeon provided us with an escort, two good men. We travelled at night, hid in caves during the day, for there were Roman soldiers everywhere. Once I saw a Roman camp in the distance teeming with soldiers, horses, supplies, a large city with streets and squares. I had never seen the like of it. My heart sank.

We reached Sepphoris in two weeks' time. We found the house there in good order, our relatives and friends were happy to see us. We spent many evenings telling them about the war, our victories and also, alas, our losses.

During our trip, and while in Sepphoris, I constantly worried about Shimeon and the situation in Bethar. Before leaving, I made him promise that, whenever possible, he would send couriers with news to us, so that I would always know what was happening at Bethar.

The courier usually turned out to be Hillel of Cyrene. When he first came, he told us about the events during the weeks after our departure from Bethar.

"It went just as Shimeon expected," he reported to us. "The Romans thought that they would mount a surprise attack, but we knew it was coming, and the town was evacuated. They quickly took Bethar town. But they could not come close to the fortress."

"But how did all those people fit inside?"

"Not easily. There are now two thousand five hundred fighters inside the fortress, and also many horses. It is very crowded."

"I suppose the rest are on the plateau."

"Yes, another two thousand, maybe closer to three thousand. At first there were mainly women and children there, but we are trying to move out as many as we can, and to bring in more soldiers. So that plateau is getting to be full of soldiers, too, and horses. And supplies, of course."

"And you think that the fortress and the plateau can be defended?"

"Oh, yes. The entire hill. You see, we shall have more and more people there all the time. We are getting stronger. In Bethar."

A good thing he qualified that statement, for I would not have believed him otherwise.

"How strong do you think you'll get there?"

"The Nasi is talking about ten, twelve thousand fighters, maybe fifteen thousand."

"You could not put so many soldiers onto that plateau!"

"So we'll place them just below the plateau, on the hillside. They can watch the Romans there, and shoot arrows or slings at them, if they get too close."

"But what about food for so many people?"

"We can still get through and bring in supplies. And Shimeon says there is plenty of food hidden inside."

"Well, thank you for the news, Hillel. Rest now, eat and sleep, and tomorrow ride back to camp. I will write a letter to Shimeon, so that you can take it with you in the morning. I hope that you'll come again, soon, perhaps with better news."

But good news were scarce in those days, Yose.

Peace be with you.

Hadrian's letter to Lucius Aelius Caesar

NOW REVENGE!

The Emperor Caesar Trajan Hadrian August –
to Senator Lucius Aelius Caesar – greetings.

My dear Lucius, you will notice that I no longer address you as Lucius Ceionius Commodus, rather by your new appellation, that you shall soon assume upon your adoption as my son and heir. Very soon, you shall be Emperor, leader of the greatest empire the world has ever known. It is time that you learn everything about the affairs of the empire, so that you can act correctly, should you be suddenly called to take the reigns before my return to Rome

You were surely in the Senate when my recent letter was read to that august body. It could not have escaped your attention that the letter did not start as it should have. We are used to the Emperor reporting from the battlefield to the Senate thus: "I hope that you and your families are well. The troops and the Emperor are well." I wish that I could have started my letter that way. Alas, no. The troops are not well at all, and the Emperor has never been farther from being well.

We are a few months away from having this campaign wrapped up. The war is almost over, and there is no possibility for setbacks, surprises, further losses. Now the enemy is sitting on one hill that we have completely surrounded. We shall soon begin to build the circumvallatio, the siege wall. When it is completed, we build up the ramp, bring up our battering rams and movable towers, break down the walls. That day the enemy will be finished and they will bring me the head of Bar Kokhba. Just a few more months.

So we shall be victorious. Hah, what a victory! I would not tell this to my troops, what is left of them, but this has not been a victory. This has been a defeat, the greatest defeat the Roman Empire has ever suffered.

Consider: The Legion *XXII Deiotariana* has been completely destroyed, eliminated. The other legions suffered great losses. I had to order ever more legions over here. The last three to march here during the past year were the *IV Scythica*, the *II Trajanan* and the *V Macedonica*; these are still in relatively good shape, having lost only – only! – a few thousand men. Over the last three years, we have lost at least a hundred thousand soldiers.

Consider: The reputation of the empire is in ruins. Our once glorious and feared army is not more than a ragtag group of defeated men. Sure, we won, but that was simply due to the sheer number of our legions. We have nothing to be proud of. The enemy could be proud, if there were any of them left alive. They lost 560,000, we have never killed so many in any battle, in any war. And yet I feel that they have won and we have lost.

Julius Severus fulfilled my expectations. He refused to rush into battle, took his time. He launched small attacks, only where he was sure of winning. For a while, I worried about his strategy. I had promised him, though, not to interfere with his decisions. He told me that many small victories will add up to total success, and he was right. Slowly, he eliminated all the outlying strongholds, one-by-one. He took the smaller villages, weakening the enemy with every such small step. Eventually, he felt confident enough to take Aelia Capitolina. There I decided to interfere and to order the razing of the entire city. I issued a command that no Jew should be allowed to enter it ever again. If their strength comes from that city, they will be barred from there forever!

So, little-by-little, they were cut down, their territory diminished, until, by now, they are held to this one hill just half a league from our camp. I can watch them from my tent. They are teeming there, so many men, so many horses on such a small hill, but their number is getting smaller every day. Their food supply is running low, I am told that they are already starving. Just a few more months.

I hate them. How dared they to stand up to Rome? I told Rufus Tinneius, and later Julius Severus, that there was no place for mercy. No kindness to captured soldiers, no clemency, no forgiveness. They must all die most horrible deaths. I watched their spiritual leader, Rabbi Akiva, breathe his last. I used to know the man. Now he was naked. Several of our men surrounded him, each with a rake, its prongs sharpened to an edge. They attacked him and flayed his flesh with those rakes. He was saying his prayers to the end. Let him. It was time for that old man to die, anyway. I would like to do the same to Bar Kokhba, but I have given orders that his head be brought to me. Soon now. Very soon.

I have been kind and compassionate for too long, and our enemies have taken advantage of it. Everybody has taken advantage of it. Even my fellow Romans. There is nothing new in that, our noble leadership in Rome has always been scheming, always trying to find ways to stab me in the back, figuratively or actually, like they stabbed Gaius Julius Caesar. Always spreading rumors, always planning to sabotage my decisions. The Senate is a hothouse of intrigue. I have decided to end that. When I get back to Rome, any Senator who causes me trouble will be asked, politely, to die by the end of the day. My brother-in-law, Servianus, has been particularly troublesome, stirring up trouble whenever he could. He will die. So will his grandson, who is being trained as a leader to take over from me at the first opportunity. Well, there will not be such an opportunity. The young man will go with his grandfather.

You know, Lucius, that my own wife, Sabina, has always been an irritant, and more. I married her to please my adoptive father Trajan, but there was never any love between us. Stupid woman! If she was content to live the luxurious life of an empress, I would never have bothered her. But I hear that she is also plotting, also scheming. She will have to go. I cannot ask her to die, but there are other ways.

Lucius, should the gods decide that I am not allowed to reach Rome, I want you to take care of these people for me. Do to them what I would have done. It is also in your own interest, for they would surely continue their intrigue against you, they would plot your own destruction. Don't be compassionate like I was. Be strong, eliminate them before they can do you harm.

Lucius, I am sick. I am very ill. I came to this camp to encourage the soldiers. It has always been my habit to be where the action is, to undertake the toughest training tasks together with the soldiers. I have not been able to jump on horses in full armor lately, but I thought that I could still do most of the exercises with them. But during the last year or so, my strength has just melted away, and with that my spirit. I had been frustrated by the slow progress of the war. Also, camp life has been very dispiriting. Watching one of our soldiers, captured and tortured, dragging himself back to camp on his belly, using the only remaining limb left to him – sights like that have slowly taken the vigor out of me. And everybody was sick in this camp. They all had fever, they all suffered from dysentery. Most recovered, but I have not. I am weak. I can hardly rise in the morning, need two men to get me up and dress me. I cannot walk up five steps without being out of breath. My heart is pounding, my chest aches. The doctors give me all kinds of medication, but none of them helps.

As I lie in my tent, with the front flap open, I watch the camp. They are moving the catapults and rock throwers closer to the wall, half-way between the watch towers. Those engines will be moved out of the gates the moment the circumvallatio is built. We shall also use flame-throwers. Yes, our engineers know their job. All of our soldiers do, despite everything.

They may be dispirited, but the imperial discipline is largely intact. Usually intact. Yesterday, again, one of the guards fell asleep on duty. Fortunately, nothing happened. The man has just been bludgeoned to death, as he knew he would be. One more death, so who cares? Soon I shall be added to those numbers.

Lucius, is your health good? Someone wrote to me from Rome, said that you were ill several times, and that you have not fully recovered. I hope that those are just rumors. If you have problems, see a good physician, make sure to get back to normal. I need you to continue my life's work, to punish all my enemies, be it the Jews here in Judaea or my wife and my sister's husband in Rome. It is revenge that I seek. I rely on you. In a few more months, the gods willing, we shall meet one more time. Farewell.

Shimeon Bar Kosiva's first letter to Michal, his wife

ALWAYS RABBI ELEAZAR

From Shimeon, Nasi of Israel –
to Michal bat Dosa – may your peace be great.

My dear Michal, I hope that everything is well with you and with your sister and her husband. We are well and healthy in the camp. You wrote to me a letter, worrying about me, how I eat and what I wear. Don't worry, my dear, everything is in good hands. I am being looked after very well, usually by Hillel, but there are other people here who know how to wash and mend clothes. And I eat well, at least as well as the others in the camp. I refused to have special food prepared for me, there is nothing wrong with the meals that are prepared for the soldiers.

You also asked me about the well-being of Rabbi Eleazar. I am not sure why you should care that much for him. He is also well. He set up a little area for himself in the middle of the main square. He prays there every day, from morning till night. Just sits there alone and prays.

Yes, but not always alone. People go up to him, ask him to pray for them or for their families. A soldier's wife or daughter asks a special prayer for the husband or father. Or the soldier himself may ask for advice before going on guard duty, on such matters as should he kill a Roman when the man is not about to kill him, say a water-carrier. And of course, Eleazar says don't kill him.

Then I hear about it, and I am very angry.

Do we argue a lot? All the time. Sometimes I come out to the square and make some nasty remarks about Rabbi Eleazar, so that the old man can hear them. Then Eleazar prays for forgiveness for those who sin. He also fasts a lot. I asked him why he fasted, and he said that perhaps that would influence the Lord to save the remnant of the Jews from extermination.

"The remnant?" I asked. "Who are those? My own men? Or perhaps people like yourselves, rabbis and sages?"

It was not clear what he answered. It is not always easy to understand Rabbi Eleazar.

Michal, you think that I don't like my uncle. Don't be so sure of that. Sometimes I think that I love the old man. Hillel will tell you that once I even went over to him, embraced him and kissed him, and I had tears in my eyes. I don't know why, it had something to do with his being closer to God than I am.

But there are other times when I don't like him so much, don't like him at all.

Enough of Eleazar. Let me tell you about what is happening here.

Of course, I cannot really report on the military situation. You must realize that there is a chance that, God forbid, the enemy will capture Hillel and this letter will get into his hands. I would not want them to know how strong we are here, how many men, how many horses we have, what arms. They do know already that we are very strong, they cannot just run over us, no matter how many legions they bring here.

But they know, as you know, that we have many, many fighters inside the fortress, also on the plateau and all over the hillside. We can do major damage to the Romans, we can shoot arrows directly into their camps. And, of course, when they are out in the open spaces around the hill, we can get them quite easily. They wear lots of armor, breastplates and helmets, but there are openings for the eyes and other soft spots; don't worry, we kill many of them every day.

Also, we capture some of them. We can learn a lot of things from such captured men, and then we kill them. We cannot afford to keep them and feed them. But my uncle, Rabbi Eleazar, always counsels us against it, always wants us to send the Roman back to his camp with some goodwill offering. Nonsense! He does annoy me.

But Michal, it is not true that I never liked my uncle. When I was a child, I used to love his teaching, until my father took me out of his academy. He was afraid that I would become a Hillelite. I don't think that I would ever have become that, I had too much respect for the Maccabees, I've always known that you must fight the enemy, not make compromises with him.

But lately, I have come to distrust the man. It is not because he is of Bet Hillel. There are very decent people of that school, such as your brother-in-law, Rabbi Halafta. So it is not that. But Eleazar always talks about compromises and being nice to the enemy, offering him peace, as if that would make him go away without trying to kill us all.

When he prays that the Lord should save a remnant of the Jews, I assume that I would not be included.

That kind of talk bothers me. We are going to win this war. We should not be talking about our being exterminated. Of course, we need the help of the Holy One, blessed be He, we could not win without it. That's what he should be doing, asking for the Lord's help in winning the war, not for a few to be spared some horrible fate.

Once Rabbi Akiva asked me to remember that might was useless without faith, just as faith was useless in war without might. I do remember that. He is a wise man. I hope that he is not suffering, wherever he may be.

So I accept that it is good to have somebody around with perhaps more faith than the rest of us, to augment our might. But I refuse to accept when he counsels people to rely on faith alone, giving up might as something almost offensive to the Lord. Believe me, it is not offensive, it is necessary.

That's why I distrust Rabbi Eleazar.

He does not understand that we must win this war. We have no alternative. There is no room for compromise with the enemy. They want to kill us all, and will if we give them the chance. So we must continue fighting, all the way to the end, whatever that may be. It will be good, we shall win.

We manage to kill many Roman soldiers, despite their armor. In close fighting we are still superior with the sword. We also know how to use spears, and the pike. Of course, our men have very little in the way of armor, only shields, that's not quite enough. They are quite vulnerable, but we don't lose too many. When it comes to arrows, we know how to hide. Often they hide behind horses. So we lose horses. I am not sure that we shall need so many of them in the near future. I am told that many eat the meat of the horses. That is, of course, against the commandments, but an exception may be made now, I think.

But Rabbi Eleazar does not think so. He is getting worse, really obnoxious. There is another thing that bothers me: When he prays, he attacks me; he asserts that I hinder his efforts by praying to the Lord incorrectly, using the wrong expressions. Of course that's nonsense.

What is he talking about, you ask? I'll explain. Of course I pray, too, I always have. Last week I used the text of the sixtieth Psalm. I quoted, correctly: 'Ha-lo ata Elohim zenachtenu ve-lo tetze Elohim betziv'otenu.' Now while we talk Aramaic, surely I understand enough Hebrew to know that this means 'You have not rejected us, God? And so would not go forth, God, with our armies?'

But he says my words amounted to saying, 'Do not, God, reject us, and do not, God, go forth with our armies.'

How could I ask the Lord for something like that? If I'll ask at all, of course I'll ask for His help.

I worry sometimes that I turn to Him too often, perhaps annoy Him with my prayers. But I would never ask Him *not* to help us.

Yet Eleazar now threatens, not that I care, that he will write to members of the Sanhedrin about my perilous behavior. Sanhedrin, ha! What Sanhedrin?

He does not understand the situation at all, does not see where we are, how difficult it is to defend this hill. We shall defend it, but it will not be easy. We are surrounded. We have a vast number of fighters inside; if the Romans try to break through, we can stream out and massacre them. But it will not be easy. There is no way to deny it: We are in a very difficult, very precarious position, where nobody can know the outcome, except the Lord. We are asking for His assistance, no matter what Rabbi Eleazar says.

And I am confident that He will assist us. After all, He did send His Messiah here, did He not? Rabbi Akiva said I am that Messiah. That did not cheer me. When he announced it, it frightened me. How could I carry such a heavy load? But then I understood that I just have to lead the people, fight the war to the best of my ability, and then divine help will come. Or it will not, as He may decide. Blessed be the Lord.

But it is also possible that I was mistaken. Perhaps Rabbi Akiva was mistaken. Apparently, that is what Eleazar believes.

Now he accuses me of having prayed thus, in Aramaic: '*Riboniyah d'Olmah, lo tas'od ve-lo tachsof.*' He translates it, this time to Hebrew, to mean 'Master of the World, neither help us, nor shame us.' Of course that's not what I meant at all. What I asked the Lord was this: 'Master of the World, if you won't help us, at least don't shame us.' Maybe I did not take care to phrase it correctly, but I was talking to our Father in Heaven, not to listeners who then run to Rabbi Eleazar.

I admit that I am somewhat reluctant to ask for the Lord's help too much, too often. I always worry that He will tire of me and will punish instead of help me.

I don't know where this thing will lead, this problem between me and Rabbi Eleazar. One of us won't be able to stand the other much longer.

Be well, Michal. I shall write to you again soon, hope to be able to send you better news.

Peace be with you.

Shimeon Bar Kosiva's second letter to Michal, his wife

I WAS ANGRY

Michal, I must tell you that, at the moment, the situation does not look favorable at the camp. We are not surrendering – we shall never do that – but we may be losing.

The Romans have completely surrounded us. They are digging ditches everywhere, and I am certain that they are getting ready to build a circumvallatio, so that we shall be completely walled in before long. Of course, it is very easy to get them while they are working, they are not protected as the soldiers are. I think that these are foreigners, not Romans, probably people from other occupied countries. They may be slaves. I am truly sorry for them, but we must kill as many as we can.

I was thinking about this, Michal. The Romans have occupied so many lands, they have oppressed so many people. Perhaps what we should have done is to coordinate our efforts with all of those people, or at least several, so that we would all have attacked at the same time. The Romans could not then have sent over all of these legions. But we were too sure of ourselves, we thought that the more legions they send, the more we destroy, and the weaker Rome gets.

Food is scarce in the camp. We still manage to bring in some, until that circumvallatio is completed, we should be able to obtain food. But it is not easy to find it, even when I send people out and they do get through. My commanders at Ein Gedi and other places claim that they don't have any victuals. I don't believe them, but I am not in a position to punish them now. We still have horses. They may provide enough food until we experience a turn for the better.

What may happen? The Lord may help us yet. The Romans may just decide to pack up their camps and return to Rome. Why would they do that? I don't know. The Lord may help us yet.

But why should He?

Michal, something terrible happened here last week. It's about Rabbi Eleazar, my uncle. You know why I accepted him as a representative of the Sanhedrin. Akiva wanted that; I think he needed it as a gesture, so they would not accuse him of being a Shammaite.

I had always considered him a weakling. Perhaps worse than a weakling. A sanctimonious preacher, a deceiver, maybe even a traitor. You might say that he was not that bad, that I am unfair to him. But you don't know him as I do.

He was always counseling peace, inaction, when action was clearly needed. I think that many times people listened to him, accepted his advice. No, not just other people. I may have listened to him, I may have accepted his counsel in such matters as how to treat captives, whether or not to attack the enemy at night, which some say is not fair. Many of us followed his cautionary warnings. That was a big mistake.

Maybe I should have thrown him out a long time ago, it might have made a big difference. But I thought that perhaps there was a need for such a man around, a sage, ha! I thought that I didn't want to bother the Lord with constant supplications, but if such a man did it, that might help.

I suppose that I had some respect for the man, despite everything. I may even have loved him a little bit. After all, he was my uncle. But now he has certainly robbed me of any such respect or love.

What happened was that the Romans sent in a spy, a traitor. A Samaritan. He went over to Eleazar to discuss surrender.

Somehow the Romans knew that he was the man who would want us to surrender. It would not be difficult to negotiate such matters with him. They certainly could not talk to me about surrender.

You say, what difference would it make what they discussed with Eleazar, when I am the man in charge, not he.

It does make a difference. It did. Many people have listened to him who thought that it would be wiser to negotiate with the enemy, so that we could get good terms. Idiotic! But that's how he talked, and now this Roman spy went to him and whispered such things for a long time. How do I know? I had the man captured and he admitted it. That's how I know!

You cannot imagine how angry that made me. I ran out to the square, shouting at the traitor, the so-called Rabbi, about trying to sell our nation. I attacked him. I kicked him, again and again. I did not think about the consequences, and what do they matter, anyway? He may have been a sick man, I don't know, because after two or three kicks, he just lay there. I stopped and looked at him; he did not move. So someone came over, examined him closely and told me that the man was dead. Perhaps he would have died anyway, if he was so sick.

So you say that I should not have done that. Maybe not. But I was so angry that he wanted to sell us to the enemy. And not only for that, but because he made us do many things his way, when it would have been better to do them our way. I should never have listened to him.

One should always be strong, always follow one's own ideas, never listen to weaklings who try to undermine one's efforts. I blame myself for not realizing this sooner. I just hope that it is not too late to correct the course.

But maybe it is too late now. Maybe I should not have done that. The Lord will punish me now, I fear. But why should He punish all my men with me?

Michal, I don't know what to do. I don't dare to pray, I fear that my prayer would be rejected. I should not have done it.

Michal, I don't think that we shall meet again. I wish you well, you and all of those who survive. Peace be with you.

Michal's letter to Yose

NOT THE MESSIAH?

> *From Michal bat Dosa – to my nephew –*
> *Rabbi Yose ben Halafta, may your peace be great.*

Yose, I cried when I read that letter. Cried for Rabbi Eleazar and cried for Shimeon and cried for our nation.

That evening I showed the letter to Halafta, not to Tzviyya.

He was also shocked.

"You see, Michal," he told me, "Shimeon never understood that he could only win with the help of the Lord."

"Why do you say that? Did he not always talk about how the Lord would send a Messiah to regain our country?"

"Yes, and later he thought that he was that Messiah himself, right?"

"That was Akiva's doing."

"Akiva did not mean it that way. You knew that and he knew that. Yet I think that the victories made him conceited."

"Perhaps. But he never wanted to win without the Lord's help. Eleazar accused him of that, but it was not true."

"Still, it was Eleazar who tried to save him. Believe me, Michal, Eleazar was his friend, not his enemy."

"Are you saying that he killed the only man who could have saved him from disaster?"

"Perhaps. Who are we to say? Right now, it seems as though we shall lose this war. Why? Because we did not ask the Holy One, blessed be He, for help? Because we sinned? Because Shimeon killed Rabbi Eleazar? Or maybe because that's what He wanted all along, and so we never had a chance? Who knows?"

"Should Shimeon have followed Eleazar's advice, tried to negotiate peace with the Romans? Surrendered?"

Halafta thought.

"I don't know, Michal. Perhaps it would have been better. Perhaps he could still do that. But no, I don't think so. I think it's too late."

*   *   *

Can you imagine, Yose, the tension that oppressed us during that spring? We should have been elated by the flowers everywhere, the lovely weather.

But, of course, we did not even notice such things. We had no news from Bethar in months, and I was pacing the room all day with worry.

Then Hillel arrived one day. We embraced him and did not know whether to make him comfortable, feed him and let him rest, or ask questions. But he told us the one thing I wanted to hear right away.

"The Nasi, Shimeon bar Kokhba, is well, thank the Lord. He is healthy and sends his greetings."

"No letter?" I asked.

"Not this time. We did not know that I would be coming, until an opportunity opened up suddenly, and he insisted that I must go."

"Tell us everything," commanded Halafta.

"Well, the Romans are strong and they are getting stronger all the time. As I rode through the countryside, I saw them everywhere. I talked with people. They've been telling me about a number of new legions. The Fourth *Scythica*. The Second *Trajana*. The Fifth *Macedonica*. You've heard of that already, I think. Altogether, there are thirteen legions, all attacking Bethar."

"Yes, there is not that much more left to attack," Halafta commented bitterly.

"True. But we did not expect that many troops. They are brought in from all over the world. From Arabia and Syria and Egypt; but also from Pannonia and Britannia, some place I have not even heard of."

"So there must be a hundred thousand Roman troops around?"

"More, I am afraid. Far more. You see, in addition to the legions, they are also bringing in auxiliary units. They may have as many as fifteen auxiliary units attached to each legion. These just about double the size of a legion. I would say that there might be two hundred thousand Roman men around Bethar now."

We sat in shocked silence.

"So then, I suppose that they could just run over the place, never mind any losses they suffer," commented Halafta.

"They don't do it that way. They have learned from Shimeon. This Julius Severus, he knows what he is doing. Some say he learned his profession in Britannia. They were also fighting in the hills there. He's even brought in a unit, the *Cohors* Fourth *Lingonum*, with him. They teach the other Roman commanders how to do this kind of fighting. He conducts small attacks, eliminates small groups of people, until few are left. He encircles towns and villages, starves them to death."

"Are you starving in Bethar?" I asked, very worried.

"Yes, madam, we are. Sometimes we manage to bring in food, but it becomes more difficult all the time."

I cried, thinking of Shimeon and all the other people there.

Halafta asked Hillel:

"What do you suppose are Severus' plans? To starve Bethar, too, to death?"

"No, he is not that patient. They have started to build a circumvallatio. A siege wall. When they complete it, I suppose that they'll build a ramp across the fosse, and then they can bring up the battering rams to the walls. That's how they did it at Masada at the end of the previous war."

"But surely you don't let them build that wall in peace. Do you just sit there and watch?"

"Of course not. We attack them all the time. We send out small groups, kill some of them, destroy a section of the wall. But there are so many more of them. They are now also split up into small fighting units, but all of them are connected, we cannot eliminate many of them, except maybe at night, when we see better than they do. Oh, we kill more than they do, they have lost maybe as many as they have brought in by now. This is the fourth year, after all."

"Yes, the fourth year. Shall we last a fifth one?" I should not have asked that. Halafta did not wait for an answer but turned to Hillel:

"So you can no longer bring in food and supplies?"

"Yes, we still can, but how much longer, who knows. We can get food and other things from Ein Gedi and a few other places. But the other problem is that, even if we could get the food inside, they won't always send it."

"What? Why not?"

"I don't know. I just know that Shimeon is trying all the time to get food in, writes letters to his governors in those places, and they won't even reply, sometimes. You see, I am the one who writes the letters. He just tells me what to write, and I do and make sure that, somehow, a courier can get out and deliver it."

"What kind of letters does he dictate? Just demanding food?"

"No, there are other kinds. Just last week, I wrote a letter to the governors at Ein Gedi, demanding that they arrest everyone who won't cooperate, confiscate their properties."

"And will they do it?"

"That I don't know. Then we wrote to the governor at Beth Mashko, demanding that he destroy certain Galileans who are staying there."

"Who could they be?"

"I would not know. But what struck me is a letter to Masabala and Yehonathan, the governors at Ein Gedi. The Romans are all over there now, but Shimeon still expects to receive produce. He has been demanding fruit, something about a boat full of fruit, docked at Ein Gedi, that they have not unloaded. I remember the last letter word-by-word, for I found it painful. What he dictated to me was this: 'In comfort you sit, eat and drink from the property of the House of Israel, and care nothing for your brothers.'"

"Is he desperate?" I asked him.

"Desperate? Not really, no. But he is thinking all the time how to turn the situation around. He still thinks that he can win."

"But you don't?"

"Frankly, no. I think it's impossible now. But Shimeon says that there are miracles, the Lord can help. That's true, of course. But then, he mutters sometimes about the Messiah."

"What does he say about that?"

"Once I heard him saying something to himself. I thought he said 'So it was not true, after all. Akiva was wrong.' I asked him how was Rabbi Akiva wrong, and he was surprised, he would not tell me anything. Another time he told me that he will win because he is the Messiah, after all."

"He actually told you that?"

"Yes, but soon afterwards, when he heard of more people dying, he told me to forget what he said, it was silliness. Then, quite recently, he said that one did not have to be the Messiah to win, one just had to hit the enemy at the right time, at the right place, then hit him again and again, that might turn things around."

"Does he pray a lot?"

"He does, but not like Rabbi Eleazar used to pray. He kind of discusses the matter with the Lord, but I don't think he asks Him anything. He is afraid to ask for favors."

Hillel seemed very tired, so we let him sleep. Next day he told us that he wanted to leave right away.

Halafta asked him:

"Hillel, have you considered not going back to Bethar?"

He seemed shocked at the idea.

"Of course I'll have to go back. The Nasi is expecting me."

"But what can you do to help him?"

"Oh, all kinds of things. I am his assistant. He is always so relieved when I return. He needs me for very many different tasks."

"But Hillel, have you considered that you won't be able to hold out very much longer at Bethar? When the Romans come in you may all be killed. You might want to get away at that time, but it may be too late. Now you are out, so why go back? Oh, I know. Shimeon is expecting you. But think about it."

"There is nothing to think. He will also want to know about all of you, his family. I must go back immediately. It may be that now I can still get in, but once they finish building the circumvallatio, it may be impossible. So I must go back right away. Do you have food that I can take with me?"

Of course we gave him all the food we had, all the food that he could carry.

And shortly thereafter, he was gone.

That was the last time we saw him.

*   *   *

We did talk to another man, about a year later. Apparently, he was the only one who got out of Bethar alive. He was seriously wounded, the Romans left him for dead, but somehow he survived. He told us about the last days of Bethar.

There was famine and pestilence. The nights were dark, with no oil to put in the lamps. At least there was still water from the spring. But there was no food at all.

Even though Rabbi Eleazar was dead, more and more people wanted to surrender. They organized themselves as a peace party. They wanted to send a message to the Romans, give up on any terms. Shimeon would not hear of it. He had the leaders of the party executed.

It was late in the summer when the Romans finished their wall. Then they started to build the ramp and may have been surprised at how little resistance was offered. Within a few weeks it was complete. They brought up battering rams and, in no time at all, there was a huge hole in the wall.

They poured in and murdered everybody inside the walls and beyond, on the plateau. The man thought that by that time they could probably have mounted the plateaus directly, from the bottom, as our soldiers were too weak to resist.

They killed Shimeon bar Kokhba, my husband.

*   *   *

He died, along with everyone else at Bethar, on the ninth day of the month of Av, in the fourth year of the war, sixty-five years after Jerusalem was destroyed by the Romans.

But Shimeon and his people were not the only ones killed. The Romans destroyed nearly a thousand villages, massacring the whole population. They say that in all of Judaea, 580,000 of our people perished by the enemy's sword; even more succumbed to famine and disease.

There is not that much comfort in knowing that the Romans themselves lost about two hundred thousand. That won't bring my husband back, nor any of the other hundreds of thousands.

There were apparently many people from the Judaean hills who took refuge in caves on the hills, large groups of people, whole families. They wanted to outwait the legions. But the Romans learned about them, set up camps on hilltops above the caves, watching them patiently for many months. Nobody could get in or out. Those people, too, died slowly of starvation.

Suffering, death everywhere.

Michal

PERSECUTION

From Michal bat Dosa – to one of my grand-nephews –
may your peace be great.

I have now finished writing many letters to your father, my nephew, the great Rabbi Yose ben Halafta, about the life and times of my husband, Shimeon bar Kosiva, and about my own life. I have reached the place in those letters where I cannot tell anything to Yose that he does not know himself; for these last twenty years we have all lived together in the Galilee. But I don't want to stop writing. I want to finish my own story; maybe one of you grand-nephews, one of Yose's boys, will one day be interested in finding out about the life of that old woman whom they perhaps liked when they were small children. If not, then let us say that I am writing for myself. But it is better to believe that I do have, will have, a reader.

Dear Reader: It is my desire to tell you all that has happened to us since the end of the war.

That first year was excruciating. We received more news about Bethar from Samaritans who went there after the Romans had done with the killing. They saw blood everywhere, torrents of blood. They saw children's brains on rocks. Other children were burnt alive. They saw dead bodies everywhere, but they could not bury them – even if they wanted to, of which I am not sure – for the Romans were still around. As a matter of fact, the Romans insisted on the dead remaining unburied for a long time.

All of Judaea was made desolate. There were no Jews left in Judaea at all. Those who stayed alive had been sold into slavery, except the ones who had escaped earlier. Fortunately, some of the best young scholars were abroad, such as Meir, Yohanan HaSandelar and others.

Then, the Romans started to punish those Jews they found alive elsewhere. We were not permitted to enter Jerusalem or even the surrounding area. They reserved that honor for the Notzrim, who refused to support our struggle.

They actually renamed Judaea as Syria Palaestina. So now only the Galilee was left of Eretz Yisrael.

I suppose the Emperor Hadrian was bitter about the war. I am told that never have the Romans suffered so many losses as in Judaea, not even in their Parthian adventure. Some people expected the emperor to lose his throne but, in the end, he did not, for he prevailed against us and punished us severely.

What Hadrian wanted to do was to abolish the Torah and to make sure that Israel, as a nation, would no longer exist. He simply prohibited the practice of our religion. Of course, that was futile, for Jews will always practice their religion, with permission or without.

He also wanted to eliminate all Jewish institutions, such as schools, synagogues, meeting places, burial societies and so on. They issued decrees against observing any of the commandments. How stupid they were. When a person does not murder his neighbor, he is observing one of the commandments. How could they stop that?

But we could not gather anywhere for prayer or study. The courts were not allowed to function. It was very important to the Romans, that there would no longer be any Jewish judicial autonomy. We had to go to their own useless courts. Of course, observance of all of the holidays and customs was banned, such as building a sukkah, kindling Hanukkah lights, wearing tefillin, collecting Terumah, going to the mikve, observing the sabbatical year and so on.

We were now called *dediticii*: oppressed individuals, with no collective aspect at all.

Also, they expropriated large parcels of our farmers' land again and leased them to non-Jews. Our peasants could, at best, become subtenants. If a farmer violated any one of the myriad regulations, or was accused of doing so, he lost his land.

Worst of all were the *quaestors*. The Romans employed these spies everywhere. They sneaked up on us, trying to find evidence that somebody was secretly practising the Jewish religion. There were also *speculatores*. Those had the right to arrest anyone pointed out to them by the *quaestors*. They handed those people over to the Roman legions for execution, or they could execute those poor victims themselves, if they felt like doing so.

* * *

Enough of those horrors. Let me tell you a little about ourselves, our life in Sepphoris.

Within a year after our arriving there, our dear mother, Martha bat Shimeon, the granddaughter of Rabban Gamaliel the Elder, died. May her memory be blessed. Under other circumstances that would have been a great shock to me and to Tzviyya; but in those days, death was all around us, our feelings were dulled.

Rabbi Halafta became the head of the local court. True, no court was allowed to function for some time, but of course there was a court, just as there were prayers and Torah study and everything else that Jews need. We only had to be careful to do everything where no *quaestor* could see us.

Soon after that, my favorite nephew, of whom I have always been proud, secretly returned from Babylonia. Yose ben Halafta was now ordained as a Rabbi.

He told us about that ordination: How it had to be done in a clandestine manner; how Rabbi Yehuda ben Baba did it secretly, in the hills between Usha and Shefaram; how Rabbi Yehuda ordained him and Shimeon bar Yohai and others; how Rabbi Yehuda was caught by the Romans, tried and executed for doing what he had to do.

By then, everybody was talking about Yose as the most outstanding scholar of the times, surpassing even his father. Rabbi Akiva would have been proud of him. But Akiva had been killed by then.

We received more information about his death. They took him out to a public square. As he was about to say his morning *Shema*, they attacked him with iron combs, tearing his flesh out, but he continued to say the prayer loudly, almost joyously, until, with the last word, *ehad*, he gave up his soul. May his memory be blessed, blessed manifold.

Compared to such news, our own lives were rather humdrum. We had to survive. Most of the money left to us from both sides of the family was gone. We all worked. Yose worked in the tannery, as did his mother and I. Some people said that the descendants of a Rachabite family, not to mention the Nasi, really Hillel, should not do such lowly work. But we had no alternative but to perform our labors.

RESTORATION

You may have heard that the Emperor Hadrian died two years after the collapse of our freedom, two years after he killed my husband. He started his career as a friend of our people and ended it as our most cruel, most hated enemy. Yet when he died, there was no rejoicing. We were too tired, too broken to rejoice. We thought that one emperor was just like another, it would not make much difference who was the emperor in Rome.

At first it did, indeed, not make any difference. The new emperor, Antoninus Pius, approved all of Hadrian's evil decrees. But as he slowly learned how to be an emperor, he began to make changes. And those changes were good ones! Well, relatively good ones.

He abolished most of the oppressive edicts against the Jews. We were allowed to circumcise our sons! We, the Jews, and no other nation.

In fact, all of the laws prohibiting the practice of our religion were annulled. That was great news.

It is true that other decrees, those that had to do with our independence as a people, remained in force, but we were grateful for the little we received. Antoninus declared the Jewish religion legitimate again.

So now our sages no longer needed to meet in secret, two or three at a time; they could convene as before, even if only for discussing religious matters, not affairs of the nation. They sent messages around, and before long it was agreed that they should meet in the Valley of Rimon to intercalate the year; that was very important, since errors had increasingly crept into our calculations. Afterwards, they were to assemble at the small village of Usha, hometown of Rabbi Yehuda bar Ilai, in the Galilee. That was five years after the end of the war.

I knew all about that meeting and what followed it; I heard it first hand from my brother-in-law, Rabbi Halafta. He was very enthusiastic when he came back.

"Finally, we could get together and talk freely. Everybody had a story to tell. They had all been hiding, like Yose, but for many more years. Shimeon bar Yohai. Yose the Galilean, not my son, but the old man. Many more had fled abroad, some have just returned. Others have been back for a while. My Yose. Meir. Yohanan the sandal-maker. Many more."

"But was anything important discussed?" I asked him.

"Of course. But not very specific things, not yet. We must consider how to restore our nation."

"What kind of nation shall it be?"

"Well, that's just the question we have struggled with. It seems that we shall call it Eretz Yisrael, but for the time being it will be not much more than the Galilee."

"And who shall lead it? Will there be a Nasi?"

Halafta hesitated.

"Yes, I suppose, there will be one, soon. For now, there is no official leader."

"Official, you say. But there must be some one or two persons who are leading the discussions."

"Oh, there are, but not one or two. It's more like ten."

"Are you one of them?" I challenged him. "You should be, you are the respected judge around here."

He waved that away.

"No, I would not aspire to such a role. There are many others, natural leaders. For instance, there is Rabbi Shimeon bar Yohai, he would like to be the leader, or Rabbi Eliezer, the son of Yose the Galilean. Then there is Rabbi Meir, young, but very intelligent. Rabbi Nehemiah, Rabbi Eliezer ben Yaacov. Even my son, Yose, he may be a leader one of these days."

"Let's hope so, he may be the best of all."

"Yes, but there are still others. We paid special tribute to our host, Rabbi Yehuda bar Ilai. We let him be the first speaker on almost every occasion, he remembers commandments and customs that are nearly forgotten."

"Yes, great man. Everybody likes him."

"Not quite everybody. I think Meir does not really like him."

"No? Why?"

"I am not sure. I think that for some reason he resents Meir's coming back from exile. They were both students of Akiva, Meir is much younger, of course. He senses this resentment and it annoys him very much."

"Pity. But then, are you not going to enact specific new laws, legislation?"

"We shall, to the extent possible. Remember, the country is still run by the Romans. But we plan to have a formal Sanhedrin, with judicial responsibilities, and legislative ones, too, as soon as that can be done. And we are going to re-establish the office of the Nasi."

"But that's what I asked before. Who shall be the Nasi?"

"Ah, that's another question. We can have the office, but not the person."

"I suppose everybody is thinking of the man whose role it naturally should be."

"Yes, they do. Shimeon ben Gamaliel."

"Where is he? Is he alive?"

"Oh, yes, he is alive. But he is still hiding, he is worried about being arrested by the Romans, if he appeared."

"Would they?"

"Perhaps. They are concerned about a Jewish leader, almost like some princeps. The last one…" He stopped in some embarrassment.

"Yes, I know. Shimeon bar Kokhba."

"Well, yes. Of course, this is a different situation. Shimeon ben Gamaliel may come out of hiding one of these days, and then we may decide to make him Nasi."

*   *   *

Shimeon ben Gamaliel did return after a while, and they did make him Nasi, somewhat reluctantly. Halafta told us about it.

"It looks like Shimeon has become a very strong-willed man, quite aggressive. Some call him arrogant."

"Why did the Romans permit him to take power?"

"I think that they somehow consider him a safe man, they think that they will be able to co-operate with him. Of course, they retain the right to approve or disapprove his appointment, but it looks like it will be approved."

"And the sages? Why would they want to elect him Nasi?"

Halafta pondered in his careful manner. He always gave the right answer.

"Well, you see, in a sense the office was always his. By birth. I know, that should not be enough, if the person is not right for the job. But in some ways he may be exactly right."

"What ways?"

"As I said, he is strong-willed. I think that this is what's needed now. A strong man, to lead the nation. But there are those who don't like him at all. Meir, for one."

"What will Meir do? Quit the Sanhedrin?"

"Oh, no, not at all. He is a fighter. He has his own supporters. As a matter of fact, he was appointed *Hacham*, the third post, directly behind the *Av Bet Din*, Rabbi Nathan haBavli."

"And Shimeon ben Gamaliel does not like that, does he?"

"No, he hates the idea. But he was forced to compromise."

I did not quite like what Halafta said about Shimeon ben Gamaliel. I thought that the situation was not healthy, there would almost certainly be some further development soon.

Sure enough, a short time later, the new Nasi tried to grab all power himself.

"He's enacted a new rule today," Halafta told us. "When the Nasi enters, everybody must stand until he tells them to sit down."

"Is that so bad?"

"Nathan and Meir don't like it. They were not at the session, and they consider that this diminished their position, especially that of Meir."

"What can they do about it?" asked Tzviyya.

"Not an awful lot. They are trying to stir up trouble, get the majority to protest, perhaps even to impeach the Nasi. It won't work."

"Why, are the sages generally in favor of Shimeon?"

"Well, perhaps not in favor, but they respect him. No, they don't like him. Few people like him. But he is not only a strong leader, but generally a fair one, except when it comes to Nathan and Meir."

"Being fair is not enough. The Nasi should be strong and knowledge-able."

"Oh, he is that, and more. He knows all about agriculture, about medicine, about anatomy. But when I say fair, it shows in his treatment of the gentiles. He says gentiles should not be judged differently from Jews in court. When it comes to the Samaritans, he claims that they are really Jews."

"My husband would have objected to that, vehemently."

"I know. But he goes out of his way to be nice to all kinds of people. Perhaps he thinks that, in the end, they will all like us."

"Not much chance, if you remember our past."

Halafta shrugged. "You tell him that. But his leadership does produce some good results. We now have some national institutions, courts, schools, synagogues, funeral societies. And Shimeon is certainly friendly, he knows how to build a consensus even as he asserts the authority of his office. He asks everybody's opinion, tries to accommodate them, yet is willing to make a decisive action when needed. He is not at all bad as a Nasi."

*   *   *

Nathan and Meir were not successful in their attempt to unseat the Nasi, but Shimeon could not dispose of them either, not for a while.

But he kept gaining strength and was biding his time. His opportunity came when Nathan and Meir thought that they might be able to humiliate the Nasi. Halafta told us about it, as usual.

"Meir and Nathan don't think highly of the Nasi's learnedness. So they decided to ask him a series of questions that he wouldn't be able to answer, and thereby show him up as an ignoramus. They wanted to ask him questions about how the stems of fruits affected their ritual cleanliness."

"What happened?"

"Someone warned Shimeon, I think it was Rabbi Yehuda bar Ilai. The Nasi studied the subject matter thoroughly, then just to be sure, he prevented Nathan and Meir from entering the Sanhedrin that day."

"Could he do that?"

"Apparently he could. He still had to accept their questions, which they submitted from the outside, in writing."

"And he answered them?"

"Yes, as best he could. But then, when Meir and Nathan did not consider the answers appropriate, they sent in their own responsa from outside."

"Ridiculous!"

"That's what my son told Shimeon. He said 'The Torah remains outside, while we sit calmly within.'"

"Brave young man. What happened?"

"Eventually, Shimeon permitted Nathan and Meir to return, but ruled that henceforth any new laws enacted based on their opinion shall not mention the two by name. The formula will be 'some say' for Nathan and 'others say' for Meir."

"Is that fair, as you said?"

"No, I would not say fair. He is a strong man, and he defends himself this way."

"And what do the sages have to say?" I asked.

"Some support him, and some oppose him vehemently."

"Yose?" Tzviyya was worried.

"Yes. You know that he is a friend of Meir's. He keeps defending him and criticizing the Nasi. Don't worry, Tzviyya, Shimeon won't be able to harm Yose, he is already too strong for that."

"I hope you are right. Talk to him, anyway. There is no need to cause trouble for oneself."

*   *   *

Some time later Nathan and Meir were told – some say in a dream – to reconcile themselves to the rule of the Nasi. Nathan complied, and accepted severe punishment. Meir refused, and a court of the sages, set up by Shimeon,

excommunicated him! There was such an outcry, that the Nasi was forced
to revise his ruling, but Meir had to leave the land.

He visited Yose before he left; we were all there that evening. He was
a pleasant young man, not very tall, with wide, smiling face, curly beard,
and he had such a lovely young wife, Beruriah.

I asked him: "Meir, where will you go?"

"We shall travel to Asia Minor," he replied. "Life is good there, and there
is always a need for learned rabbis."

"Won't Beruriah mind it, having to leave her home?"

"No, she says that she is proud of being the first woman scholar in Asia
Minor." We all laughed at that. Beruriah was certainly a gifted scholar, few
men knew more of the sacred books, *Mishnah* and *Gemarah,* than she
did.

"Still, it will be tough to live in the Diaspora, won't it?"

"Why, Aunt Michal, you lived in Africa for a while, did you not?"

"That was different. It was just for a short time, preparing for our return
to Eretz Yisrael."

"Perhaps this will be just for a short time, too. But there are lots of
Jews living in the Diaspora now. People are coming and going all the time.
Why, many Babylonian communities feel free to come to Sepphoris and
Tiberias, establish their own synagogues there, also people from Tarsis and
Cappadocia. There is really no such thing as a permanent exile. Everybody
travels freely all the time these days."

"I suppose we should feel grateful to Antoninus for that. But it is still
a long trip, from here to Cappadocia or Babylonia. Will you live at Cappadocia?"

"We are not yet sure. That's where we'll travel at first, but then we shall
see where the greatest need might be."

"What languages do people use there?"

"Generally, Greek. The Jews speak Hebrew, of course, and Aramaic."

"But don't they slowly forget their own language?"

"Not in Cappadocia, which is close to Eretz Yisrael. Of course, I hear
that the immigrants who escaped our troubles and went to live in distant
lands, in Gaul, in Hispania, in the lands of the Rhine river, they don't speak
much Hebrew by now. They use Latin and other local languages."

"Yes, and I suppose that's true for Rome, as well. Many of our people
live there, don't they?"

"Too many. We may be losing those people. But Asia Minor is different.
It is almost in the neighborhood. And the Jewish communities there are

very prosperous. They can afford to teach their children Hebrew, as well as Torah and everything else necessary to make good Jews out of them."

"Thank the Lord for that. I hear that there are some wonderful new synagogues all over that land."

"Yes, a beautiful one has been built at Sardis. We may end up living there."

Yose asked him:

"But Meir, surely you are not thinking of spending the rest of your life in the Diaspora?"

Meir smiled. "Not if I can help it. It will be up to the Nasi. But for now, he seems intent on not seeing me again."

Yose commented: "Yet he should be the one discouraging the growth of the Diaspora. Is that not a danger, people leaving the Land of Israel for an easier life elsewhere?"

His father, Halafta, nodded. "Yes, that is a serious problem. Shimeon bar Yohai has recently been railing against those who leave the country."

Meir added: "Not only Shimeon bar Yohai. Also, Rabbi Meir. What can be done? One thing definitely can be done: I shall be able to persuade people in the Diaspora to return home. I expect to be quite successful at that. But then, when they arrive here, efforts must be made so that they shall feel welcome. And not only that, they have to be provided with a way to make a living."

Yose answered: "We shall make sure that they won't lack for anything."

Brave words from a young man who works in a tannery to make a living.

When Rabbi Meir left, Yose said of him: "He is a great man, a holy man and a modest man."

*   *   *

Working in the tannery was not an easy job. We had no other choice. There were so many taxes we all had to pay to the Romans: *tributum capitis*, *tributum soli* and, of course, the two drachma Jewish tax. They certainly did not eliminate those.

One morning my nephew, Yose, was working alongside myself in the tannery. I was somewhat surprised to see him there, I thought that he was in Usha, at the Sanhedrin session.

I used the opportunity to ask him a question that I had been thinking about.

"Yose, don't you find it a disadvantage, working in such a bad-smelling place?"

"No, Aunt Michal, it is not worse than any other work. We all work. Rabbi Yitzhak is a smith. Shimeon is a weaver. Nehemiah is a potter, Yehudah a baker, Yohanan a cobbler. It is just work. We must do our share."

"Once we were a wealthy family."

"Is wealth so important, Aunt Michal?"

"It is certainly useful. Who gets buried at Beth Shearim? The family of the Nasi, certainly. But any other sages? Have you attended the burial of any of your colleagues or their families there?"

"No, I cannot say that I have."

"Of course not. But the families of the rich merchants, here in Sepphoris and in Tiberias, they can afford that illustrious place. So can wealthy tradesmen from abroad."

Yose shrugged. "One place is as good as another, especially for the dead."

"I suppose it is, yet it just goes to show how much honor is given to the best scholars."

"Aunt Michal, you worry about the wrong things. It is the Roman oppression that we should care about, not money."

"Yose, I have spent my life talking about the Roman oppression. Let others worry about it now."

"We do, Auntie, we certainly do."

"Don't tell me that you are starting something again?!"

"Starting? No. We are just talking. But that is bad enough, in the view of the Romans."

"Has anything happened?"

He lifted a load of skins to the table before answering.

"Well, yes. Just a few days ago. Four of us were sitting together at the academy – Rabbi Yehuda bar Ilai, Rabbi Shimeon bar Yohai, Rabbi Yehuda bar Gerim and I. We were talking about the Romans."

"Did you say anything wrong?"

"Wrong? No. Actually, I did not say anything. It was Yehuda bar Ilai who started the conversation by praising the Romans."

"Praising them?!"

"Yes, he is very friendly with the Roman authorities, maintains close contact with them."

"I did not know that!"

"Well, on that day he praised them for paving roads and building bridges and baths. So Shimeon bar Yohai jumped up, shouting at him: 'What is there to praise? Whatever the Romans did, they did for their own benefit. They paved streets in order to settle their harlots; they built bathhouses in order to anoint themselves; they built bridges in order to collect tolls."

"I think he is right. I don't much like the man, but in this he is absolutely correct."

"Of course he is. But Rabbi Yehuda bar Gerim talked about that incident in front of others, and the Romans eventually heard about it."

"Oh, no. What have they done?"

"They praised Yehuda bar Ilai, but they issued orders that I must remain here, at Sepphoris, permanently, never step outside the city."

I was shocked.

"So you can no longer participate in the Sanhedrin sessions?"

"Not unless they move to Sepphoris. But that's nothing. They sentenced Rabbi Shimeon bar Yohai to death."

"Do they have him then?"

"Fortunately, not. He escaped in time. He went into hiding, along with his son. Who knows how long he must stay in that place, wherever it may be."

*   *   *

Yose remained in Sepphoris for many years. We all live here, and it is not a bad place to dwell in. Somebody once said that Herod Antipas made Sepphoris an ornament of the Galilee. It has been peaceful for the last one hundred and sixty-two years. It was indeed re-established in the last century by that hated Tetrach and settled with Jewish people; yet somehow the town always remained friendly with the Romans, never participated in any of the revolts.

There has been much improvement in living conditions here. The Romans destroyed the olive plantations, but young trees have been planted again; for several years now, they have been yielding good harvests. We export oil to many other countries. Landowners are among the most respected families, even the peasants with very small holdings, if they have at least a little olive grove and a vineyard.

The Romans actually renamed Sepphoris, they called it Diocaesaria. But the name did not take root, everybody has continued to call the city by its old name.

So Sepphoris is now the capital of the Galilee, practically the only Jewish land left. Well, it could be worse. People here are good Jews, they observe the commandments and traditions.

In some ways, we Galileans are better people than the Judaeans used to be. For example, here they give the widow the right to continue occupying her husband's home, supported by his estate, all her life. In Judaea, the relatives could give her the amount specified in the *Ketubah* and kick her out of the house. Well, that does not apply to me: Shimeon had nothing and I have been living in my sister's house. The little money I have was left to me by my father and my grandfather.

But my love for the Galilee – I suppose I inherited that from my great-grandfather, Rabbi Hanina ben Dosa, who used to live very near to Sepphoris, in a little town called Arav. His father was a convert, as was my own grandfather Archinas.

These days, again, gentiles are turning to our faith, more and more of them are becoming Jews, and good Jews at that. Many others also sympathize; they are not ready to convert, but they observe the seven Noahide commandments and are called 'God-fearers.' Some of our sages welcome people like that, others want nothing to do with them. My father, grandfather and great-grandfather would have liked them very much. People of the Galilee also like them.

They say that the men of the Galilee are more concerned for their honor than their property, while in Judaea they were more concerned for their property than their honor. People here are much more caring, more sensitive.

The Galilee. A good place to live. And Rabbi Halafta, my brother-in-law, is still the head of the local court.

I shall finish this memoir by writing down a little more about his son, Yose, about other members of our family, and also about some other people that I have been thinking about lately.

PEACE?

Rabbi Yose ben Halafta was certainly not in danger of being punished by the Nasi, Shimeon ben Gamaliel, for supporting his friend, Meir. Yose was, and is, too important a man.

Why, the Nasi establishes all laws according to the decisions of Yose.

His arguments are called *nimukim*, deeply considered convictions.

So one should think that Yose is a proud man, thinking a lot of himself, as he well might. But no, he is very modest. Pious, guarded. He always speaks with the greatest respect about his colleagues.

I am glad to report that the decree against him, confining him to Sepphoris, has now been annulled. He is free to participate fully in the sessions of the Sanhedrin.

And this dear nephew of mine, Yose, is married to Shoshana bat Yaacov, and has five wonderful children: Ishmael, Eleazar, Halafta, Abtilas and Menachem. The youngest is three years old, the oldest is eighteen. Eleazar in particular seems to have the making of a great scholar one day.

I also promised to write down a few words about other members of our family.

I am afraid that there has been some bad news, sad news.

My brother-in-law, Yose's father, Rabbi Halafta of Sepphoris, died eight years ago. May his memory be blessed.

His wife, my sister Tzviyya, followed him two years later. May her memory be blessed.

We also lost my aunt Elisheva, the wife of my uncle Yonathan. May her memory be blessed.

And the best friend of my brother-in-law, Rabbi Yohanan ben Nuri, also passed away, quite recently. May his memory also be blessed.

I have just turned eighty years old, and feel quite weak. Before long, I think, someone might bless my memory.

*   *   *

But I wanted to write to you a little about Rabbi Shimeon bar Yohai. A friend of the family? Hardly that.

He is still in hiding. I hear that he may soon return. His son has already come back and accepted the position of Director of Public Safety from the Romans, to protect them from the *listim*, the highwaymen. From people like my husband's troops were once. His grandfather held a similar position with the Romans.

This Shimeon was a pupil of Rabbi Akiva for thirteen years. I hear that he forced himself into that position by threatening that his father would report Rabbi Akiva to the Romans. When Akiva expressed a preference for another student of his, Meir, Shimeon was very upset. Later, he declared some of Akiva's interpretations incorrect.

Still later, he criticized scholars like Yose, who worked in some profession while studying the Torah.

While he is in hiding, he feels very sorry for himself. Is he the only one who has suffered? People go and visit him, and he tells everyone that he is a saint and a top authority on everything. He claims that his merit and that of his son, the Director of Public Safety, are sufficient to redeem the world from all the sins since the Creation.

He has also declared that, as long as Jews are in exile, nobody must laugh wholeheartedly. My husband was killed, yet there are occasions when I laugh.

Rabbi Shimeon hates the Romans, so he must be a good man. Yet I must be allowed a personal bias.

It was Rabbi Shimeon bar Yohai who came up with that despicable pun on my husband's name.

He said: "A star came out of Yaacov? A lie came out of Yaacov!" He used the word for lie, *koziva*, instead of Kosiva, my husband's name. And ever since, many who study Gemarah, learn that expression, and they think that my dear husband's name was Shimeon bar Koziva. I have been fighting this for years, but I have no strength left, while this man is still around.

He has suffered, but so have we all.

He has lied and has accused my husband of lying.

Still, Eleazar, the son of my nephew Yose, likes him, so maybe there is some good in the man. There must be, many respect him greatly.

*   *   *

And now, perhaps, we have peace.

Or do we?

The Romans are still everywhere. Their Sixth *Ferrata* legion watches over the Galilee from Legio. They are now afraid of us, they know that if we decided to fight, our armies could challenge the entire Roman Empire, destroy legion after legion, even if we destroyed ourselves in the process. They respect our potential.

They really have two full legions now in our land. There is also the Tenth *Fretensis* in Jerusalem, which they now call Aelia. And they have all kinds of other troops around, *auxilia* of infantry and cavalry, all over the country.

Somebody told me that fully one fifteenth of their army is kept here, in such a small country. That must have been very inconvenient for them, and that's probably one reason, the main reason that Antoninus Pius chose to appease us, make peace with us, or at least a semblance of peace.

And so, we have peace.

Peace, but not freedom.

Most of our people, the Jews who have survived, are in exile. The ones who have remained here live without too many restrictions. But our dream of an independent land of Israel remains just that, a dream for the future.

Was it in vain? Shimeon's fight for freedom, for a Jewish nation in its own land, were all those things in vain?

Did Shimeon bar Kokhba sacrifice his own life and that of hundreds of thousands, all in vain?

I don't think so. I know it was worthwhile.

Hadrian wanted to make a Greek nation out of us, and he would have succeeded. We would have prayed in secret for a while, but how long can you do that? Our sons were no longer circumcised, yet that's how they must join the covenant our father Abraham had made with the Lord. We would have bowed down before alien gods. We would have adopted their language and their culture and their customs, just as Hadrian wanted us to do. That was intolerable. Somebody had to prevent that.

The whole nation wanted to prevent that, and Shimeon led the way.

He lost, true. Yet he did not. We are fewer now, most of us are in exile, but we have remained Jews. And we await the time the Lord shall lead all of us back to Eretz Yisrael, to give us the freedom and the strong independent nation that Shimeon and his troops struggled to achieve.

If that's what the Holy One wants.

Blessed be His name.

Peace.

Notes

In the following I wish to indicate for the reader what is historical fact and what is invention in the book.

Historical personages: Just as in *Hanina My Son*, my book to which the current one is a sequel, all the Tannaic Rabbis mentioned existed. However, most of their family relations are invented. Thus, there is no historical evidence of Rabbi Halafta being related to Rabbi Dosa ben Harkinas or to Rabbi Hanina ben Dosa; nor do we have reason to believe that any of these sages were related to Rabban Gamaliel. Other relations described are equally fictitious.

None of the female characters is historical, with the exception of a brief reference to Rachel, wife of Rabbi Akiva, to Imma Shalom, sister of Rabban Gamaliel the Second, and to Beruriah, wife of Rabbi Meir; as well as to Poppea, wife of the Emperor Nero.

All the major Roman functionaries, emperors, governors and generals are, of course, historical personages. So are Bar Kokhba's commanders specifically named. Even Hillel of Cyrene is mentioned in one of the Bar Kokhba letters.

As to **events**, all military and historical occurrences described are historically correct, as far as can be determined based on sometimes spotty and indirect documentation. The only qualification from the above statement is the placement of Shimeon Bar Kosiva in Africa during the 115–117 revolt. There is no historical evidence whatsoever that he actually participated in the North African campaign. There is no reason to believe that he was there; neither is there any reason to believe that he was not.

Many of the **letters** mentioned, all but the personal ones, have actually been found, buried in the caves of the Judaean hillside near the Dead Sea. See reference to Yigael Yadin's explorations, below.

The following **source material** has been consulted by the author:

Alexander, P.J. "Letters and Speeches of the Emperor Hadrian." *Harvard Studies in Classical Philology* 49, (1938).

Alon, Gedalia. *The Jews in their Land in the Talmudic Age, Vol. 2* Translated and edited by Gershon Levi. Jerusalem: Magnes Press, the Hebrew University, 1980.

Applebaum, Shimon. "Prolegomena to the Study of the Second Jewish Revolt (C.E. 132–135)." *B.A.R. Supplementary Series* 7 (1976).

———. *Jews and Greeks in Ancient Cyrene.* Leiden: Brill, 1979.

———. "Points of View of the Second Jewish Revolt." *Scripta Classica Israelica* 7 (1983/84).

———. "The Second Jewish Revolt (C.E. 131–135)." *Palestine Exploration Quarterly* 116 (1984).

Avi-Yonah, Michael. *The Jews of Palestine.* Oxford: Blackwell, 1976.

Barnard, L.W. "Hadrian and Judaism." *Journal of Religious History* 5 Oxford: Blackwell (1969).

Baron, Salo W. *A Social and Religious History of the Jews, Vol. II* N.Y.: Columbia University Press (1952):57.

Benoît, P., Milik, J.T., et de Vaux, R. *Les grottes de Murabba'ât.* Oxford: Clarendon Press, 1961.

Bowerstock, G.W. "A Roman Perspective of the Bar Kokhba Period." *Approaches to Ancient Judaism 2.* Missoula, Mont.: Publ. by Scholars Press for Brown Univ., 1980.

Büchler Adolf. "A Szamaritánusok részvétele a Barkochba felkelésben." *Magyar Zsidó Szemle,* 14:36 (1897).

Dio, Cassius. *Roman History.* Edited and translated by E. Cary Cambridge: Harvard University Press, 1954–1961.

Eldad, Israel. *The Jewish Revolution: Jewish Statehood* N.Y.: Shengold Publishers, 1971.

Eusebius. *Ecclesiastical History.* Translated by Kirsopp Lake. London: Heinemann, 1959–1964.

Frankel, Yonathan. *Bar Kokhba And All That Dissent* 31. New York: Foundation for the Study of Independent Social Ideas, 1984.

Harkabi, Yehoshafat. *The Bar Kokhba Syndrome.* Chappaqua, N.Y.: Russel Books, 1983

Isaac, Benjamin. *Roman Roads in Judea.* Oxford: B.A.R., 1982.

———. "Cassius Dio on the Revolt of Bar Kokhba." *Scripta Classica Israelica* 7 (1983/84). Jerusalem: Israel Society for the Promotion of Classical Studies.

———. *The Limits of Empire: The Roman Army in the East.* Oxford: Clarendon Press, 1990.

Isaac, Benjamin and Oppenheimer, Aharon. "The Revolt of Bar Kokhba: Ideology and Modern Scholarship." *Journal of Jewish Studies* 36 (1985). Oxford: Centre for Postgraduate Hebrew Studies.

Kolits, Hayim I. *Rabbi Akiva, Sage of All Sages.* Woodmere, N.Y.: Bet-
    Shamai Pub., c. 1989.

Mantel, Hugo. "The Causes of the Bar Kokhba Revolt." *Jewish Quarterly
    Review* Vol. LVIII (1967/8). Philadelphia : Center for Judaic Studies,
    University of Pennsylvania.

———. *Studies in the History of the Sanhedrin, v. 9.* Cambridge, Mass.:
    Harvard University Press, 1961.

Midrash. *Lamentations Rabbah 2.5*

Mildenberg, Leo. *The Coinage of the Bar Kokhba War.* Aarau, Frankfurt
    am Main, Salzburg: Verlag Sauerlander, 1984.

Moore, George Foot. *Judaism in the First Century of the Christian Era*
    N.Y.: Schocken Books, 1927.

Mor, Menachem. "The Bar Kokhba Revolt and Non-Jewish Participants."
    Journal of Jewish Studies, v. 36 (1985). Oxford: Centre for
    Postgraduate Hebrew Studies.

———. "The Samaritans and the Bar Kokhba Revolt" In *The Samaritans,*
    ed. Alan D. Crown Tubingen: J.C.B. Mohr (Paul Siebeck), c. 1989.

Reznick, Leixel. *The Mystery of Bar Kokhba: An Historical and
    Theological Investigation of the Last King of the Jews.* Northvale, N.J.:
    J. Aronson, 1996

Rosenthal, Monroe. *Wars of the Jews: A Military History from Biblical to
    Modern Times.* New York: Hippocrene Books, c. 1990.

Shafer, Peter. *Rabbi Akiva and Bar Kokhba: Approaches to Ancient
    Judaism 2.* (1980). Missoula, Mont.: Publ. by Scholars Press for
    Brown Univ.

———. *The Causes of the Bar Kokhba Revolt Studies in Aggada, Targum
    and Jewish Liturgy. In Memory of Joseph Heinemann* Jerusalem:
    Magnes Press, 1981.

Schuerer, Emil. *The History of the Jewish People in the Age of Jesus
    Christ.* Revised by Vermes, Geza and Millar, Fergus T. and T. Clark.
    Edinburgh: Clark, 1973–1987.

Smallwood, E. Mary. *The Jews under Roman Rule.* Leiden: E.J. Brill, 1976.

Stern, Menahem. *Greek and Latin Authors on Jews and Judaism Vol. II.*
    Jerusalem: Israel Academy of Sciences and Humanities, 1974–1984.

Talmud Yerushalmi. *Ta'an. 4.8 (24a–b)*

Yadin, Yigael. "Expedition D – Nahal Hever." *Israel Exploration Journal,* 11
    (1961) 36–52.

———. "The Finds for the Bar Kokhba Period in the Cave of Letters."
    Jerusalem: *Israel Exploration Society* (1963).

———. Bar Kokhba. N.Y.: Random House, 1971.

Yadin, Yigael and Greenfield, J.C. *The Documents from the Bar Kokhba Period in the Cave of Letters.* Jerusalem: Israel Exploration Society, 1989.

Yardeni, A., Levine, B. (eds.) *The Documents from the Bar Kokhba Period in the Cave of Letters.* Jerusalem: Israel Exploration Society, 2002.

Yourcenar, Margaret. *Memoirs of Hadrian.* Farrar Straus & Giroux, 1963.

Zerubabel, Yael. *Recovered Roots.* Chicago: University of Chicago Press, 1995.

And finally, I wish to express my thanks and appreciation to Professor Menahem Mor, of the University of Haifa, for the time he spent with me and the assistance he offered during the research stages of this project; and I wish to apologize to Professor Mor for the fact that my final conclusions are significantly different from the valuable opinion offered.

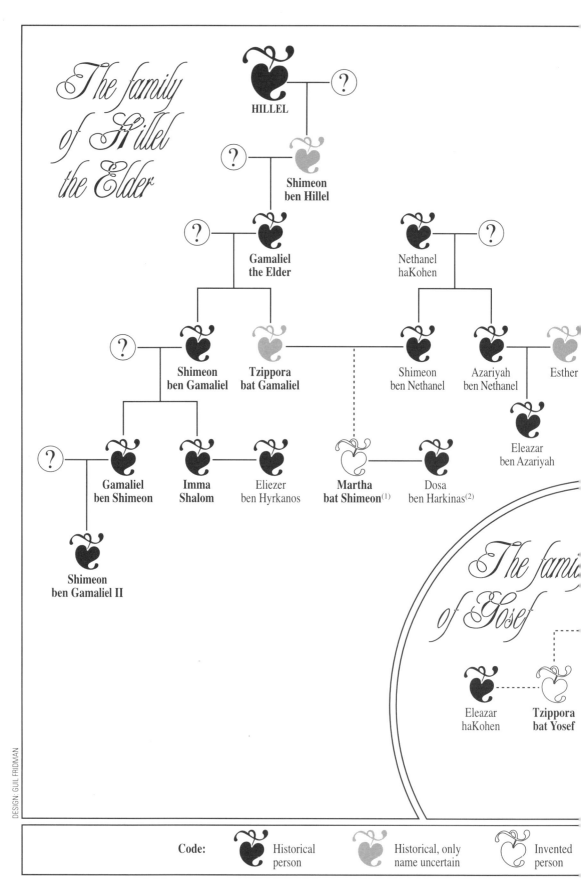

The family
of Hillel
the Elder

HILLEL — ?

? — Shimeon
ben Hillel

? — Gamaliel
the Elder

Nethanel
haKohen — ?

? — Shimeon
ben Gamaliel

Tzippora
bat Gamaliel

Shimeon
ben Nethanel

Azariyah
ben Nethanel — Esther

? — Gamaliel
ben Shimeon

Imma
Shalom — Eliezer
ben Hyrkanos

Martha
bat Shimeon[1] — Dosa
ben Harkinas[2]

Eleazar
ben Azariyah

Shimeon
ben Gamaliel II

The family
of Yosef

Eleazar
haKohen — Tzippora
bat Yosef

DESIGN GUIL FRIDMAN

Code: Historical person | Historical, only name uncertain | Invented person